house
swap

Olivia Beirne is the bestselling author of *The List That Changed My Life*, *The Accidental Love Letter* and *House Swap* and lives in Buckinghamshire. She has worked as a waitress, a (terrible) pottery painter and a casting assistant, but being a writer is definitely her favourite job yet.

Also by Olivia Beirne:

The List That Changed My Life
The Accidental Love Letter

house swap

swap

olivia beirne

REVIEW

First published in eBook in 2021 by
HEADLINE REVIEW
An imprint of HEADLINE PUBLISHING GROUP

First published in paperback in 2021 by
HEADLINE REVIEW
An imprint of HEADLINE PUBLISHING GROUP
1

Cataloguing in Publication Data is available from the British Library

ISBN 978 1 4722 8445 7

Typeset in Bembo Std by Palimpsest Book Production Ltd, Falkirk, Stirlingshire
Printed and bound in Great Britain by Clays Ltd, Elcograf S.p.A.

HEADLINE PUBLISHING GROUP
An Hachette UK Company
Carmelite House
50 Victoria Embankment
London EC4Y 0DZ

www.headline.co.uk
www.hachette.co.uk

To my wonderful dad,
for keeping me laughing and cheering me on.

PROLOGUE

From Rachel Dower to Katy Dower
Sent 4 January 18:01
Hey Katy, how are you? How was Christmas in the end?
Sorry I left you with Mum, Danny wanted to spend it
with his family. What did you think of your present? I
thought the plant would look great in your rooftop garden!
   Love, Rachel x

From Katy Dower to Rachel Dower
Sent 5 January 00:45
Hey, didn't want to spend Christmas with Mum and her
massive new family so went to Dad's. He asked about you.
I said you might give him a ring in the new year?
   Thanks for the plant, yes, it looks fab on the rooftop. It's
right next to the Shard. What did you think of that vegan
cookbook? I use it all the time.
   K xx

From Rachel Dower to Katy Dower
Sent 6 January 08:07
Love the cookbook! The sweet potato brownies are great. x

From Rachel Dower to Katy Dower
Sent 15 February 08:06
Hey Katy,

Just got a notification to say that your membership to
Food Glow hasn't been used, remember you need to sign
up by the end of Feb otherwise it automatically cancels? I
did say to the girl that you had been into the shop so she's
looking into it.

Love, Rachel x

From Katy Dower to Rachel Dower
Sent 15 February 08:07
Hey,

That is weird because I have used it? Look, I made this
spelt spinach cake.

From Katy Dower to Food Glow
FAO Kelly
Sent 15 February 08:15
Hi Kelly!

Thank you so much for all your help on the phone! As
I said, my sister bought me membership last year to Food
Glow, which I was super excited about, but when I came
to register I couldn't (because of my ex-fling Larry
working there, and yes, you're right, he is a total shit).
Anyway, Rachel will never understand that, so if you could

please send her an email saying that there's been a mistake and I *have* registered then that would be so great! I know you're worried about your manager, but please feel free to forward him my email!!!

With very best wishes,

Katy Dower

From Rachel Dower to Katy Dower
Sent 15 February 08:20
Wow, that cake looks amazing. It's like something out of a book! What recipe did you use?

From Katy Dower to Rachel Dower
Sent 15 February 08:30
I'll post it to you.

From Katy Dower to Rachel Dower
Sent 3 March 22:15
Hey!

Know you love running, and just saw an advert for Super Bike, have you seen it?!? Looks amazing and an easy way to get fit. Thinking of buying it! What do you think?

K x

From Rachel Dower to Katy Dower
Sent 4 March 07:45
Hi Katy,

Have you bought this?!

No, I haven't seen these advertised, but just looked them up and seen they are two thousand pounds! They look like a total con, and I would 100% say not to buy one. Why don't you start jogging? That's free!

Also if you are rich enough to spend two grand on a bike then please can you transfer me your half of Mum's birthday present.

Love you,

Rachel

From Katy Dower to Rachel Dower

Sent 4 March 09:08

Hey,

Thanks for the advice. Don't worry, I didn't buy one.

K

CHAPTER ONE

KATY

I glance anxiously back at the house, the bedroom window flickering from the reflection of the television. The fat van crunches over the gravel, casually trampling one of Fiona's precious rose bushes and dragging the plump pale pink flowers under the tyres. My eyes flit back up to the window, waiting for Fiona to fling it open and demand me to tell her what the hell is going on.

I bite my lip, willing the driver to hurry up as the engine rumbles with enough force to awaken the Kraken.

I had no idea he would be this late! What sort of courier delivers a bike at ten thirty at night? Not that I'll say that to him. I've been waiting since three o'clock for this bloody bike to arrive; there is no way I am saying anything to piss him off. If he drives off with it, I'll cry.

The driver hops out of the van, slamming the door behind

him with a loud thwack. I jump as the echo reverberates through me and force myself to smile at the man. His head is a perfect circle and completely hairless, and he has large folds of skin gathered under his eyes that pull his entire face downwards like anchors. He looks exhausted.

He'll be even more exhausted when he realises where I need him to carry my bike.

'Are you Katy?' he says, his voice thick with a Scottish accent.

'Yes,' I say, my hand twitching as I fight between the awkward urge to wave or shake his hand.

He stomps towards the back of the van and I scuttle after him, trying to make as little noise as possible. He reaches forward and flicks a tab at the bottom of the metal door, triggering it to shoot up with a rattle as though it's holding an army of pot-wielding tap dancers. I feel my hands clench into fists by my side.

Oh my God, why is it so loud?

He catches my stricken face and scowls at me.

'You did order a bike?' he says, pulling out his phone and squinting at the screen. 'The Super Bike?'

My stomach twitches.

Yes, yes, I did order the Super Bike. I did sign up for a finance plan for the next two years to pay for a bike I can only afford if I eat Tesco own-brand food until I die and never use fabric softener and wear the same pants for the rest of my life even if they have an unfortunate hole or fall down every time I sneeze.

But who knows? Maybe I'll use this bike every day and look so fantastic that a billionaire will fall in love with me who has shares in fabric softener and then I'll be glad I bought the bike. Thank God I bought this bike, I'll say. And then I'll send Rachel a photo of me sat on a yacht with my new beau, smiling smugly into the camera whilst subtly showing off my new, perfectly ripe arse.

'Yes,' I say, 'yes, that is for me. I live down the bottom of the garden.'

I feel my face flush as it always does whenever I admit to anyone where I live, which is very rare. Don't get me wrong, I don't live under a flowerpot like Bill and Ben, I just live in my boss's back garden (in the annexe) so I can be the perfect PA to her highly successful events company.

Oh, and so I can also be the perfect nanny. Not that it was part of the job description, nor in the small print of my contract. No, it was more that Fiona literally pointed at my little home and told the children that I would love nothing more than to play hide-and-seek, and now, three years later, I'm trapped like a hostile Mary Poppins who's run out of places to hide.

I look over my shoulder at the narrow path that winds down to my small home, and then back at the man. He doesn't look impressed.

'Right,' he says. 'Can I move my van closer?'

If he got any closer to the house, he'd be parked in Fiona's front room.

I chew on my lip. 'Er,' I say, 'no. Sorry. But I can help you carry it!' I add brightly, offering my matchstick arms towards him as if I'm the answer to all his problems.

He cocks his head and climbs inside the van. 'You're going to have to,' he says, and my arms wilt.

I peer inside the van, which is practically empty apart from one large box glowering at me from the corner.

I watch as the man slams his body weight onto the box, shoving it towards me.

I feel myself tense.

Was it a good idea to offer to help lift this? Am I really going to be able to do it?

'Right,' he puffs, 'ready?'

I jump to attention as the box suddenly tilts towards me. My hands grip the edge of it and I feel a surge of heat rush through my arms.

I shall not drop this box. This box contains the reason I'm not having takeaways for the next two years (minimum). I must carry it to safety. It is literally my most prized possession.

The delivery man eases himself out of the back of the van and the box lunges towards me, and before I know what's going on, I'm hobbling backwards down the drive like an unenthused crab. An unenthused crab with a serious yeast infection.

This is not the luxury experience I was hoping for when I ordered this bike. Honestly, why don't they have more than one delivery driver? He's lucky I'm a naturally strong, independent woman. What would he have done if I had broken my arm? Or was heavily pregnant? Or, you know, just didn't want to carry it?

'Is it just straight on?' he says, his gruff voice reverberating around the garden.

'Yes,' I hiss back, willing him to be quiet.

The last thing I want is for Fiona to hear a mysterious man's voice following me down the garden path in the dead of night. I don't want her to think I'm sneaking Scottish men into my flat like a secret temptress.

Not that she'd care. If anything, she'd love it and pluck me raw for all the juicy details over coffee the next morning, using code words the children can't understand.

I say the children; the first time it happened, she kept asking if I had 'captured the goat', and to this day I have no idea what she was talking about.

(I said I had, as this seemed to be the answer she wanted. She was delighted.)

I try not to shriek as my foot lands in a patch of mud and slides off to the side.

Bloody hell, how does anyone walk like this? The Chuckle Brothers made it look so easy! It is totally unreasonable for anyone to be expected to walk backwards in this weird position. I mean, there is a reason why it's only crabs that walk sideways.

A gust of wind whips my thick hair in front of my eyes and I shake my head about like a distressed horse.

'Just down here,' I manage between puffs of air.

'Oh yeah,' he replies. 'I can see it. Cute little place.'

'Thank you,' I say, craning my strained neck to see, to my relief, that we have arrived at my cabin.

That's what I call it: 'The Cabin'. It's a beautiful little lodge, with my own squashy armchairs and perfectly fitted kitchen. Fiona and her husband Tristan had it built just before I arrived, in hopes of an au pair appearing and casually teaching them all French. She was thrilled when I applied to be her PA and told her I was moving from Wales to start a new life in London.

I mean, I was applying to be PA to the events director. Not PA to Fiona Cunningham and her entire family. But whatever. It has its perks. I mean, there is a reason I'm still here three years later.

'Okay,' I say, 'so if we just put it down, I'll open the door.'

I've barely finished speaking when the man starts to dip into a deep squat. I fight the urge to scream in pain as my poor thighs tremble under the weight of the box.

Christ! Who does he think I am? The only time I squat is when I'm avoiding a toilet seat!

The box lands on the ground with a thump and I fumble around for my keys.

'Do you need help bringing it inside?' he says, looking back up the garden, not bothering to hide his desperation to leave.

I click the door open and flash him a smile.

'Just through the door, please,' I say. 'I'll set it up.'

He gives the box a final shove with his shoulder, and it slides through my front door. He pulls himself to standing and turns his iPhone towards me. I push my long hair off my face, shoving it behind my ears roughly, and scribble my signature, then look at the bike, my heart thumping in my ears.

'Thanks.' He shoots me a thumbs-up and stomps back down the garden. I watch him leave and then slowly push my front door shut, the familiar silence of the cabin falling around me.

I just won't mention it to Rachel again until I'm sure it's a good idea. That's the way I've been living for the past three years, and it's been going pretty well.

It's not lying; it's just that there are some aspects of my life I've never told her about.

What's the big deal?

★

I feel myself stir as the bright white light of the sun streams over my face. Every night for the past three years I have slept with my face next to the window. It means I wake as the sun rises each morning.

It makes me feel quite peaceful and at one with nature, like Snow White. Although I bet Snow White didn't consider murdering a pair of foxes who thought that outside my bedroom window was the perfect place to start a family.

I open my eyes, shielding them from the sun as I peer up the garden towards the main house. I can see William's shadow against the blue blind, sitting up on his bed and scratching his head. He's probably reading; he knows he's not allowed out of bed before six. Jasmine will still be asleep, which isn't unusual.

I roll onto my front and pick up my phone, feeling a tingle of nerves as I look at the date: 13 March. Two days before the charity ball, the first event Fiona has let me properly work on. Which means that today, I am going into the office.

I look down at my outfit, perfectly laid out on the chair beneath me. My bed is made up of a large mattress and duvet, with about thirty old pillows, tucked away on the mezzanine section of the cabin. I've stuck some photos on the wall next to my pillows, and sometimes pull a string of fairy lights up if there is a storm outside and the place gets particularly dark.

They're all photos Rachel took – she's always had a knack for photography – which means they are from our teenage years, when we spent real time together. There's one of me and Dad grinning over a birthday cake, a photo of the four of us standing on a cliff edge in Pembrokeshire, the Welsh air pinching at our cheeks and our arms linked around each other as our shiny sunburnt faces beam at the camera. Then there's one of Rachel, me and our grandma, with Rachel's arm stretched out in front of us holding the camera. That's my favourite one. Our cheeks are pressed to either side of Grandma's face, my teenage braces glinting in the light and Rachel's circular glasses propped on her button nose. Grandma is grinning mischievously at the camera. There was always a light in Grandma's eyes, a certain twinkle of naughtiness. Even when she was really sick, she'd look at you as though she was sitting on the most delicious gossip, or about to burst into ripples of giggles at a prank she had in store for one of the neighbours.

As twins go, Rachel and I are practically identical. Although Rachel now has a blunt fringe, and my nose turns up slightly at the end whereas hers sits neatly on her face. Which sums us up really. Rachel has always been perfectly organised and in control, with nothing out of place, whereas I'm the flyaway. Grandma never let us take ourselves too seriously, and she certainly never let us fight. Although I think if she could see the stilted, rehearsed version of our relationship now, she'd say that was worse. At least when we were fighting, we were being real.

I pull myself up to sitting, being careful not to hit my head on the low ceiling, and swing my legs round to find the ladder.

I go into the office about twice a week, as Fiona says the rest of my work can be done at home. I have helped her with events before – I mean, I am the PA to the director of events – but in the past that has just meant ordering flowers or sending invitations that someone else has picked out. A lot of the time, the biggest help I seem to be to her is keeping the children entertained when she's on a business call.

She knows I want to work in the office and be a proper employee. She's made excuses over the years about my experience, and talked about me building my 'repertoire' (all the other staff seem to have come straight from fancy agencies), so I've waited patiently for my time to prove myself, and now this is it. Out of nowhere, Fiona let me organise the auction at the charity ball. The most important part of the event! I haven't mentioned it to her, but I know that if I get it right, she'll have to offer me a position within the company. You know, an actual I-have-a-desk-and-nobody-dare-use-my-prized-mug employee, taking part in the absurd office polls about who is the most outrageous person on *Love Island* and the correct way to make a cup of tea. Caitlyn, one of the junior event executives, left last month to work in Canada, so it's as if everything is lining up for me and finally my entire fantasy of what my London life should be is about to come true.

I flick the kettle on. Today I'm wearing my leopard-print dress, black court heels and my new hoop earrings. I can barely stand in heels, but there is no way I'm sauntering into the edgy east London office in flats. I already feel like an outcast every time I walk in.

I pour the boiling water into a mug over the dark coffee granules and pick up my phone as it vibrates in my hand. Three emails pop onto the screen. Two from Fiona and one from Rachel. Rachel and I used to text, and occasionally we still call, but she worked out that the quickest way to get a response from me was to send an email. She stopped picking up the phone months ago.

I mentally note the two emails from Fiona, a reminder of what time the taxi will be outside, and have I remembered to bring my laptop? (Yes.) I take a sip of coffee as I open the email from Rachel.

Hi Katy,

Hope you're having a nice Monday.

I thought I'd email your work address to remind you to triple-check with HR that you can have the time off to come and house-sit next week. Bruno is very excited to see you, and I've attached a schedule with his meals and exercise regime. I'm sure you'll have lots you'll want to do when you're here, but I'll leave the fridge full and my Sky password is on the remote.

Good luck for your big event. Maybe I can see you before you go. I'll try and leave Paris a day early.

Love you,

Rachel x

I drop the phone back to my side.

Urgh.

Six months ago, Rachel asked if I would house-sit for her and look after her giant, slobber-ridden dog/bear Bruno, while she spent a week at a work conference in Paris. I wanted to ask why her husband, Danny, couldn't return from the boat he's been on for the past ten bloody months to look after his dog, but I thought that wouldn't be very sisterly. (He's not a pirate; he just works on a cruise ship.)

Anyway, she asked me in the depths of a hangover when I didn't have the energy to make up an excuse, and she's been reminding me every other Monday since with a brisk email or novelty countdown tag on Instagram. I don't know why she's so excited; it's not like she's going to be there.

I take a sip of my coffee, squinting towards the house, where I notice William throwing his cereal across the table.

I wince as the coffee burns my tongue.

Obviously when I agreed to house-sit, I didn't know I was going to be organising the single most important event of my entire career the week before. In an ideal world, I wouldn't be going. It seems ridiculous to take a week off when I am finally on the cusp of a promotion. Really, I need to be in the office bright and early on Monday morning after the ball, ready to schmooze Fiona with light titbits and stories of how fabulous the evening was while everybody chips in with how much fun they had. Not being dragged around soggy Wales by a dog that always tries to hump my leg.

I did toy with the idea of cancelling. I even found a nice-looking doggy hotel that I thought Bruno might enjoy (with female dogs he could 'socialise' with), but quickly dismissed the idea when Rachel sent me a list of his favourite walks, with a sloppy picture attached of Bruno 'smiling' because he's so excited about seeing me.

I begged Fiona to give me the time off (even though I haven't had a holiday for the entire time I've worked here), and she agreed on the condition that I took my laptop with me so I could work remotely 'if required'. I didn't ask whether this included some awful virtual babysitting.

So I replied to every one of Rachel's incessant emails about my stay, assuring her that *yes* I was definitely coming, *no* I didn't still own a pair of walking boots, and *no*, I one hundred per cent did not want to buy a pair, especially that hideous pair that were fifty per cent off in the sale.

I down the final dregs of my coffee and check the time. Right, one hour before we have to leave.

Rachel doesn't know my real work situation. It wasn't a complete lie. I told her I work at Hayes Events (which is true) as PA to the director (also true). She knows I live in a flat in west London (almost true) and I live by myself (true!).

But she doesn't know that I live in my boss's back garden, and I actually spend eighty per cent of my working week looking after her children and sometimes feel like I was hired as an accidental nanny who just happened to apply for a job as the annexe was finished.

There would be no point telling her any of this. She already doesn't understand why I wanted to move away from our precious childhood village to live in London. She's never wanted to understand. So I leave her to it, with her perfect marriage and her perfect little life in our family cottage. We normally see each other once a year, at Christmas, and send the routine birthday cards and Lush vouchers, and that's fine. Neither of us asks for anything more.

I mean, sure, perhaps there have been times when I've exaggerated the glossiness of my life in answer to her asking an innocent question like 'How is your job going?' But what am I supposed to do? Tell her the truth?

But yes, even I can see that telling her that I hosted an after party in my rooftop garden with everybody from *Heat* magazine was a bit extreme. And that Kem from *Love Island* was there. And that I may have got off with him.

But I did say 'may'! I was very clear on that.

My phone buzzes in my hand and a second email from Rachel pops onto my screen.

PS I'm having a piece of bara brith for breakfast for Grandma. Hope you're okay today x

My heart squeezes as Grandma's warm, doughy hands fill my mind, pulling another bara brith from the oven and laughing as Mum exclaimed how we'd only just finished the last one. 'You can never have too much cake!' she'd say, giving Rachel and me a wink as we grinned over our cereal. If we did well in school or helped her around the house, cake for breakfast was our treat.

Bara brith was her favourite. The heavy fruit loaf was a constant staple of our kitchen, sitting right next to the kettle. None of our friends from school liked it, but Rachel and I couldn't get enough.

My eyes sting at the memory. How has it been two years since she died?

I drop my phone onto the sofa and pluck a fondant fancy from the cupboard, shoving the entire thing in my mouth before I start crying.

I can't start the day in tears.

I catch sight of myself in the mirror and give myself a goofy grin. I wince as I notice my large teeth, and the bags that threaten to swallow my eyes. I pull a more serious face, with a small, subtle smile. The kind of face I need to fit in with Fiona's dreadful cool employees.

Except every time I pull that face, I look like I'm trying to hide the fact that I'm the person who's just farted.

I relax my face and pad into the bathroom. As I shut the door and switch the shower on, I continue to practise my face of indifference.

CHAPTER TWO

RACHEL

I swing my legs against the back of the chair, remembering the feeling of being a child and only being at the doctor's for something minuscule, like a routine injection that resulted in a sticker from the doctor and a secret McDonald's from Grandma.

My eyes scan the room, lingering slightly on each person as I find myself trying to guess what they're in for. After flitting over each unsuspecting patient, my eyes land on a young couple and I feel my heart jolt. The woman has caramel skin and thick braids, twisted together over her shoulder. She is leaning against the back of her chair, her stomach stretching out effortlessly as her manicured hand rests lightly on her bump. The man next to her has his arm wrapped around her shoulders, speaking quietly and making her giggle. He places his hand on top of hers and gives the bump a light rub. The woman beams up at him and I have to clench my jaw to stop myself from vomiting.

Isaac spots me holding my hand over my mouth and jerks to attention, his pale eyes alert.

'What is it?' he says quickly. 'Do you want the doctor? Or the toilet?'

He looks at me nervously and I almost want to laugh at the pure terror etched on his face.

Poor Isaac, I don't think he'll ever recover from seeing me throw up in my pyjamas seconds after opening the front door to him. I don't think his shoes will ever recover, either.

But I mean, really. Who shows up at their pregnant neighbour's front door at 8 a.m. with a fresh bag of wet dog food wafting through the air?

Still, I should really buy him a new pair of shoes. And socks.

'I'm fine,' I say, taking a deep breath and forcing myself to look away from the giggling couple, stealing one final glance at the gold band wrapped around her finger.

'Rachel Dower?'

A petite receptionist with a thick Welsh accent pokes her head around the door. I raise my hand and she gives me a quick once-over before realising that I'm not going to stand up. Like clockwork, Isaac leans forward and takes the form. The woman gives him a kind smile and I can almost see the lovely thought bubble pop out from her head.

How sweet. He'll make a great dad.

Without quite meaning to, I scowl at her.

This must be the tenth form I've filled out since I've been pregnant. I swear the receptionist just collects them for fun.

'Right,' he says, leaning back into his seat. 'Have you got a pen?'

I raise my eyebrows at him. 'I can fill out my own form, Isaac,' I say. 'Assuming you have a pen I can borrow?'

19

He looks down at my expectant hands and shrugs.

'Pen? No. I do have a trowel in my bag, and,' he pats his pockets, 'some dog biscuits and perhaps a tissue?' He yanks out an old red sock from the depths of his pocket and I grimace as dust flies off it like icing sugar.

'You need to bin that,' I say, trying not to laugh as the woman sitting opposite looks at him as though he's just produced a squirming rat.

Isaac glances at the sock, shrugs, and shoves it back in his pocket, where it will undoubtedly stay for another two years.

'I'll grab a pen from reception,' he says.

I smile after him and make the stupid mistake of catching the eye of the pregnant woman across the room, who is beaming at me, her hands still placed delicately on her bump. Much like the receptionist, I watch her thought bubble pop out of her head.

You must be as blissfully happy as I am.

I stare down at my hands, heat prickling my cheeks.

If only they could see my thought bubble.

'Rachel, are you ready?'

The receptionist reappears and I snap out of my thoughts. Slowly I grip the chair and push myself to standing, trying to ignore the splats of black that squirm in front of my eyes from the effort. Just as I take a step forward, I feel Isaac's arm link into mine.

'I'm fine,' I say quietly.

'This is for me,' he mutters. 'I need to regain some credit after the sock incident.'

I notice him look over at the woman opposite, whose head is now cocked in approval.

For goodness' sake.

'Right,' the nurse says as we sink into identical chairs in her office and Isaac finally lets go of my arm. 'So, Rachel . . . and partner?'

My stomach drops. I haven't met this nurse before.

'No,' Isaac says, as though she's just asked whether he'd like a cup of tea.

'He's not the father, either,' I blurt, unable to bear to wait for the inevitable question. 'He's my neighbour.'

'Friend.' Isaac shoots me a look. 'Childhood friend. Sister's ex-boyfriend,' he adds to the nurse as an aside.

Oh God. He's making it worse. Why does she need to know that? She doesn't even know Katy.

'He's here to support,' I say quickly. 'It's just me, I'm doing this all by myself.'

A horrible, awkward laugh tinkles out of my mouth and I rest my hands on my round stomach, my face burning as my thought bubble finally stretches out for everyone to see.

I'm doing this all by myself.

★

The rest of the appointment goes quite quickly. I nod and smile and answer the questions politely, all the while chewing on the inside of my cheek whilst fighting the urge to tell the nurse my entire life history to stop her from potentially thinking I'm sleeping with my sister's ex-boyfriend. An image of myself blabbering out my thoughts creeps in front of my eyes:

Isaac really is just a friend, he's actually never got over my twin sister. I was married up until last year, but then he sort of left me. Or, well, I guess we kind of left each other. He works on a cruise ship so I haven't seen him since. And I was stupid and sad and let myself get sucked in by a guy from work and somehow ended up pregnant. He didn't even pretend he wanted anything to do with it, so he's gone too. So here I am, all by myself, which I am totally fine with.

I catch hold of the imaginary dialogue steamrollering through my mind as the last few words judder to a halt. In my mind, I am chirping these words to the nurse as though I am chatting about the weather, but just thinking them causes my stomach to churn like a vat of cream cheese.

Isaac is the only person I've actually allowed myself to spill all my secrets to. Well, Isaac, and Peggy from work, who caught me crying in the toilets and has been showering me with unexpected gifts ever since to try and get me excited about the baby, with varying success. Let me tell you, one thing to get you suitably mortified about childbirth is being sent a breast pump.

I mean, what is she going to send next? Anal cream?

Actually, I shouldn't joke about that. Her daughter Tabitha has just had a baby, and Peggy told me a *highly* personal story about her 'post-birth piles' that made me want to rip my ears off. A week later, Tabitha popped into the office and I spent the entire conversation bright red fighting a horrible urge to ask her if the cream worked, and did she prefer the scented one after all the fuss?

I lean back in the car seat and check my watch. The appointment was over in five minutes flat, just a routine check-up. I shooed Isaac out of the room before the nurse could ask me anything too personal.

He reappears around the corner, strolling towards the car as though he's in a mid-nineties boy-band slow-mo. Sometimes I wonder how he and Katy ever worked together as a couple, considering Katy is the most impatient person I know and does everything at one hundred miles an hour. Neither of them has ever found anyone else who matches their speed.

'All right?' he says, opening the driver's door. I drop some change into the cup holder for the parking and he grins. 'Thanks. I'd say don't bother, but the parking here is extortionate. I mean, it's a hospital!' He clicks his seat belt on and judders the rusty old Clio into life. 'It's quite clever actually,' he adds, leaning over the wheel as he pulls off. 'I suppose if someone has lost an arm, they'd be so desperate to get inside that they'd pay anything for parking.'

'I don't think someone who'd lost their arm would be driving themselves to hospital,' I laugh.

'No, you're right.' He grins, flicking his indicator on. 'They'd find a kind-hearted neighbour and guilt-trip them into giving them a lift.'

'And buy them lunch?' I add pointedly. 'And offer to sort their recycling to stop them getting an enormous fine?'

'Yeah, yeah,' he says, 'and all that.'

My ankles knock together and I glance down at them. For a horrible second I almost see them wobble.

Urgh. What are you doing, ankles? Why on earth are you getting fat? No part of the baby is being stored anywhere near you; you have absolutely no reason for swelling up like baked potatoes.

I pull my phone out of my bag and let out a sigh before I can stop myself.

Are you going to speak to Dad today?

Isaac frowns at me. 'What?'

23

'Katy,' I say, rubbing the palm of my hand against my forehead. 'She just text me about Dad.'

'Ah.' Isaac nods, keeping his eyes on the road. 'It's your grandma's anniversary soon, isn't it?'

'Well remembered,' I say. 'It's today.'

We fall into silence and I stare down at the message. I haven't spoken to my dad in years. I didn't think I'd ever speak to him again.

'When is it Katy's coming down again?'

I lock the phone and look up at Isaac. Although he's trying to act normal, two red patches have formed on his cheeks.

'Sunday.'

'And are you going to tell her before she arrives that you're pregnant, or see how long it takes her to notice?'

He swings the car around another corner and I roll my eyes at him.

'I'm eight months gone,' I laugh. 'I know we hardly see each other, but I think she'll notice.'

He smiles, waiting for me to answer the bigger question.

'I'm not telling her before,' I say quietly. 'I don't want to risk her cancelling on me. I need to tell her while she's here so that she can get used to the idea.'

'But you are telling her that your conference has been cancelled?'

I nod, staring out the window at the flashes of green as we shoot down a narrow country lane.

'Yes,' I say. 'The day before. I'll tell her it's cancelled and suggest we spend the week together instead.'

'Then when she gets here, you'll surprise her with a niece.'

'Or nephew.'

24

'And then you'll mend your relationship and go back to being best friends rather than weird estranged sisters?'

My throat tightens as Isaac casually announces what's lying underneath my heart.

'That's the plan.'

★

It's a good plan. That's what I keep telling myself. Or rather, it's the best plan I could think of.

Katy is a flight risk. She hates Pembrokeshire and anything that reminds her of Grandma, and has been happily burying her head in the sand for the past three years. And by burying her head in the sand, I mean sipping posh cocktails and flouncing around London as an elite events something-or-other and pretending she's far too busy to come home.

And what am I going to ask of her? To come home permanently? To leave her glamorous London life and move back to live with me and the baby as a happy little family in our childhood cottage, where we'll spend our weekends baking bread (which I'll do, as Katy is terrible) and making pottery (Katy's forte)?

I lean back against the sofa and slot a piece of bara brith into my mouth. The sharp, sweet taste of currants floods my senses.

That's my happy place, imagining Katy flinging her arms into the air in delight and rushing back home. In the depths of my fantasy, she tells me how she's actually hated London all this time and has been desperate to move back. She settles into the family cottage and everything goes back to how it was when we were fifteen, thick as thieves like twins should be. Not how we are now, only speaking via cold, professional emails and never answering the phone to one another.

The mug in my hand starts to burn and I peel my fingers away. As the steam rises and sticks to my glasses, I lose my grip of the happy fantasy and the cold, dark, nightmare version creeps into my mind.

This is the version that keeps me awake at night. Just as I'm falling asleep, it seeps in front of my eyes and curls around my throat until I'm so deep within its clutches that I can barely breathe. Katy is furious with me for lying to her about my conference being cancelled and for tricking her into coming home. She can't understand why I would leave Danny, and how I could be so stupid as to have got myself into this mess. She loves her London life too much to let it go, and worst of all, she doesn't really care. She leaves, and we go back to sending the yearly gift card on our birthday and making awkward small talk at Christmas, and I'm left with this baby and our old house, really alone.

I catch myself as my eyes start to sting and pull myself back into my living room.

That won't happen. She won't do that. She would never be that heartless. She loves you.

I close my eyes as I repeat those words in my mind, but each time I say them, they somehow weigh a little less, until they might as well be made of dust. Because the truth is, no matter how much I tell myself that Katy won't leave me for London again, I'm not sure what she'll do.

I sip the tea and the hot, sweet liquid burns my throat.

I don't really know anything about her any more.

The baby gives a determined wriggle and I smile down at my bump.

'You're right,' I say, 'you are much more exciting than London.'

I wiggle my finger on the mouse pad of my laptop and watch the email come to life, the same email I've been reading for the past two weeks and editing at 4 a.m. when the baby decides it's ready for a rave.

Hi Katy,

I hope your journey is going well! My business trip has been cancelled, so I'll be here after all. I thought it would be nice to spend some time together, as I now have the next week off too. I need to talk to you about something.

Love you,

Rachel

I steady my breathing as my eyes scan the final sentence. It's perfect, and all ready to send on Sunday at 5 p.m., when Katy will already be on her way. I have to add the last line about needing to speak to her about something (even though every time I read it, I nearly throw up) so that she knows it's important. She won't cancel on me if she thinks something has happened. Although God only knows where her mind will go, considering I've been spouting the same rubbish to her for months about how everything is fine, Danny is great and life has never been better.

I chew the inside of my cheek.

I should have told her months ago. Why didn't I tell her?

I turn my phone in my hand and reread the message she sent.

Are you going to speak to Dad today?

My fingers tense around the phone. I didn't speak to Dad on the first anniversary of Grandma's death. I haven't spoken to him in years. Why would I speak to him now?

Katy speaks to Dad, that's the deal. She speaks to Dad and I speak to Mum. Not that I've been able to for the past few months, seeing as she lives in France now with her new family and I have a stronger relationship with her answering machine than I do with her.

But it was Dad who had the affair. Dad broke our family. I've never forgiven him for that.

My phone bleeps again and my heart stutters as I read a second message from Katy.

Also, in response to your email, all fine with HR. So stressed with event, will just work for the week on my laptop while I'm at yours! Wish I had time for a holiday LOL.

Hope conference goes well. Can't believe they're sending you to Paris for a week. To be honest, if you come home a day early I'll probably just leave, got so much to do and will need to get back to London.

Don't forget to tell me where you're leaving the key. Love you xx

As I finish reading the message, I notice my eyes are wet.

Well that's that then. She doesn't even want to spend a day with me; how could I expect her to want to spend an entire week? How could I expect her to want to spend, oh I don't know, the rest of her life here with me?

The baby wriggles again and I rest my damp hand on my bump.

She doesn't need me like I need her.

I close my eyes, trying to fight the hot tears that are seeping out.

I never thought I'd have a baby without Katy here. I thought we'd have got over this weird rift by then. But then why haven't I called her? Why can't I just pick up the phone now and tell her everything?

My heart jumps as I hear my front door crash noisily open.

Bruno, my ungraceful St Bernard, comes thundering from the kitchen, sounding his battle cry and crashing straight into Grandma's lamp. My head snaps round; for one wild second, I think Katy has let herself in using her old key. She's here as a surprise, or she somehow guessed that I need her, using that twin intuition that everyone talks about. I don't even need to ask her to move back and help me; she's already here. Everything is going to be okay.

'Yoo-hoo! Only me!' Peggy's thick Welsh trill sings through the door and I quickly wipe my eyes, trying to ignore her shrieks as Bruno leaps all over her.

Peggy insisted I give her a spare key when she found out I was going on maternity leave by myself. (As opposed to what? Going on it with Bruno?) She didn't even try to hide her shock when I told her Mum wasn't rushing home from her second family in France to be by my side, let alone that my dad and sister didn't know a single thing about it. So she appointed herself my surrogate mother and, by extension, my birthing partner. Both of which meant it was crucial that she had her own key cut and matching T-shirts ordered to wear on the big day.

I mean, crikey. This time last year I was mentally calling her Polly.

She bustles in backwards, her body half bent over an enormous carrier bag and her face red and shining. I'd guess she's in her early sixties, although I'll never find out, as I once heard my manager ask her when the 'big six-five' was and Peggy looked as if she'd been shot. Her cheeks are always flared with deep rouge patches and she's the type of woman who has a constant ear-splitting smile on her face. She's been going to some form of weight-loss class for as long as I've known her, and was kicked out of Weight Watchers after she was caught dropping Kit Kats into her opponents' handbags.

She calls me her 'little duck', and as much as I hate letting anybody in (especially someone who is trying to shoehorn their way into the gaping parent gap in my life, something I've been quite content with for the past ten years), I've grown strangely attached to her.

She scooped me under her wing as soon as she found me crying in the toilets at work, and has barely let me out of her sight since. The moment Tabitha had her baby, she printed out photos and stuck them to the office corkboard (taking down the fire procedure notice to make space). When the baby was four weeks old, she told me over a bubbling kettle that Tabitha and her husband had decided to move to Leeds and that they'd had an offer accepted on their perfect house. Although her voice was bright and laced with *Isn't it exciting?* and *What an adventure!*, I could see the hurt glistening from behind her eyes. At that moment, an unusual friendship was formed. I knew what it was like to feel like everyone had left you behind. To be honest, the more time she's spent letting herself in and giving me top tips on birthing plans, the more I've wondered how I ever survived without her.

She beams at me, her auburn hair spun on top of her head like a Danish pastry and her cheeks glowing with pride as she gleams down at my bump. She keeps doing this. One time she caught me throwing up in the office toilet and dabbed her eyes as though I was the Virgin Mary.

'Hello, pet,' she says.

'Peggy,' I say, trying to look stern but failing instantly, 'how often are you going to let yourself into my house with no warning? One day you'll walk in on me on the toilet.'

'And good thing too!' she cries, plucking the empty mug out of my hands and marching into the kitchen. 'Soon you'll be needing my help getting back up. You don't want to be one of those girls who have their babies on the toilet, do you?'

I open my mouth to reply and close it instantly.

Great, well now there's something else for me to obsessively worry about every time I go for a wee.

I hear Peggy flick the kettle on.

'Oh!' she coos. 'That smells nice. What are you cooking?'

I allow my heavy eyes to shut as I rest my hands on my bump.

'A big batch of chilli,' I reply. 'I read a blog that said the best thing to do is fill your freezer with food, as you'll be too tired when the baby comes. So far I've made a bolognese, a curry and a— Peggy!'

My eyes snap open as Peggy plonks down next to me cradling a small bowl of chilli.

'That's for when I've had the baby!' I cry, trying not to laugh as she blinks back at me innocently, holding the spoon towards me. I shake my head, but she looks at me like I'm a child being fed Calpol. Reluctantly I take the spoon and taste the chilli.

She winks at me. 'Delicious, darling, but it could do with a pinch more salt.' She springs to her feet and disappears back into the kitchen. 'I've been doing some batch cooking for you too. Lots of hearty stews and a lovely cottage pie.'

The lingering taste of chilli dances on my tongue. I'll need to somehow tell Katy that I gave up veganism last year. I say 'gave up', but can you really give up something you only tried for two days? I didn't mean to lie to her about it, but she was so into it and doing so well, I felt guilty. I mean, last month she sent me a photo of a spinach cake she'd made. A spinach cake!

Maybe I'll just tell her that veganism is bad for the baby so I was forced to give it up. She won't know any different.

'I'll drop it round next week.'

I jump out of my thoughts as I realise Peggy is still talking.

'Not next week,' I say quickly. 'That's when Katy is here, I'll be a bit preoccupied.'

Peggy pokes her head out of the kitchen and gives me a knowing look. She has been desperate to meet Katy and cannot understand why I'm worried about her reaction. 'Of course she'll want to help you,' she told me. 'That's what families do for each other. They help each other.'

But my family isn't like every other family. We don't stick around to help each other. We run away.

And although Katy is the one in London, I ran from her first.

CHAPTER THREE

KATY

I catch sight of myself in the reflection of the revolving doors and fight the urge to flick my hair like I'm in a shampoo commercial.

The good news is, this outfit looks just as fantastic outside as it did in my living room when I tried it on last week. The dress skims my body, not too fitted but fitted enough to show off my figure and my toned legs (the only benefit to racing after screaming children for entire weekends at a time). I'm standing effortlessly in my gorgeous new court shoes, as if I wear heels all the time like every other city girl. Honestly, even my hair has stayed in place and—

'Katy? What are you doing?'

I feel my face pinch with embarrassment as Fiona appears behind me, catching me admiring myself in the reflection. I thought she'd already gone inside.

'Nothing,' I say quickly, turning to face her with a big smile. She gestures for me to enter the building first and flicks her sunglasses onto the top of her head. I scuttle in obediently, trying to force a cool expression onto my face when all I want to do is grin with excitement at how fantastic my dress looks.

I hope someone takes my photo today. Or if there's good light in the bathroom, maybe I'll take a photo when nobody else is in there. My mirror at home is covered in smears of make-up and dust, which makes all my photos look as if someone has sneezed on them. I glance down at my Apple Watch; it beams 08:57 back up at me.

'Morning!' I say brightly to a receptionist, who shoots me a limp smile back.

I follow Fiona into the lift and she pulls out her phone. Fiona has caramel hair, which always glows in the sunlight thanks to the fresh highlights that she gets done religiously every six weeks. She's tall, almost six foot in heels, with slender arms and a pointy face. She describes herself as a 'city bitch' to anyone who will listen, but I've seen her in dungarees and Converse, rolling around in the garden having a tickle fight with William. Not that I'd ever tell anyone that for risk of being fired. Actually, no, not fired. Assassinated.

'Right,' she says, without looking up, 'so I'll be in a meeting this morning. I'm sure you have plenty to do regarding the auction. Diane has been put on the team, so she'll help you with whatever you need.'

I feel my bright smile twitch at this new piece of information. Urgh, Diane.

I really try to like Diane. Every Sunday night, I feel a wave of guilt and vow to be kinder to her. I'm sure she means well, but spending time with her is like taking a bath filled with leeches.

She sucks the life out of you.

'Great!' I say, as I realise Fiona is waiting for me to respond. 'I do need to leave at five today, if that's okay. I'm seeing my dad.'

She snaps her head up from her phone, her eyes full of worry. 'Oh, I'm so sorry!' she cries. 'God, what type of person am I? I told myself not to forget that it's your grandma's anniversary today, I even wrote it on my bloody fridge, and here I am blabbering to you about a bloody auction.'

'It's fine,' I say, 'really.'

'Do you want to be here? You can go home, I'll be fine.'

'No,' I say quickly, 'I need to be here. I'd like to have something to take my mind off it.'

She blinks at me for a second, and I raise my eyebrows back at her. Eventually she nods.

'Okay,' she says, 'if you're sure. We'll catch up later, okay?' She gives my arm a squeeze as the lift pings open and she glides out.

Although I have seen Fiona collect snails with William, nobody can deny that she makes an excellent city bitch. She skims through the office like an overly important swan, like she was placed in her five-inch heels the moment she was born with her smartphone in her hand, ready to go.

I force my face into the rehearsed expression of indifference everybody here permanently wears, and make my way after her with my head held high, trying not to wail in pain as my shoes stab my feet like I'm walking on razor blades.

I spot an empty desk in the corner and sit down, pulling my

laptop out and quickly making myself at home, as if I sit here all the time and me being here is no big deal whatsoever. Actually I should try and take a picture of myself at my desk to put on Instagram. You know, while I'm here.

'Oh Katy! You're here!'

Vanessa's sickly-sweet voice fills my ears as she stops right next to my desk, coffee in hand. Vanessa is one of the event executives, and even though she's met me several times over the past three years, she always looks surprised to see me, as though I have crawled in through the fire exit undetected. Needless to say, she fits the Hayes mould perfectly. She has smooth skin and long, shiny hair that reaches her waist and swings perfectly when she walks. She always wears tailored suits, and I once saw her run in a pair of Jimmy Choos.

I mean, if that's not the sign of a dangerous woman then I don't know what is.

I feel my top lip quiver as I meet her eye.

Don't you dare start sweating now, upper lip. That is not the sign of an important, in-control woman. Stay dry, goddammit.

'Morning,' I say. 'Good weekend?'

Vanessa flicks her hair and sinks into the seat opposite. I feel my body stiffen as her wide eyes survey me. I straighten my spine, waiting for her to comment on how sweet I look. She always smiles when she says it, as though it's a compliment, but it never feels like one. It feels more like somebody giving you a lemon meringue pie made with rotten eggs. And arsenic.

'Yeah,' she says, 'just a quiet one. Brunch Saturday, gig in the evening. Hung-over roast in Putney and casual date on Sunday.'

Casual date? What's an intense one?

Actually, I definitely know what an intense date is. I'm looking at you, guy who invited his mum.

Her piercing eyes flick up to me as she finishes her sentence, as if daring me to challenge how perfectly cool and effortless her weekend was.

I feel my tight smile mirror hers.

'Oh lovely,' I say smoothly. 'I went to an organic painting class, and then did some light yoga on a rooftop in Dulwich. I had a heavy one in Soho Saturday night with an old beau, and then Sunday went to an abandoned cinema to watch David Attenborough documentaries.'

Without quite meaning to, I feel my eyebrows slide up my face in triumph. I mean, I do have an unfair advantage. I knew at least one of Fiona's staff would ask me this question, as if to prove that I'm not cool enough to work here and should just focus on bringing everyone coffee and fixing the photocopier. So in preparation, I practised the answer while drying my hair this morning.

And how is she to know it's a lie? The weekend was my weekend off from looking after the children. I could have done whatever I liked. And just because doing whatever I liked actually consisted of sitting in my pants and watching *Friends* doesn't mean I have to tell anyone that.

Vanessa's poised expression stays in place as she looks down at her phone, obviously annoyed that I didn't give her the dull answer she was hoping for.

'That sounds nice,' she says coldly, hooking one leg over the other. 'So why are you here today? Are you not with the children?'

I feel myself flinch as she bats her hand across her face as though I'm a fly. I wish Fiona hadn't told everyone that I help with the children. I am employed by Hayes, just like the rest of them.

'I'm assisting Fiona with the charity ball,' I say, lifting my chin. 'I'm organising the auction.'

Vanessa raises her eyebrows. 'Oh,' she says, her voice sliding up at the end. 'I had heard that you were helping with that.'

I open my laptop, trying to hide my pink cheeks.

'Yes,' I say, 'I'm very excited.'

But as I look up, I notice Vanessa has already left and is now throwing her head back in a loud laugh with Sasha, another perfect human who works here.

Sasha is far nicer to me. She at least always offers me a coffee when she's making one, and we did once bond over who Hedgehog might be on *The Masked Singer*. Although she kept suggesting people I'd never heard of and thought I was joking when I said I thought it was Philip Schofield.

I flick open my notepad and start compiling a list, trying to ignore my disappointment at Vanessa's obvious dismissal of me once she'd found someone more interesting to talk to.

It's okay. That is the level of conversation I have with ninety per cent of the employees here. I'm fine with that. When I work here properly, I'll have a better relationship with them. I'll go for drinks with them on a Friday and then I'll laugh with them over a Monday-morning coffee about what a riot we all had. It's just because I don't see much of them at the moment. That's why I don't fit in.

'Morning.'

I look up at the sound of Diane's slow voice as she slumps into the chair next to me.

'Fiona said you wanted to speak to me,' she says, her head drooping into her shoulders as though her neck is made of tissue paper.

My shoulders sag.

My God. She's like Eeyore with a hangover.

'Hi, Diane,' I say, flashing her a grin as I click open a highlighter to colour-coordinate my list. 'Nice weekend?'

Pink for secondary work, orange for urgent, green for done. Lovely.

'Not really,' she says, picking up my fluffy pen and turning it between her fingers. 'I was ill all weekend.'

I try not to roll my eyes.

Of course she was.

'Really?' I say. 'Well I'm glad you're feeling better now.'

There is no point asking her what was wrong. I've made that mistake before. It's like opting in to a three-hour special of *Holby City*.

'So,' I say, smiling at her with such force that she might feel obliged to smile back, 'I think I have everything ready for the auction. We've got all the prizes, and I've completed the seating plans for the tables.'

'Where am I sitting?'

I pause.

Why does she want to know that?

'Oh,' I say, pulling open my ring binder, 'I'm not sure. I think you're at the back.'

'Oh. That's a shame.'

My fingers tighten around my pencil.

'Would you like to be at the front?' I say.

'No.'

39

'Fine.'

I flick through the folder and hand Diane a sheet.

'What would be really helpful is if you could type up the table settings for me, please.'

Diane takes the paper from me reluctantly and slouches back through the office. I watch her, my smile staying firmly in place as I catch Vanessa looking at me over her shoulder.

This event is going to be perfect, and I'll finally prove my place here. I'll be offered the full-time job in the office and I'll be able to slot in with everybody else with ease. Maybe I'll even buy myself a pair of Jimmy Choos.

*

I hold my thumb to the discoloured buzzer, number 18 blinking orange as the low rumble of sound echoes from the speaker.

'Hi, Dad, it's me,' I say, leaning my weight on the door as it clicks open. My hands tighten around the Tesco carrier bags and I start the climb to the fourth floor, my eyes on the brown carpet as I count the stairs. God knows how Dad deals with these stairs every day. I mean, he's only sixty-two, and he is in good shape. But still, this would be enough to make me move, and he's lived here for years. There isn't even a lift!

Dad moved to London a few years after he and Mum separated. He'd lived in Wales for the majority of his life, but he was the one who had an affair, so he had to leave. He said he didn't want to stay in Wales anyway, and once Rachel stopped talking to him and I moved to London, it seemed like the natural place for him to live.

I puff the air from my cheeks as I start on the next flight, my thighs burning. Have they added extra steps since I last came here? Or have I got more unfit? Christ, maybe buying the Super Bike was more important than I thought.

For years I tried to convince Rachel to forgive Dad. I know he did a terrible thing, but he is our dad, for goodness' sake, and people make mistakes. But she refused to listen. Although I don't know why I ever thought she could understand, considering she never makes mistakes. She's bloody perfect. It's her worst trait.

I rap my knuckles on the door, and within seconds it swings open and Dad appears in front of me, his arms wide in a *ta-dah!* motion and his mouth pulled into a beaming smile, as though he's just performed a magic trick and climbed out of a top hat. Even though he always answers the door this way, and I've seen him every other week for the past two years, I still laugh.

'Hi, Dad,' I say, as he pulls me into a hug, shaking me from side to side as though I'm a wet dog being quickly rubbed by a towel.

'Hello, my girl,' he says, finally letting me go. 'Come in, what have you bought me? Any cakes?'

I push my shoes off my feet as Dad clicks the door shut behind me. His flat is light, with pale walls and a shiny wooden floor, and it would be as neat as Rachel's teenage bedroom if it wasn't for the pet tornado that he insisted on buying when he moved, even though I warned him that a dog in a London flat would be a terrible idea.

As I open my mouth to reply, Betsy, the feistiest dachshund I've ever met, charges round the corner, yelping madly.

'Oh come on, Betsy,' Dad laughs, flicking the kettle on as I sink into one of his wooden chairs, 'you know Katy well enough by now. Oh,' he turns to face me, his bushy eyebrows raised, 'when is the big event? I haven't missed it, have I?'

I feel a spike of nerves as I start unpacking the shopping. 'No,' I say, 'it's Saturday.'

He nods, tapping his head as if to try and retain the information. 'Saturday,' he repeats. 'I'll try my best to remember.'

'I bought us some Battenberg,' I say, plucking the cake from the depths of a carrier bag and waving it at him. 'I couldn't find any bara brith.'

Dad cocks his head, pulling two mugs down from the cupboard. I feel a flicker of embarrassment as I look at them. They're both mugs I made (badly) as a teenager. I have tried to make him buy a new set, but he refuses. I once bought him a mug for Father's Day and he told me it was the worst present he'd ever received. He wasn't joking.

'Ah well,' he says, spooning sugar into his mug and dropping three heaped spoonfuls into mine. 'Your grandma loved cake, didn't she? I'm sure she wouldn't mind what sort. You spoken to your sister today?'

My stomach fizzles with guilt as he turns his face away from me. He always tries to laugh and smooth over the fact that Rachel hasn't spoken to him in almost ten years, but I know what it does to him really. Sometimes I think that if she could see him now, she would forgive him.

'Er, yeah,' I say, 'briefly.'

'Is she okay?'

'Yeah,' I say, unwrapping the Battenberg. 'Think so.'

'Good,' Dad says, dropping the tea bags into the bin. 'And your mum?'

I shrug as he puts the mugs down on the table. 'I've left her a voicemail,' I say. 'I don't know if I'll hear from her today.'

Dad picks up a barking Betsy and settles her on his lap. 'Ah well, it's a hard day for her, isn't it,' he says. 'I'm sure she'll appreciate the message. Any news on the ashes?'

I hold the steaming mug to my lips and try not to scowl. Mum has kept hold of Grandma's ashes since the funeral and refused to give them to Rachel for us to scatter.

'No,' I say. 'Rachel said she still won't let them go. I don't bother asking her.'

Dad catches my expression and smiles, sliding a knife into the thick marzipan of the cake and handing me a piece.

'Everyone grieves differently, love,' he says kindly.

He holds his piece of cake in the air and I grin, copying him.

'To Violet, your lovely grandma,' he says. 'May she be eating cake in heaven for all eternity.'

I smile, sadness prickling through me as Grandma's face creeps into my mind, the dull ache of missing her banging against my heart.

'To Grandma.'

CHAPTER FOUR

RACHEL

Steam billows against my face and sticks to my glasses as I open the oven door, the sweet smell of vanilla sponge filling the kitchen. I smile as I pull out another perfect cherry cake and place it on the cooling rack. Even though I know the recipe by heart, I check it one last time.

Step 7. Put the kettle on, gather the family and enjoy!!!

Grandma's neat handwriting flows across the page, each exclamation mark bigger and more exaggerated than the one before. I can hear her excited, upbeat voice calling us, finally breaking the cold silence that was cast after my mum had slammed the door for the final time that day. Every time Mum and Dad argued, Grandma would scoop the two of us up and try and pretend nothing had happened. A lot of the time this ended in us eating cake, until Katy got told off at the dentist so Grandma started making soups instead. They weren't nearly as exciting.

I catch sight of my reflection in the toaster and try not to flinch at my distorted face.

Katy and I are practically identical. We're both five foot six with dark hair and dark eyes. My face is round, just like our dad's, whereas Katy inherited our mum's pretty heart-shaped face. She also has a tiny point on the tip of her nose where it turns up, like a fairy-tale creature, whereas mine sits plainly on my face. We have fairly ordinary lips, but where Katy's teeth gleam in perfect formation after years of braces, my teeth crowd together, slightly crooked.

I turn my misshapen mug in my hands as I rest against the counter. Cherry cake is Katy's favourite, and she's always said that she'll never find another version as good as Grandma's. I've followed the recipe precisely.

The thought of Katy cues my stomach to tighten.

I think Grandma thought that once Dad had left and Mum had moved to France, the arguing would stop in our house. But it turned out that Katy and I were ready to step into their angry shoes. We went from being joined at the hip to disagreeing on almost everything – worst of all, our parents. Grandma made us apologise and forgive each other every time, her stern eyes boring into us until we mumbled an embarrassed apology.

But then, right before we were about to move to London, I told Katy that I didn't want to go with her. That time it didn't matter that Grandma forced us to apologise and forgive each other; I could tell neither of us meant it. I know Katy has never forgiven me for leaving her, just like I've never forgiven Dad for leaving us.

I smile as Bruno pads over to me, flopping down by my feet.

'It could just be me and you, boy,' I say, 'and the little one. Do you think we'll— AARGH!'

I scream as a face appears at the kitchen window. Bruno scrabbles to his feet and begins to howl, launching himself at the back door. I am about to drop to the floor and pretend to be dead when a hand appears next to the face and begins to wave.

It's Isaac.

I wrench the door open, 'You scared me half to death!' I cry, gripping the door frame as Bruno barrels past me, immediately forgetting that Isaac could have been a mass murderer.

God, that's the only thing about living in a tiny village: everyone just pops by whenever they feel like it.

'Sorry,' Isaac grins. 'Catch.' He throws a packet of Smarties at me and I catch them ungracefully.

'You need to stop buying me these or the baby will be born bright blue,' I say, cracking open the tube. 'Are you coming in?'

Isaac nicks a green one and pops it into his mouth. 'No thanks,' he says. 'I just wanted to say that you won't see much of me for the next week. I'm going to spend a lot of time at the farm to stay out of your way.'

'To stay out of my way, or to avoid seeing Katy?' I say, raising my eyebrows at him.

Isaac hasn't seen Katy since she left for London. I wasn't the only one she argued with.

'She'll be happy to see you,' I tell him, knowing full well that I have no idea what Katy feels about anything these days. 'She'll probably be happier to see you than to see me.' My thinly veiled attempt at a joke falls flat as my voice quivers.

Isaac shakes his head. 'You need to have some faith in her,' he says. 'This is Katy, she'll be fine.'

I crunch an orange Smartie viciously.

'Anyway, it's about time you put this rift behind you,' he adds.

A gust of wind shoots past him and I drag him into the kitchen and shut the door.

'It's freezing,' I mutter as he looks at me in surprise. 'And if you're so into mending rifts, then why are you planning on hiding from Katy on your farm?'

He tucks his hands into his pockets.

'I'm not hiding,' he says gruffly. 'I have a lot to do, and anyway, it's best we don't see each other. We don't get on.'

He can't even meet my eye, and before I can argue, he swings the door open and slips back outside.

'Have fun with Katy,' he says. 'I'll see you in a week.'

CHAPTER FIVE

KATY

My foot taps against the floor, the sharp heel of my pointed shoes clicking against the marble as I watch the waves of expensive-looking people swan through the hotel reception. All chuckling and tittering to each other, focusing intently on pronouncing their 't's and adding an extra 'r' into every word to make it very clear that they too are exceptionally posh.

My smile aches. I've been standing here in shock for what feels like hours.

I pretend to scribble something on my clipboard as a glamorous couple glide past me.

I can't believe how many people are here. I mean, I've seen the guest list. I know everybody arriving (not that a single person will know me), but I can't believe so many of them *came*.

I feel a bubble of excitement rise inside me. Fiona is going to be *thrilled*. If all these rich people bid at my auction, we're going to make a fortune!

I catch sight of myself in a mirrored pillar. I'm wearing a gold sequinned dress that fans out into a skirt just below my knees. My skin is sparkling under the glitz of a spray tan, and my freshly blow-dried hair is falling down my back like a water-fall. They say 'dress for the job you want', and so tonight, Matthew, I am successful events executive, professional woman and social butterfly. I look fantastic, and so I should, considering this dress cost almost an entire month's pay packet.

The best part is that I didn't even pay for it! I found this great website that lets you rent designer dresses for one night, for fifty quid! So I can glide around the hotel like an effortless socialite who wears designer dresses that cost hundreds of pounds like it's no big deal whatsoever.

I can't wait for Vanessa or Sasha to see me. They'll go, oh, your dress is nice. And I'll go, oh, this old thing? It's just a casual Gucci number. And then I'll do a big swoop off onto the dance floor, where Fiona will flamboyantly open a bottle of champagne with a novelty sword and crown me CEO of Hayes.

Or, you know, just give me my promotion at long bloody last.

'Hi, Katy.'

I look up to see Diane, who has slouched over to me.

I feel a bolt of fear as she slumps her weight against the pillar. The only problem with everything going so well is the fear that something is about to go catastrophically wrong.

'Hello, Diane,' I say, clicking my pen. 'Everything okay?'

Not that anything bad is going to happen, because I have organised this event to a T under Fiona's beady eye. Nothing has been ordered without her prior approval. Each flower has been picked, each item for auction has been screened; there is nothing I am not prepared for.

Apart from Diane, that is, and her compulsive love of disaster.

'Not really,' she sighs. 'I quite wanted a canapé, but they don't have any gluten-free options.'

I feel a jab of irritation.

'There are gluten-free options,' I say briskly, feeling my face flush. 'We have vegan, nut-free, gluten-free, dairy-free and vegetarian.'

I can't help but shoot her a look out of the corner of my eye.

Don't mess with me, Diane. I have thought of everything.

'Oh,' she says, 'well maybe you should tell the chef.'

My smile tightens. 'I have.'

I need to get rid of her. If she keeps standing next to me and whispering rubbish in my ear, then I might kill her. And that's a sure way to ruin any high-class ambience, Gucci dress or no Gucci dress.

'You're going on holiday tomorrow, aren't you?' she says, folding her arms. 'I wish I was going on holiday.'

I try not to scoff. A week in my tiny childhood village in Pembrokeshire is hardly a holiday.

'I'm going to stay with my sister,' I say. 'Well,' I add, 'she won't be there. I'm house-sitting for her.'

Diane shrugs and mumbles her catchphrase: 'That's a shame.'

'Not really,' I say brightly. 'We're not that close. Anyway,' I fix my smile back in place, 'why don't you go in? Remember, it's an auction, so people need to be taking an interest in what's on offer so they're ready to bid later. Make sure the drinks and canapés are circulating nicely. People are more generous if they're a bit drunk. I'll come through in ten.'

She blinks at me as if I've asked her to scrape the gum off the bottom of everybody's shoes.

Instinctively I reach forward and grab one of the champagne flutes sailing past me.

'Have a drink,' I instruct, handing it to her. 'It's important that we have a good time tonight, Diane. This is a fun evening. It's for charity.'

I stare into her watery eyes, trying to mask the stench of my desperation.

Please, Diane. Just chill out and have a good time. Please.

She takes the glass nervously and I feel myself relax slightly.

'Great.' I smile. 'You like champagne, right? Everybody likes champagne.'

She nods, and I feel as if I could punch the air.

Oh thank God for that.

I squeeze her shoulder and gently push her towards the door of the ballroom, taking in her outfit as she goes. She's wearing a floor-length black dress with long lacy sleeves. Her dark hair is pinned off her face and she is even wearing low heels.

If she didn't look so miserable all the time, she'd be a catch.

As she vanishes into the ballroom, my phone vibrates in my hand. Immediately a million panicked thoughts zip into my mind.

Email from Fiona? From Vanessa? Something has fallen through? The compère has called in sick? The charity items have been revoked?

Hi Katy,

Sorry to email you this evening, but are you around for a chat?

Would quite like to speak on the phone before you come up tomorrow. Need to talk to you about some bits.

Love you,

Rachel x

I reread the email, trying to control the annoyance spiking through me.

Am I around for a chat? She knows it's the charity ball tonight, the event I've been working on for the past six months. How can she think I could be around for a chat?

I stuff the phone back into my clutch bag and try to shake off my scowl.

Why does she want a chat now, when we never speak on the phone? She stopped answering my calls months ago, so I stopped bothering to call. On the rare occasion she's called me, I've been with the children and she always follows up the missed call with an email anyway. A part of me thinks she only calls to prove that she's done it; she'd probably hang up the second I answered.

Guilt squirms in my stomach and I squash it down.

She'll only want to talk about dog food or something.

I mean, I did grow up in that house too. I know how everything works. What could be so important that she feels the need to speak to me now, when I'm in the middle of the most important night of my entire year?

★

A smattering of light applause skims around the room as the guests chuckle lightly at the compère's latest joke and the weekend retreat to a five-star spa is sold to an elegant woman in an emerald dress. I lean against the bar, positioned at the back

52

of the room, and glug the dregs of my champagne, immediately swiping another one from the passing waiter. My third glass.

Or is it my fourth?

Anyway, it's enough to stop me from panicking about what a roaring success the event is and what could be about to go wrong. It's also enough to make me laugh quite loudly at every joke the compère tells, so I'm trying to zone him out. I don't want him to think he's being heckled.

'Going well, isn't it?'

I jump slightly as Fiona appears next to me at the bar. She's wearing a figure-hugging pillar-box-red dress, with slick black heels that flash a red sole when she walks. She takes a glass of champagne from a passing waiter and leans next to me. I can't stop the grin creeping onto my face. I don't bother trying to look cool in front of Fiona. She's seen me with emergency tissues stuffed up my sleeves.

'Yeah!' I say, keeping my voice low as the compère launches into his next joke. 'I think it's going brilliantly. Everybody seems to be having a great time.'

I want to add what a brilliant team we make and lightly joke about how we should plan all the events at Hayes together, but I don't. Perhaps I'll mention it after the next school run; at that point in the morning she's usually ready to agree with anything I say.

She massages her forehead with her free hand and shuts her eyes. For a second, the high-powered-businesswoman facade slips and I see the real Fiona, sinking against the bar and being swamped by the thousands of errands buzzing around her like small flies.

Tristan was supposed to be looking after the children this

evening, but he called last minute to say that he couldn't get back from Manchester. Apparently he was there on a business weekend, or so Fiona said. I don't tend to ask her too many questions.

'Are you okay?' I say, edging closer.

She pulls her head out of her hand and smiles, giving a large fake sigh.

'Oh yes,' she says. 'Just thinking about how cross my mother will be for dumping the children at hers with practically zero notice, though I'm sure it's nothing a spa gift card can't fix.'

She holds her champagne glass to her lips and I smile weakly.

'It really is a wonderful evening, isn't it?' she adds, as she surveys the swarm of glamorous people, all laughing and chinking their glasses with one another. 'You've done very well.'

I take another champagne flute from the bar and fight the urge to neck it in one.

This is brilliant! The fantasy I've had playing in my mind for the past six months is coming true! Fiona must be thinking about how well I'd fit in at the office. Finally, after all this time and late nights and—

'It's a shame about the auction, though.'

I gulp my champagne.

What?

'A shame?' I repeat. 'What do you mean?'

My eyes fly frantically over the sea of guests. Every item has gone so far! What is she talking about?

She swirls her drink and shrugs. 'Well,' she says, 'they're just not bidding very much, are they?'

I stare at her.

Aren't they? That horrible old painting that looked like it was commissioned by a serial killer went for almost two thousand pounds!

She leans on a stool and pulls out her phone.

'I mean,' she says, 'it is for charity after all. Maybe they're just not feeling it.'

I feel a cold rush in the pit of my stomach. I tip the champagne into my mouth and place the empty glass on the bar.

'I'll be right back,' I mutter, before sweeping through the room.

I will not have my promotion sabotaged by some tight-fisted aristocrats! I'm sure they all have buckets of money. They'd probably clean their toilet with my Gucci dress. They just need a little help, that's all.

I stop behind a pillar and check the time.

Right. It's almost eleven. There's one more item to bid for. I can do this. I just—

'Katy?'

Diane pops up next to me, her wide eyes blinking up at me desperately. I feel an instant surge of irritation.

Oh for God's sake, what? What *now*?

'Yup?' I say, glancing over her shoulder as the compère congratulates the winners of a mini break to Prague for two. As he starts to introduce the final item, I grab a wooden paddle from the nearest table, tucking it behind my back.

'I think there's an issue,' Diane says, stepping closer.

'Right?'

Is there really an issue? Or is Diane just upset because someone accidentally trod on her foot?

'So!' the compère calls, leaning into the microphone. 'We're finishing off the auction with a fun prize, great for a night out with friends.'

I glance back at Diane and feel myself double-take as I notice that she's swaying, and one of her eyes is half shut.

A bolt of fear shoots through me.

Oh God, Diane doesn't drink. She once told me that she got drunk at university and was barred from the student union and hasn't drunk since. I thought she was joking! Oh God, what have I done?

I shut my eyes and say a silent prayer.

Please let her have been joking. Or perhaps the reason she got barred was because she was mistaken for another girl, or requested her favourite song of all time, 'My Way', and totally spoilt the mood like she did at last year's Christmas party.

'Right then,' the compère calls, 'we're going to start the bidding with a very reasonable one hundred pounds. Do I have one hundred?'

A jolt of electricity shoots through me as I ram my paddle into the air and then duck back behind the pillar.

'Ah!' he cries. 'I saw one hundred; do we have one fifty?'

Come on, somebody else bid. Come *on*.

'We have one fifty!'

Yes!

I'll just bid a couple of times to get the ball rolling. Just once or twice.

I turn back to Diane, and notice that she has begun to slide down the pillar. I grab her shoulders and haul her back up.

Oh God.

'Diane,' I say quickly, 'how much have you had to drink?'

What have I done to her? Please let her be a happy drunk, at least. Or a quiet one who just wants a little sleep. I could find her a nice broom cupboard to have a nap in until everybody goes home. Nobody would ever have to know.

She pulls her wandering eyes up and to my alarm starts to glare at me.

'I don't know,' she slurs. 'Whatever. Loads. I want another one. *Waiter!*' She swings her body around the pillar and throws her arm in the air. Her voice echoes around the room, and to my horror, the compère pauses mid sentence.

I yank Diane round to face me and grip her shoulders.

'Listen, Diane,' I mutter, 'just give me five minutes for the auction to finish, okay? Then I'll find you a nice taxi.'

'I don't want a taxi!' she barks. I flinch as the thick stench of alcohol hits me in the face.

Wow. She's been drinking more than champagne.

'I want to get off with one of these businessmen.' She shoves me as she tries to get past.

'Right,' I say quickly, pushing her back against the pillar, 'whatever you want, okay? Just wait one minute.'

I can deal with Diane after I've finished the auction. She is not costing me my promotion.

'Let's get this going!' the compère calls. 'Do we have two hundred?'

I launch my paddle in front of the pillar and then jump back behind it. I almost want to laugh. It's working!

'Okay, we have two hundred!' he calls. 'Oh, and there's two fifty! Can we get this up to three hundred?'

I look back at Diane, who is glugging down a glass of champagne like it's water. My arm jerks my paddle back into the air.

Well, one more glass won't hurt.

'Bleurgh!' She spits loudly. 'Champagne is disgusting!'

I shoot her a look. That champagne cost two hundred pounds a bottle; it is not disgusting.

'Can we get it to three fifty?' The compère laughs. 'Three hundred and fifty pounds, anyone?'

I grip Diane's arm as she attempts to follow a waiter skimming through the room.

'Anyone for three fifty?'

Come on, someone else bid so this auction can bloody end and I can shove Diane in a taxi. With or without a businessman, I don't care.

'Sold for three hundred and fifty pounds!' The compère bangs his hammer down. 'And that is the end of the auction, folks.'

I feel a wave of relief as I turn back to Diane. I need to get her out of here before she has a chance to pounce on one of these unassuming, married businessmen.

'Right,' I say, locking eyes with her. 'We're just going to walk together into reception. You can hold onto my arm and—'

'Katy!'

I turn on the spot, smile in place, as Vanessa and Sasha glide over to me, looking like fresh-out-of-the-packet Barbie dolls. They're both holding champagne flutes, and their perfect noses are turned up suspiciously, desperate to sniff out a flaw they can comment on.

Luckily for them, Diane has started singing the National Anthem.

Urgh. Why do they have to see me like this? I wanted us to chat at the bar whilst clinking our champagne glasses so they could marvel at my lovely dress and discuss going shopping together.

'Hi, girls,' I say, trying to keep my voice aloof while Diane latches onto my arm like a baby koala.

'I want to go to the bar,' she whines in my ear. 'I want a drink. I'm thirsty.'

I shake her off. 'In a second,' I hiss.

'Or a cig,' she persists. 'Do you have a cig?'

Since when does Diane smoke?

'Great event,' Sasha says as they reach us. 'Everybody seems to be having a good time.'

I meet her eyes as she smiles at me, feeling a slight relief as Diane finally lets go of my arm.

'Thank you,' I say. 'Yes, it seems to be going well.'

'And you won something!' Vanessa giggles, nudging me with her champagne flute. 'Fancy bidding at your own auction.'

Shit, I did win, didn't I? Where am I going to find three hundred and fifty pounds?

She flicks her eyes over to Sasha and they both laugh. I feel my face flush.

'Yes, well, I just thought the prize sounded fun,' I say, trying to squash their giggles, 'and it's all for charity, isn't it? So just doing my part.'

I look around and suddenly realise that Diane has vanished. For God's sake, where has she gone?

'Well, we should all go!' Vanessa says. 'A work night out on you for charity sounds great.'

She raises her champagne glass to me and I shoot her a limp smile, desperately trying to spot Diane.

'Yeah,' I mutter, 'sure.'

Where is she? Where *is* she?

My eyes scan the room, latching on to any businessman to check Diane isn't trying to lick their ears.

'Also, Katy,' Sasha says, leaning in as if she's about to tell me a juicy secret, 'I love your dress. It's Gucci, right?'

For a moment I forget almost entirely about my mad hunt for Diane, and shoot Sasha a smug smile.

'Yes!' I cry, unable to hide my giant grin. 'Isn't it great?'

Vanessa looks at Sasha and then back at me, her eyebrows raised.

'Really?' she says, not bothering to suppress her shock. 'Gucci?'

I go back to searching the room. 'Yeah,' I say, 'just thought I'd—'

Oh my God, she's there. I feel my stomach turn over as I spot Diane, leaning against the bar smoking.

What is she doing?

'Anyway,' I say, my voice strained, 'I'll catch up with you guys in a bit.'

I'm going to kill her.

I need to get to her *now*.

I storm across the bar, trying to keep my smile fixed as I slip past the smattering of socialites. As I reach Diane, she takes an almighty suck on the cigarette and glares at me defiantly, like a toddler about to lose their dummy. I lurch forward to grab the cigarette from her hand, but she sticks it in her mouth again and turns her back on me.

Oh my God, am I going to have to wrestle her?

I glance over my shoulder. Thankfully Fiona is surrounded by people and clinking her champagne glass with a man wearing an enormous hat.

'Diane,' I hiss, trying to grab her arm as unobtrusively as

possible. 'Diane, you can't smoke in here. You need to put that out!'

I notice another swirl of smoke float from her mouth and wrench her round to face me. She pulls the cigarette from her lips and launches her arm into the air.

'No!' she snaps. 'You can't tell me what to do. I'm allowed to smoke!'

I feel a surge of anger.

'Not inside!' I cry. 'Look, just put it out and I'll get you another one to smoke outside.'

She sticks it back in her mouth and takes another furious drag. I take my chance and clamp my hands onto hers, trying to prise the limp cigarette from her mouth.

'Diane!' I grunt, as she swivels around in an attempt to knock me off balance. 'Diane, please, you can't smoke inside! You need to put it out, you need—'

But suddenly the screeching sound of the fire alarm reverberates around the room and an almighty spritz of water fans down from the ceiling, showering the guests. Their high-pitched squeals join the fire alarm and I yank the cigarette furiously from Diane and stamp it on the floor. She blinks back at me, her eyes finally looking sorrowful, but I quickly work out that it isn't because of what's just happened.

It's because she's about to throw up all over my designer dress.

CHAPTER SIX

RACHEL

I flop onto my bed, feeling a small tingle of warmth as the fresh waffle duvet attempts to swallow me, and for a minute it's as if I'm about to fall into Wonderland. I take a deep breath, pushing the air into my lungs as I try and ignore the gentle ticking from the wall clock hanging over my head.

I don't need to look at the clock; I know what time it is. I've felt unnaturally in tune with the time all day. I've tried my best to ignore it. I've changed all the bedding, I pottered about in the garden, and I even took Bruno on an extra-long walk along the cliffs at the end of the village, which almost gave me a heart attack when he charged after a bird and tried to throw himself off the edge. All day, the slow ticking of the clock has clouded my brain like a faint mist, because I know that at six o'clock, Katy will arrive. An hour before that, I need to send the email telling her the conference has been cancelled and I'll be here after all. Two hours after that, we'll be spending more time together than we have done in three years, and I will have forced her into it. I'm not even giving her the choice.

Nausea rolls through my body and I clamp my eyes shut.

I don't know if I can do this.

I rest my hand on my bump as the baby wriggles around as though it can sense my nerves.

I was almost grateful that Katy didn't email me back last night. In a mad state of loneliness I suddenly felt the need to call her and tell her everything in one go. This urge vanished as soon as the email had sent, God knows what I would have said to her if she had called me. Some lie about Bruno or something.

She'll be so angry that I lied to her about needing her to house-sit and tricked her into coming home. There's a high chance that she won't even stay the night. She'll be here long enough to hear my explanation and slowly unpick each of my lies: Danny, the baby, my life. And that's when I lose the ability to predict what she'll do or say next. I don't know her well enough any more.

I try and conjure up the happy fantasy where Katy is hugging me, delighted. But although she is there, her eyes are blank and withdrawn, and somehow I can't hear her voice in my mind.

I feel panic shoot through me and snap my eyes open.

The clock hands click into a new position and I look back at the ceiling.

It's ten to five.

I can't keep living this fantasy. I need to know what the real Katy will do. I need to find out. I'm running out of time.

I push myself to sitting, scrunching up my face as a head rush swims in front of my eyes. I grab my laptop and open the lid, bringing the prepared email back onto the screen.

My heart quickens as I read it again. My fingers curl around the duvet and I try to keep myself calm.

As terrifying as it is to picture being alone, the reality of it is much worse. If I'm right, and I've already done too much damage for Katy to forgive me, then I won't have anyone else. My husband has gone, Mum has a new family, I drove Dad away and Grandma died. Katy is all I have left, and even though the door is barely open, if she slams it shut, I don't know how I'll survive.

Before I realise what I'm doing, my hand closes the laptop. I jump up and open the wardrobe, dragging out a suitcase and hurriedly throwing clothes into it. Once it's full, I wrench the zip shut and ease myself back to standing. With the bulging suitcase in my hand, I catch sight of myself in the mirror. My ankles are swollen, my hair is scrunched above my head and my face is red and blotchy. My stomach, which looks bigger than ever, sticks out like a beach ball, screaming to be noticed. I take a moment to look at myself, my head throbbing as a new idea spins through my mind like silk. Before I can pull the plan apart, I step out of sight of the mirror and race down the stairs.

I don't know how Katy will react, but I'm not ready to find out. I need more time.

CHAPTER SEVEN

KATY

Okay, so it was bad.

I can't really escape that. There is little point trying to convince myself that it wasn't actually that bad and perhaps I'm dramatising things because I'm so hung-over I feel as though a rat has died in my mouth and the juices of its rotting carcass have stained my insides for all eternity. It was just very, very bad.

The train jolts over a bump and my clammy hands clench onto my Evian water bottle.

You know when you're worried about something and your brain does that fun trick of listing every possible thing that could go wrong? And then you go, 'Oh, you're just being silly! That will never happen! You're worrying about nothing!'

Well, what happens if the thing that actually happened was so bad that it didn't even make it onto the list? I didn't fall off the stage after announcing the bar would be closing. I didn't accidentally sneeze into the open mouth of a very important investor. I didn't even get the dates mixed up and arrive at the venue to find that I had missed the entire thing.

The man next to me pushes his shoulders back and I fight the urge to hiss at him as his elbow knocks mine.

Instead, I wrestled a cigarette from my colleague who has a 'weak ribcage' and had to go to A&E because she suspected I'd cracked one of her ribs (which I'm sure I'm not capable of, but even if she's fine, it's enough to start a rumour that I'm an absolute brute).

The fire alarm sent a shower of water over all the guests, which might as well have been acid by the way everybody reacted, and all the designer outfits were ruined, including mine, which I now have to pay for. God only knows how much that bloody dress will cost me. Obviously I have nothing of value to sell to pay for it, and since I single-handedly flushed my promotion down the toilet, I'll have no choice but to sell one of my stupid kidneys.

The staff had to treat the fire alarm as a real emergency and insisted on evacuating the entire hotel. I begged them to just turn it off and put it down as a blip. I even offered them champagne for their silence (*not* a bribe, as the manager cruelly suggested, but a kind gesture. Who doesn't love champagne?) But twenty minutes later, our glamorous party were out on the King's Road being splattered by sheets of rain and wincing at the crowds of drunken teenagers staggering about. Hardly the high-class ambience I was hoping for.

Oh! And then Diane's ambulance arrived.

Needless to say, Fiona didn't offer me the job in the office with a large bottle of Dom Perignon. She barely looked at me until an hour later, when we were the last two left on the street. Then she turned to me and said:

'And now you're off for a week, aren't you?'

Before we climbed into an Uber and travelled home in silence.

I take a dubious sip of my water.

I barely slept last night. When I got back to the cabin, I ordered a Chinese, ate it in bed and slept in my stupid soggy Gucci dress. I was so defeated I didn't even care when I spilt soy sauce down the front. I woke up this morning feeling as if my organs were sitting on a bed of pins, and every breath I took pierced my insides a little. The torrential fear of a hangover is multiplied when the things you were worried about actually happened, and I have nobody to reassure me that it wasn't that bad. Who was I going to tell? I could hardly call Rachel when she thinks I've already been promoted.

I threw whatever I could find into my suitcase and dragged it along the grey street until I got to the Tube station. After chugging along on perhaps the most rickety Tube I have ever experienced, I am now safely cushioned in the warm corner seat of a train on the way to Wales. I've tried sleeping, but every time I shut my eyes, I feel as if I'm falling down a rabbit hole. So I'm staring out of the window instead, watching the world turn slowly into colour as we roll into the countryside.

'Any snacks or drinks?'

I look up and see a kind woman at the end of the carriage chatting to passengers and handing out Kit Kats. For some reason, this makes my eyes swell and for a horrible moment I feel as though I could burst into tears.

Look at her. Look at how clean and put-together she is. I bet she didn't get disgustingly drunk last night and wake up this morning with a half-eaten spring roll lodged in her cleavage. Why can't I be more like Train Lady? What's wrong with me?

I think I'd like to be Train Lady.

'Anything from the trolley?'

I feel myself jump slightly as she reaches me, as if she can read my thoughts and is suddenly aware of what an enormous creep I am. My stomach twitches as I look at the snacks. I am starving. The time shines at me from my phone; it's just gone five. No wonder I'm hungry. I've barely eaten today.

'Yes please,' I say, digging my hands into my pockets to try and find my bank card. 'Can I please have a bacon sandwich and a Crunchie?'

'Sure, would you like any sauce?'

'Ketchup, please.'

As I pull my card out of the depths of my pocket, trying not to fling an old tissue across the carriage, my phone vibrates loudly. I glance down at the flashing screen and see Rachel's name.

Why is she emailing me now? Maybe she's checking I'm actually on the train and that I haven't forgotten. Honestly, I've never known anyone so obsessed with sticking to a plan.

I mean, yes, I was going to cancel two weeks ago with some elaborate fake business conference, but like the absolute moron I am, I forgot, and there is no way I'd cancel on her this late. She'd march up to London and drag me to Wales herself.

I pick my phone up and open the email. As I read it, I feel as if I'm about to throw up.

Hi Katy,

Sorry, last min change of plans. Conference has been moved to London, so I'm going to stay in your flat. Your spare key is still under that fake rock I sent you, right?

Let me know you get to the house okay.
Love you, Rachel

I glare at the phone, my mouth hanging open.

What? She's going to *what*?

She can't just turn up at my place! What is she thinking?

I scrabble at my phone to try and call her, just as a large tunnel swallows my last bar of signal.

Rachel thinks I live in a flat! Which I do, sort of, but at the bottom of my boss's garden, something I've never mentioned to her. Why would I? How was I to know that she would one day decide to trick me into leaving my home so that she could move in for a week?

I type a manic text to Fiona trying to explain that my sister is planning to show up and move into the cabin for the foreseeable future and to please not call the police. As soon as it sends, I jab a frenzied response to Rachel and take a giant bite of my bacon sandwich.

I can't let Rachel stay in my cabin, but how the hell can I stop her?

★

My eyes glue themselves shut as another wave of sickness rolls across my body. I've given up trying to determine whether it's hangover sickness, hangover fear, anxiety over possibly losing my job, or anxiety over my highly strung, perfect twin sister arriving at my hellhole of a home and realising that not only am I not actually a real adult like I've been pretending, I may not even be a real human being. Although I think she'll only realise that if she finds the egg-fried rice under my pillow.

The taxi lurches over another bump and I clamp my jaw as the urge to vomit tickles the back of my throat.

'What number did you say you were?'

My stomach turns over as I feel the car slow down. My eyes pull themselves open and I look around. I haven't been back in two years. Me and Rachel spend every Boxing Day nibbling through turkey sandwiches at our aunt's house, when Mum can be bothered to come back from France, and that's the only time we see each other. Not that I saw her this year, she said that she was spending Christmas with Danny and Mum said she'd like to spend the holidays in France, so I spent it with Dad. We watched old rugby highlights and ate roast lamb, which was great.

The place is still filled with fat cottages sitting in wild, lively gardens that pop with colour and almost wave for your attention. The village pub, the Sailor's Ship, stands proudly at the end of the main street, by the cliff that overlooks the frothy seafront. As my eyes scan the village, they eventually fall on my childhood home, which looks exactly the same as it always did. I feel a pang in my chest as I take in the pebble-grey door, the duck-egg-blue garden fence, and finally my bedroom window. My old bedroom window.

A chill runs up my spine and my grip tightens on my seat belt as a thought shoots through me.

I don't want to be here.

I push it out of my mind and take a deep breath.

I haven't been back since Grandma died. I didn't want to; I didn't want to see my childhood home without my family sitting inside it, laughing and having fun. I never wanted to be in that house with only Rachel and the simmering reminder that the big, warm family we were once a part of doesn't exist any more. And the only thread of family I've managed to hang onto, Rachel barely acknowledges.

After she turned her back on Dad, it was never the same. I never understood how she could cut him out when we had so little family left. We could have kept a piece of our childhood alive, but she refused.

I don't want to be here.

A thick wind shakes through the hedge surrounding the cottage, like it's beckoning me inside.

Rachel has never left this house. As soon as our parents left, she invited Danny to move in, and that was that.

'It's just here,' I say, my voice hoarse.

The taxi driver clicks off the engine and hops out.

The sea air hits the back of my throat as I open my door, and for a second I feel as if it might steal my hangover away. The fresh taste of salt and the light smell of wet grass fills my senses, and I feel as though I've stepped into another dimension. I haven't had this feeling in years.

But as soon as it comes, my memory ticks into life and brings the expected next sounds and smell to my mind. The smell of the kitchen, the smell of fresh bread. The sound of Grandma laughing and the prickling feeling of peeling off damp socks and warming my feet by the fire. The feeling of her soft, pillowy arms pulling me into her chest and her familiar lavender scent.

I force myself back into the present, my throat tight as the memories float above me, teasing me to reach forward and believe it's all still real.

I don't want to be here. God, I really don't want to be here.

The driver drops my suitcase next to me and I glance down at it dubiously.

Eurgh. I'm sure there is absolutely nothing useful in there. I bet I didn't even pack any clean pants.

'Thank you,' I mumble, fishing around in my pockets for cash and handing him a ten-pound note.

He gives me a thumbs-up out of the window and pulls the car away. I rub my forehead with my sleeve and drag my suitcase towards the house. My head continues to throb, and I feel my ponytail droop with every step, like a disappointed horse's tail.

At least I can rely on Rachel's house to be clean and warm. I can crawl into her fresh sheets and maybe, just maybe, her fabric softener and freshly lit candles will soothe my hangover away and I'll wake up a new woman.

Wouldn't it be great if I woke up as Rachel? I'd have a flat stomach, perfectly conditioned hair and teeth free of red wine stains. I'd probably cartwheel out of bed and spend the entire day happily tending to my lovely bush (not a euphemism) until dinner time – or, as I'd suddenly call it, *supper* – where I'd eat one slice of vegetable pie with a glass of still water because that is all I need to satisfy my lovely, perfect life.

I feel another flurry of worry as I picture Rachel arriving at the cabin and realising I live in a back garden like a slightly important gnome. I did compose a mad email confessing all my secrets, saying how I didn't actually have a high-flying job in events after all and actually spent eighty per cent of my week looking after my boss's children. Oh yes, and I live in her garden.

But I couldn't send it. So instead I'm choosing to believe a new fantasy where she doesn't even notice. She thinks I just live in a nice little field and Fiona and the children disappear for a week and they never even cross paths.

I did think about immediately getting on a train back to London and shoehorning Rachel out of Chiswick before she could even reach the cabin. But by the time she landed her lovely bombshell, the last train to London was chugging through Gloucester and the next train I could catch wasn't until tomorrow morning. So I'll just have to wait this one out.

I reach the front door and pull my phone out of my pocket. Right. Where did Rachel say she was leaving the key?

I finally find the email where I asked her where she kept her spare key, and feel a small stab of panic as I realise she didn't answer the question.

She never told me? She's been pestering me about this trip for months. She had the time to send me a 'selection of recipes that Bruno enjoys', but it didn't cross her mind to tell me where she kept her spare key?

I jab her name into my phone and hold it to my ear, my heart thumping in time with my head, which is starting to feel as if it might explode.

Rachel's automated message kicks in, and I fight the urge to throw my head back and scream.

I shove the phone back into my pocket and step towards the living room window.

God, I really don't want to have to break in, but maybe Rachel left a window open?

I mean, I know I'm not the same size as I was ten years ago, but I definitely climbed through the odd window as a teenager. It can't be that hard, surely, and I—

THWACK!

I almost collapse in shock as a large dog throws himself at the window with a bang. His paws scrabble at the glass, then he slides back down out of sight.

'*Jesus*,' I manage.

He leaps back up at the window again, loud barks echoing through the house like a battle cry. I try and flash him a smile, and to my relief, I notice his tail wagging.

Okay, good. He doesn't look like he wants to eat me.

Bloody dog.

'This is all your fault,' I mutter under my breath. 'You're the reason I'm stuck here and Rachel is at the cabin. This whole disaster would never have happened if it wasn't for you.'

Bruno leaps up again, the force of his wagging tail causing his whole body to ripple like a belly dancer.

Actually, this is great. Maybe he can help me get inside. What's that film where the dog is actually super intelligent and helps the humans? Lassie? Tarzan?

Oh no, Tarzan is about monkeys, isn't it? Well, they're still animals. It must be partly based on fact.

I fix my eyes on Bruno determinedly.

'Right,' I say, 'we both want the same thing, mate. I want to get inside the house and you probably want some food or, like . . . a piss. So I need to get in.'

At this, he throws his head back and begins to howl.

Okay, great. I'll take that to mean he's on board.

I feel a zap of adrenaline.

Christ, if this works, I'm going on *Britain's Got Talent*. Screw Fiona. I could be a star!

I mean, I'm not actually expecting him to pad over to the

front door and let me in, but if he can just show me an open window or a loose door frame, that would be great.

'So how do I get in?' I say, raising the pitch of my voice. 'Where's the key? Where's the key, boy?'

I slap my legs with my hands and Bruno launches himself back at the window.

I wince as it rattles.

Actually, if he breaks the glass, that would be amazing. I can climb through the window and Rachel won't even be able to blame it on me. She'd never get mad at her beloved dog. It would be the perfect crime!

'Come on, boy!' I say loudly, grinning at him like a lunatic. 'Show me where the key is! Let me in the house!'

At this, he shoots out of the living room and I feel a wave of excitement.

Of course, the back door! Why didn't I think of that? It will be much easier to get in the back. Rachel might even have left it open!

I skirt round the side of the house, dragging my suitcase behind me.

I almost want to laugh as I drop the case and grab hold of the door handle. I pull at it, and the door shakes back at me stubbornly.

Okay, well maybe it was a bit naïve to assume Rachel would leave the back door open. This is the woman who was so shocked at me leaving my spare key under the mat that she sent me a fake rock and made me promise I'd keep it there.

I glance around the garden dubiously, looking at the hundreds of pebbles.

Please don't let the key be hidden in one of those. I don't

want to spend the next week on my hands and knees surveying rocks like a crazed geologist.

I drop my hands back to my sides as Bruno reappears at the door, bouncing up and down with pride. My face pings back into the big fake smile.

'Hi, Bruno,' I say. 'How do I get in? Where did Rachel leave the key? Where did she leave it, boy?'

He stops bouncing and stares at me. I feel my heart turn over as I stare into his big goofy eyes, and for an exhilarating moment I feel as though he's understood me. Then all of a sudden, he shoots off again and disappears.

Next minute, I hear a loud bark above me, and feel as if I could cry with happiness as I spot his head sticking out of the window of the upstairs bathroom.

Oh my God, he's actually done it.

'Bruno!' I cry. 'Oh my God, you are so clever!'

Why did I ever want a cat when dogs can do *this*? The only trick my cat used to do was vomit on my carpet and bring me dead birds.

Right, now all I need to do is get through that window.

I look back up at Bruno, shielding my eyes from the sun as I start a mini pep talk.

Okay, Katy. You can do this. If you can climb through this window then nobody can call you a failure. It doesn't matter what has happened over the past few days. It doesn't even matter that Rachel will probably find your chicken chow mein from last night and work out that you've been lying for the past year about being a vegan. If you do this, nobody can deny that you are a proper functioning adult.

I grab Rachel's two bins and push them together, then step back to survey them.

Okay, the window isn't that high, and I'm already five foot six. Once I've climbed on the bins I should be able to pull myself through the window. I did a pull-up at the gym last month and it wasn't even that hard. I can totally do this.

Also, don't people get a super zap of strength in times of need?

I swing my leg up and plant my trainer on top of one of the bin lids. Immediately I want to do a little cheer.

Okay, that part went very well.

I lean forward and grab hold of the bin, and then, before I can talk myself out of it, swing my other foot onto the second bin. The bins wobble wildly and I will myself not to let go.

Stay calm, Katy! You've got this. It's all about your core! All you need to do now is get yourself to standing. You've done the hardest part. You've—

'Katy?'

My head whips round in shock as I hear a male voice. The sudden movement makes the bins skid apart, and before I know it, my head has smacked against the floor.

As the hot pain bleeds through me, my brain fires one more furious thought.

What the fuck is Isaac doing here?

★

A heavy throbbing echoes around my head as I will myself to stay perfectly still, like a child pretending to be asleep, while I try and work out the best way to deal with this situation.

Right. So about ten seconds ago, I did the splits off two bins because my ex-boyfriend, who I haven't seen in three years and who is supposed to be living it up in Cardiff, appeared unannounced and uninvited. Which has left me strewn across the garden like a half-eaten chicken carcass with my poor, humiliated face pressed into the mud like an old tissue.

My mind spins with questions as I try to stay focused on the situation. I would be lying if I hadn't occasionally thought about the moment I might see Isaac again. I imagined I might be strolling round Tesco, wearing my ripped skinny jeans and heels in a 'casual sexy shopper' kind of way. I'd bump into him in the fruit and veg aisle, my basket overflowing with fresh vegetables for that tart I'm making, and he is shocked at how fantastic I look. I am elegant and demure (naturally) and pretend that this is what I always wear for my weekly shop, considering I am a high-flying events manager in the city. He asks if we could go for a drink and I say I need to check my schedule, before handing him a business card and slinking into the baking aisle. Because yes, dear reader, I am also making my own pastry.

Instead, I'm lying face first in possible dog poo wearing my worst hangover clothes with enough grease in my hair to cook a vat of chips.

I feel him kneel down to my level and try to ignore his familiar earthy scent. He must still wear the same aftershave.

What do I do? Pretend to be passed out? At least then he might get help and I can make a break for it. Although what if he then files a missing person report and I have to go on the run?

I need to do something. If I keep lying completely still, he might think I'm dead and try to resuscitate me, and I can't have the first time Isaac touches my breasts in three years being now. When I'm not wearing a bra and my boobs are flopped in my armpits like old plums.

I feel a shadow creep over my face and my heart jolts as I realise he must be leaning over me. I can feel his breath on my face.

Oh God, he's not about to *kiss* me, is he? Not like this! I haven't even brushed my teeth!

Okay, right. I'm going to open my eyes. I need to pretend I passed out briefly and now I'm fine. No, not completely fine, I need to be a bit delirious to distract him from the fact that I look like an old troll.

Maybe I can do it in a sexy Sleeping Beauty way.

Slowly I pull my eyes open and move my lips into a subtle pout. As I focus, I see Isaac leaning over me. His curly hair is flopped forward, and I notice a smear of mud on his cheek. His green eyes meet mine and I involuntarily jump as if I've been caught in the act.

'Katy,' he says, moving his hand to my face, 'are you okay? Can you hear me?'

I try not to snort. Someone has clearly been watching *Casualty*. You don't lose your hearing from falling off a bin. The only thing I've lost is my dignity, which thankfully was already in short supply.

'Yeah,' I say, trying to keep my voice weak and slightly unwell, like the voice you put on when you're calling in sick because you stayed up late watching *RuPaul's Drag Race* and can't be bothered to go to work.

Not that I've ever done that.

I see him smile down at me, and try and reposition myself; at the very least, I need to slightly close my legs.

'Are you okay?' he says again. 'I think you hit your head. Do you know who I am?'

I open my mouth to respond, but then clamp it quickly shut. I cannot chirp Isaac's name straight away like he's the man of my dreams. No way.

'I'm not sure,' I say feebly. 'Is it you, Jonathan? Or . . . Gerard?'

Ha! Look at me and all my possible men. I mean, yes, perhaps Gerard wasn't the best choice of names, but who cares?

The kind smile on Isaac's face vanishes and he moves his hand away from my face.

'No,' he says, 'it's Isaac. Your old neighbour.'

I feel myself glare at him.

Old neighbour? How about 'ex-boyfriend of four years'?

'Come on.' He springs to his feet and holds out a hand towards me. 'I think you're fine. Up you get.'

I feel a stab of humiliation as he pulls me unceremoniously upright. My head thumps painfully as I steady myself, and I catch sight of my reflection in the kitchen window. Mud has flattened my hair to my head like wallpaper paste, and my cheeks are flaring.

I'm not sure I've ever looked worse.

Isaac glances back at me. 'You all right?'

I lift my chin. 'Yes,' I lie, 'I'm fine, thank you.'

He nods curtly, and is turning to walk away when I hear myself shout after him.

'Wait! Sorry, do you know where Rachel keeps her spare key? She didn't tell me. I was trying to climb through the window when you . . . er . . . appeared.'

He looks up at the window, his eyebrows raised.

'You were going to try and climb through that window?' he says, as though I've suggested coming down the chimney like Father Christmas.

'I've done it before!' I say defiantly. 'I used to do it all the time.'

He crosses his arms. 'When?'

'All the time.'

He shrugs. 'Okay,' he says, 'fine. Well, have you knocked? Rachel might be asleep.'

If Rachel was in the house, does he really think I wouldn't have thought to knock on the door?

'She's not here,' I say. 'She's gone to stay in London. In my flat.'

I notice a shadow pass over his face.

'She's not here?' he repeats. 'Are you sure?'

I fight the urge to throw my shoe at him.

'Of course I'm sure!' I cry, slapping my hands against my sides. 'If she was, I'd be inside having a cup of tea, not climbing on bins and—'

I break off before I can add 'talking to you'.

'Right,' Isaac says, looking around. 'Well, I have a spare key. I'll go get it.'

I gape at him as he starts walking down the side of the house.

'You have a spare key?' I echo. 'Why?'

Why does my ex-boyfriend have a key to my sister's house?

Isaac looks back at me, and for a second I see a small smile reappear on his face.

'Didn't she tell you?' he says. 'I live next door.'

CHAPTER EIGHT

RACHEL

I lean back into the leather seat as the Uber driver swings round another corner, and look out the window at the line of street lamps, blinking in time with the cars skirting underneath them. A yawn stretches onto my face and I feel my eyes sag. It's almost midnight and we're not even at Katy's flat yet.

I pull up her latest email and read it again, feeling a pang of guilt. I knew she'd hate the idea of me turning up at her flat with no warning. As chilled out as she pretends to be, we are twins.

Hi Rachel,

I'm confused ?! I thought you were meant to be in Paris! I don't think you can stay in my flat, it's not ready and I know you're allergic to cats and I used to have one?! Actually, I think the neighbour has a cat too? Why don't you stay in a nice Travelodge instead? There is one literally around the corner, which is super cheap, here's the link.

I roll my eyes.

I mean, honestly, suggesting I can't stay there because I might sneeze once an hour? Each time she's called, I've let it roll into voicemail. There is little point answering just so she can shout at me. I'll call her tomorrow when she's calmed down and realised that I'm not going to her flat so that I can set it on fire.

All I need is a bed to sleep in for a week and a place where nobody knows who I am. She won't even know I was there.

I stopped replying to messages from my friends the moment Danny left. I told myself that I would tell them everything as soon as I knew how to deal with it. But then it turned out that the way I wanted to deal with it was to pretend that Liam would slot into the space Danny had left with no problem, and I knew that if I told anyone that, they would tell me I was lying to myself. I already knew that, but I didn't want to hear it. It was all that was keeping me going.

By the time I found out I was pregnant and Liam had left, I didn't know how to tell anyone. So I cut them all out completely. The last time they saw me I was married to someone they knew and loved. How could I tell them I'd messed up everything I had? So I didn't.

The car winds down another one-way street and I rest my hands on my bump as rain slits across the sky and slashes against the pavement with angry slaps.

London never looks like this in photos or on TV. It's always set against the bright backdrop of a blue sky, with the odd cloud skirting behind like a child doing backstroke in the sea. Now that I'm here, everything seems grey.

I try to get comfortable in the car seat. I will never take being comfortable for granted again. Don't even get me started about the ease of being able to get on and off your own sofa unaided.

83

Honestly, there are articles about how strong and admirable single mothers are, but does anyone mention the sheer determination and skill it takes to get out of a comfy chair by yourself when you're eight months pregnant?

'This is it.'

The car crunches over gravel as we pull into an elaborate driveway, and I frown. Katy always says she lives in a flat, but as the driver yanks up the handbrake, I notice that we've arrived outside a house.

I clamp my mouth back shut as I realise it's hanging open.

This is where she lives? It's huge! It's not a flat; it's a bloody mansion. Why didn't she want me to stay here? I could live here with her and we'd see less of each other than we do now! The baby could have its own wing.

'Are you sure?' I say, pulling out my phone to check. 'The address is The Cabin, 38 Elmwood Road, Chiswick.'

The driver slouches further into his seat and I see his thick shoulders shrug.

'This is 38 Elmwood Road,' he says.

'Oh.'

Gosh. Well, maybe she was being modest when she told me she lived in a flat and didn't want to brag about living in a beautiful house. Maybe she thought I'd be jealous.

I can't believe she tried to ship me off to a shoddy hotel when she lives in the Ritz. And I've given her my best pillow-cases in the cottage!

I unclip my seat belt and step out of the car. Immediately I feel a slap of rain wash over my face and I push my hands into my pockets and look up at the house. Some of the lights are on and I can see a flicker of shadows.

Does Katy have housemates? Surely she would have mentioned that to me before. Although maybe that's why she was so desperate for me not to stay here; perhaps her housemates are all crazy.

Maybe she has a secret boyfriend.

I'm jolted out of my thoughts as the taxi driver drops my suitcase next to me.

'Look,' he says, gesturing to a small sign that points down the side of the house. I squint to try and read it as rain skims off my glasses like I've stuck my head inside a waterfall.

The Cabin

'Oh!' I say, turning to the driver. 'So she lives down there?'

He shrugs and climbs back into his car. I nod and step back. Right, of course. His work here is done; he's successfully dropped me at my chosen location. It is not his job to help me find the front door, and that's okay, I can manage it myself.

I drag my suitcase over the gravel, trying not to rip up the stones. It's so dark down here; is this really how Katy gets to her flat every day? There must be a better way that the taxi driver didn't know about.

My foot slips in some mud and I let out a yelp.

I take a deep breath and try and steady myself. It's okay. Soon I'll be in Katy's lovely flat with a cup of tea and a chocolate biscuit.

Or rather a vegan chocolate biscuit, which I'm sure will be just as nice. Certainly nicer than those awful sweet potato brownies I made from the recipe book she sent me. They tasted like compost.

I would do anything for a chocolate biscuit. A big fat cookie.

I feel my eyes well up.

Don't think about chocolate biscuits and tea, for God's sake, Rachel, it'll just make you cry.

I step round the final corner and suddenly a light flicks on above my head and illuminates a . . . garden. I have to scrunch up my eyes in order to see as I realise I am standing right next to a pink plastic bike leaning against a wall. I furrow my brow and look around me to check I haven't taken a wrong turn, but the path is straight.

I step forward, trying to see another sign to point me out of the garden and perhaps back onto a normal path. My suitcase knocks into another bike, which tinkles in the wind, and I mumble an apology in its direction, as if it can hear me.

This doesn't make any sense! Why am I in a garden? Does she live in the house after all? Am I going crazy?

As I peer ahead, I see a little lodge hiding behind a tree in the distance. I start walking towards it, and as I get closer, I notice one of Katy's ceramic mugs on the windowsill. I feel a wave of relief, reassurance that I am in the right place, but that vanishes almost instantly as I reach the lodge. I don't understand. Katy told me she lived in a flat.

I step under the porch to take shelter from the rain, and spot the fake rock sitting proudly next to the doormat. I feel anger bubble up inside me. How could Katy lie to me? And why? She's been singing about her rooftop garden and view of the Shard for the last three years! Surely there must be a mistake. Surely she . . .

But my anger loosens its grip on my thoughts as I begin to carefully lower myself to reach the key and spot a fat toad sitting next to the rock. Its throat bubbles and its beady eyes blink up at me, shimmering under the fat raindrops that have coated its body. I pause for a minute, not daring to move in case I scare it away. As I reach forward slowly to pick up the rock, it leaps into a bush, and just like that, it's gone.

Even though I am soaked to my bones, for a moment I feel as though I've stepped out of a warm bath.

Grandma always said she would come back as a toad. She loved them.

Feeling a fresh surge of determination, I pull myself back to standing and unlock the door.

I can work out what I'm going to do tomorrow morning, but for now, all I need is to be inside Katy's nice clean flat. Or cabin or whatever it is. To sit on her sofa with a cup of tea and watch some TV. After the long journey, I just want to be somewhere safe, warm and . . .

My heart drops as the door swings open. I step inside tentatively, feeling as if I'm climbing inside a Biffa bin as I take in the clothes, plastic bags and assorted rubbish strewn across the floor. A thick smell hangs in the air, like rotten soup, and I wince as my foot crunches on something hiding in the dark. My heavy, sodden shoulders sag and I suddenly feel myself shiver as the wetness of my clothes begins to seep into my skin.

I look around the room hopelessly, and then, before I can even work out why, I start to cry.

Vegan or not, she definitely won't have any biscuits.

★

I sink back into Katy's sofa, the only safe place to sit and look around the cabin. It's like a doll's house. The front door opens into a small living room, with the fat buttercup-yellow sofa in one corner and a built-in kitchen slotted in the other. There are stacks of magazines and books piled in various parts of the room; half-eaten containers of food are scattered across the wooden floorboards; clothes are draped across every surface, and a thick layer of dust skims the entire flat, as if Katy has sprinkled it there like fresh flour. The walls are oat white, and the only other room is a dinky bathroom that consists of a bath, a very low toilet and a smeared mirror.

I haven't dared attempt to make myself a cup of tea yet. I haven't even taken off my shoes, even though my eyelids throb each time I blink. I feel as if I'm in the wrong place. How can my sister live here, at the bottom of someone's garden? There is no grand view of the city or rooftop garden like she has always bragged about, and her designer wardrobe seems to consist of one rail of clothes standing next to the television. The only part of the flat that looks clean is the kitchen, which looks as if it's never been used.

Reluctantly I push my shoes off my sodden feet and try not to wince as they squelch to the floor. I rest my hands on my bump and feel myself scowl as my brain compiles a list of every lie Katy has told me:

1) That she is a hardcore vegan. (I literally tripped over a kebab earlier. I mean, yes, I know I also lied about this, but I spent a fortune on Food Glow membership for her! It's a bloody vegan specialist shop! And I paid extra for membership to Supper Club!)

2) That she didn't buy that hideously expensive bike that is now taking up half her bloody living room. I mean, what is the point?

3) That the orchid I bought her is thriving (it's dead).

I push myself forward so that I'm perched on the edge of the sofa, and before I can stop myself, I grab my phone and send her a message, all my frustrations pouring out into an email. Then I drop my phone back in my bag. I need to sleep. It's almost 2 a.m.

As I go to open my suitcase, it suddenly hits me. There isn't a bedroom in the cabin. Where does Katy sleep? I glance down in alarm. Surely she doesn't sleep here; she can't have spent the past three years squashed onto a tiny sofa. That would be impossible. But then where *does* she sleep? The floor?

I glance at it in disgust, trying not to recoil from the stray spring roll that's sitting by my foot.

There is no way she sleeps among all this rubbish. I mean, I know Katy can be a bit scruffy, but that's too much.

I throw myself back on the sofa and push the heels of my hands into my eyes.

This is ridiculous! I just want to go to sleep! Where the hell does she sleep? Is there a hammock somewhere? Does she secretly camp each night? Does she sleep at the foot of the bed of the people inside that big house, like their faithful cat?

I pull my eyes back open, and as the black spots blurring my vision vanish, I notice a ladder stacked behind me and feel my stomach turn over.

Oh no.

Chapter Nine

Katy

I roll onto my back, the white sunlight from the rising sun skimming through the window and spilling onto my face. The soft scent of vanilla fills my nose as I sink further into the crisp thick bedding. As I slowly wake up, I realise I can't hear a single sound apart from the faint barking of a dog in the distance saying good morning to the sea. A warm sense of calm ripples over me, as for a moment I'm thirteen again in my childhood bedroom. My parents haven't split up and my mum hasn't thrown my dad out and then run off with a new husband; my grandma is alive and all five of us live together in our little cottage. It's a Sunday, which means we'll have a roast dinner and play cards. Dad will help us with our homework and Grandma will bake a cake, hopefully cherry, my favourite, and then we'll get lost in the hills. Not that we could ever really get lost; the coast always led us back home.

House Swap

If I stay really still, I can almost hear Grandma knocking on my bedroom door with a cup of tea. She was the pin that held our family together when it threatened to fall apart. When she died, everything crumbled.

A slice of sunlight causes me to squint as I look around my old bedroom. Rachel has kept it pristine, and has even filled the vase on the windowsill with fresh daffodils, my favourite flowers. I feel like I've woken up in my own personal heaven.

It's a stark contrast to what she'll be waking up to, which will be closer to her version of the fiery depths of hell.

I pull my phone towards me and see an email flashing on my screen from Rachel, sent in the middle of the night. I feel a stab of panic.

Oh God, I hope she got there okay and managed to find the cabin. If she gave my address to a taxi driver, he would probably have dropped her off at Fiona's front door. What if she proudly knocked on the door and woke Fiona and the children? And then Fiona told her that I didn't live in the house and pointed her in the direction of her back garden.

I feel my fingers grip my phone tightly.

Rachel should never have invited herself to stay at my flat without any warning! I didn't tell her about my living situation for a reason. I didn't mean to lie to her, and I was going to tell her the truth one day, when I was finally living in a block of flats like every other twenty-six-year-old, on my own terms. I mean, I could have moved out of the cabin years ago, but Fiona likes having me around and I could never afford to live by myself in Chiswick. I don't think I could bear living with housemates now. I wouldn't be able to walk around in my pants.

I open the email.

Katy

I've arrived and I'm fine. Nice to see your 'flat' and everything in it. I'll be fine here once I've cleaned away the food and other things. Let me know if Bruno is okay. R x

I feel a wave of heat prickle up the back of my neck. Rachel is my sister, and I know her well enough to know when she's speaking in code. This is what she really means:

Katy/Scumbag

I've arrived and I'm fine, no thanks to you. Nice to see your 'flat' that you've been lying about and every other thing I disapprove of in it, especially that extortionate bike I told you not to buy, you absolute idiot. I'll be fine here once I've cleaned out all the meat and dairy products (yes, I've worked out that you're obviously not a vegan) and other disgusting things. Let me know Bruno is okay, as I don't care about you. R (no kiss)

I scowl at the screen.

I mean, she didn't even ask if I was okay! She didn't apologise for not leaving me a key so I could look after her precious dog. And yes, I know I've been lying about being a vegan, and sure, I did buy that bike, but I really think I have the right to the moral high ground here. I mean, *hello*? She didn't even warn me that my ex-boyfriend is living next door. If she'd told me that, there is no way I would have come.

I lock my phone and throw it across my bed. I have a mind to tell her that Bruno ran away. Although I don't really want to upset her. Maybe I'll tell her that he humped one of her precious pillows and I'm not going to tell her which one. Ha.

And yes, maybe I have changed and told a few white lies about some tiny details, but she's secretly changed too. I found some very odd things when I arrived last night. For example:

House Swap

1) She is suddenly obsessed with pillows. I know a lot of people really get into throws and nice cushions when they reach a certain age, but you could barely see Rachel's bed with the amount of pillows she has piled up. One of them even seemed to be one of those boyfriend pillows that you wrap your legs around and hug, which she obviously must use when Danny goes away. I mean, no judgement from me. But if she'd shared this pillow addiction, then maybe I could have got her a better Christmas present.

2) She is also obsessed with all sorts of lotions and potions. I nearly got concussion when I was searching for toothpaste and a particularly menacing bottle smacked me on the head.

3) She also has an entire clothes horse with sports bras on it. I mean, I guess that isn't that out of character considering she loves running (she once said to me 'Why walk when you can run?'), but still.

And finally, the weirdest one . . .

4) I keep finding Smarties everywhere! Rachel is the neatest person I know, and I have so far found rogue Smarties in the fridge, in the letter box and in the shower (?).

I mean, has my sister turned into some kind of hoarder?

I blink around the perfectly minimalistic room. She can't be; every inch of the cottage is meticulously perfect. Where would she be storing it all?

On the bright side, she has filled the fridge with all my favourite things. There's chocolate and sausage rolls and litres of fresh orange juice, which washed my hangover away like a dream.

I lean on my elbows so I can see out of the bedroom window. My room always had the best view in the house; you can see right down to the coast. There isn't a single soul outside yet;

they'll all be having breakfast with their families. A fluffy cloud skims through the sky and I notice someone walking through the village. It's Isaac.

What's he doing up and about so early?

Actually, come to think of it, what's he doing *here*? Why isn't he in Cardiff?

I scuttled into the cottage as soon as he handed over the keys yesterday and then immediately drew all the curtains. Hopefully that'll be the last time I see him this week. The only time I plan on leaving the house is to walk Bruno, and maybe I'll wear a big hat and dark glasses and hope he doesn't give me a second glance.

Isaac and I broke up when I moved to London. We were only twenty-three, the crushing age where love feels like a bubble you must stay in to be able to breathe. We'd barely spent a day apart since we were twelve, right back when we'd catch the school bus together every morning, pretending with our foggy winter's breath that we were smoking cigarettes.

It wasn't until Rachel told me that she wasn't coming to London with me that everything fell apart. We had spent weeks looking at flats to rent together and making lists of all the fun things we could do. The sudden burning fear of moving to a big city by myself and not seeing my sister every day scared me senseless. In that moment, I knew I couldn't go through that with Isaac, I couldn't stretch out the pain of not seeing him every day, burning through me like he was my energy source I was forever needing topped up. I couldn't have it hanging over me, my final piece of happiness waiting to be snatched away. So I broke up with him in the same week. I only had to rely on myself then. Mum and Dad had left, Rachel too. I needed to make one decision for myself.

Isaac saw right through me. He kept saying I was giving up and running away, and he was right, I was. London was my fresh start, away from the memories of my broken childhood in this house. We haven't spoken since.

Rachel tried to make it up to me, calling and sending letters, but it was never the same. The way I saw it, she'd turned her back on me just like she'd turned her back on our dad.

I lie down again, and to my surprise I feel tears prick at my eyes. I blink them away quickly.

I am *not* going to waste energy crying over something that happened years ago. There is no point.

I stretch my arms above my head, my eyes scrunching shut as I let out a yawn.

There wasn't a speck of dust to be seen when I arrived last night, and Rachel had laid out a fan of glossy magazines like they do in hotels. The duvet on my bed is thick and heavy and there was a selection of towels in a neat pile, as though she had bought them specially. The only thing out of place was Bruno, who practically roared at me as soon as I stepped inside, as if I was a burglar swinging a swag bag.

I rub my eyes with the back of my hands.

I know I won't feel this relaxed for long. It might be early, but at some point the clock will hit 9 a.m. and I'll have to log on to my emails. Fiona will have had time to process the charity ball, and I'm sure we will have had enough complaints to warrant a lengthy prison sentence.

Until then, though, there is nothing I can do, so there is little point worrying. If anything, I should savour this small pocket of time where I'm yet to find out my fate.

I climb out of bed and pad downstairs, holding Rachel's spa

Olivia Beirne

dressing gown around me. I will make a lovely breakfast coffee using her fancy machine, and maybe I'll drink it in the bath. I bet she'll have the fanciest of—

I freeze on the spot as I hear a knock on the door. Immediately Bruno skids out of the kitchen and starts barking, throwing his body at the living room window. I shoot him a look as my hand clutches my chest.

For God's sake, does he have to be so loud all the time?

The door rattles again under a knock, and I frown.

Who is that? It's the crack of dawn! Why is somebody knocking on Rachel's front door so early?

I creep into the living room and spot Isaac grinning at Bruno through the window. Instinctively I slam my body against the wall.

Isaac. What on earth is he doing here? I can't see him now! God, this is a nightmare! I haven't clapped eyes on the sodding man in years and now I've seen him twice in the space of twenty-four hours, first when I've had my face pressed into a pile of mud and now when I'm in fleece sheep pyjamas. What's he going to do next? Pop up at the window while I'm on the toilet?

He knocks again and I scowl.

How dare he? Who does he think he is? Like I haven't got anything better to do than come to the door and speak to him.

Without moving my body, I peer through the net curtains. I could never understand why more people didn't fancy Isaac at school. He's got these incredible defined cheekbones, which sit high on his face just below his bright green eyes. His hair is still as floppy and unruly as it has always been, and I smile as I glance down at his ridiculous sheep jumper.

Actually, that's why nobody fancied him at school apart from me. He always dresses like an extra from *The Vicar of Dibley*. Brown corduroys or weird waterproof trousers and some version of a thick, bobbly jumper that was knitted by a relative a thousand years ago.

For a split second I think he's spotted me, but then he gives Bruno a final wave before disappearing.

Oh thank God, he's leaving.

I peel myself from the wall, my heart rate slowing back to its normal pace. I wait until Bruno has finally calmed down, then creep towards the door. As I peer through the glass, I notice a small box sitting on the doorstep.

Has he left me something?

I scan the path to make sure Isaac is out of sight, then quickly open the door. Bruno practically grins by my feet as I grab the box and slip back inside.

'That was your fault,' I say to Bruno, skirting past him. 'You can't be that excited to see him all the time, all right? You're supposed to be on my side.'

I walk back into the living room and open the box. Six fat eggs nestled in a bed of hay smile up at me. There is a note on the top.

Fresh from the farm, enjoy.

Even if I hadn't seen Isaac drop off the package, I'd have recognised his handwriting. He used to pass me notes all the time in school.

I turn the note in my hands and sink into the sofa, my brain humming.

It's no big deal. He probably does this for all the neighbours. It might even be a subscription that Rachel has set up, a delivery of fresh eggs every morning. That sounds like something she'd be into.

Although she is a vegan, so she wouldn't eat eggs. Maybe he usually drops off a daily cluster of carrots.

Urgh. She is going to be so mad that I've been lying about being a vegan. I shouldn't have sent her all those pictures of vegan cakes I found on Google Images and tried to pass them off as my own; that was definitely a step too far. As was suggesting I was a key player in organising a vegan rally outside the House of Commons.

But she seemed to find being a vegan so easy, and what was I supposed to say when she asked me if I was finding it hard? I couldn't tell her I gave up after a day after we'd both bought that really expensive cookbook. I spotted her copy the moment I stepped into the kitchen; it still looks absolutely pristine.

I glance up at Bruno, who is sitting on the opposite side of the room staring at me. I offer him a limp smile, but he doesn't move.

I pull my laptop towards me and shake the mouse pad, making the screen swirl into life. There's no harm logging on a bit early. I doubt anybody will have sent me any emails yesterday, and maybe it will put me in Fiona's good books when she arrives at work fresh from the school run to see that even when I'm hundreds of miles away, her coffee is still waiting for her on her desk (Starbucks deliver, you know).

As I wait for my emails to load, Bruno pads past me, head high in the air, and disappears into the kitchen.

I look back at my laptop, and an email from Fiona pops up. I feel heat fizz through me as I notice she sent it two hours ago. Why was she emailing me at six in the morning?

Katy,

Need to speak to you today about this week. Also, don't mean to alarm you but we think there is someone asleep in the cabin. Do you know anything about this? My phone is broken, so please email me.

As I stare at the screen, the calm mist of relaxation I've been enjoying all morning vanishes.

Oh shit.

Chapter Ten

Rachel

I stare up at the wooden ceiling. Small planks of wood have been carefully slotted together to make the arch of the roof and a glistening nail is winking at me in the sunlight. I feel like I'm sleeping in a Wendy house.

I move my head and look at the photos Katy has stuck to the wall, right next to her pillow. I smile at the one of the two of us with Grandma. It's the best photo I've ever taken, and I somehow managed to be in it as well.

The baby grabs hold of my bladder and I wince, trying to fight my desperation to go to the toilet. It took me the best part of half an hour to climb up the stupid bloody ladder that leads to Katy's bed – if you can call it that; it's more like a nest. I'm not going down until I'm absolutely ready, and that won't be until I've worked out what I'm going to do next. Right now, I'm sleeping, or at least I'm pretending to be sleeping. Once I've got up, I'll have to be doing something else.

Sitting? Reading? Fighting off the niggling reminder that I've run away from my problems, again, and that sometime soon I'll have to confess all my failures to my sister? Or googling nice villages on the other side of the world that I could flee to without a trace, like somewhere quaint in the Netherlands?

I'm not sure if I slept at all last night. It didn't feel like I did. It's all well and good running away to London in the dead of night – it almost feels a bit glamorous and exciting, like something you see in films. But they never show the cold realisation once you arrive that you're just miles away from everything you know and still very much alone.

I move my gaze away from the walnut-brown ceiling and peer over the side of the bed. I practically tiptoed around Katy's clutter when I arrived, and now the bright sun is skimming the mess like it's going to sweep it all away. She doesn't have any food in her cupboards (I checked) and I would bet every penny I own that she doesn't possess a hoover. Or if she does, it will be a stupid Henry one.

My eyes land on the Super Bike and I instantly scowl.

I still cannot believe she bought that bloody thing.

My bladder tingles dangerously and I take a deep breath. I don't know if I can face the ladder yet. I don't have the strength.

I pick up my phone. I feel a small wave of guilt as the screen blinks up at me, free of any notifications. Katy hasn't responded to the email I sent last night. Not that I blame her; it was a bit of an attack.

I take a deep breath as my mind replays the moment I decided to run away to London. At the last second, paranoia sank in and

I scanned my house as though I were Katy, trying to spot any clues that I was pregnant. I'd been hiding all my pregnancy bits in the loft for weeks; the only thing I hadn't put up there was a tiny babygro that I keep under my pillow, and I took that with me.

My bladder spasms for the third time and I feel my body jolt in shock, as if the baby has jabbed the side of my uterus with an elbow.

Right, I need to get up before I wet the bed. Regardless of how highly impractical this weird bunk bed is for a pregnant woman, it is the only place I have to sleep for the next week. I simply cannot wee in it.

With great effort, I push the duvet off my body and grab hold of the ladder. It swings about dangerously and my stomach lurches.

Christ, and I thought getting in and out of a car was difficult.

I steady the ladder and hook a foot into it.

Come on, Rachel. It's just a ladder. You've climbed plenty of ladders before. You climbed this exact ladder last night without falling off or snapping it clean in half under your enormous weight. You haven't put on an extra stone overnight; it will still be able to hold you.

I start moving my feet, trying to count the rungs to control my fear.

That's it, just keep going, right, left, right, left.

I look over my shoulder to try and gauge how close I am to the ground, and then nearly fall off entirely as I spot two children with their noses pressed against the window, as if I'm a wallowing hippo at Whipsnade Zoo.

I cling onto the ladder, suddenly frozen to the spot.

Why are there children at the window? Are they here to see me? Am I actually in a Wendy house after all and they're here to kick me out?

Oh my God, if I've broken into a child's Wendy house by mistake, I will *die*.

I wobble down the last few steps and then turn back to the window. The children have gone.

I scrunch up my eyes, bemused, as my heart hammers in my chest.

Were they really there, or was I just hallucinating? Is that a normal thing that happens to pregnant women? Do they start picturing children wherever they go?

I step closer to the window. In the morning sun, I can finally see the house I arrived at last night. It towers over the manicured lawn, dwarfing the little cabin more than ever. I pull the curtains shut.

I really am in somebody's back garden.

The baby gives a final squeeze to my bladder and I lurch towards the bathroom.

Why does Katy live in someone's garden? Is this normal in London? Maybe everybody lives in someone's garden. Maybe it's a space thing. People are always moaning about how crowded the city is. Perhaps Katy is just really forward-thinking,

I catch sight of myself in the mirror as I pull myself back to standing. My hair is taut, jabbing out from my bun like angry blades of grass. My face is as blotchy as ever, with an ugly ruddy quality, and my eyes are slightly bloodshot. Whoever said that pregnant women are beautiful was lying. The only part of my face that doesn't look like it belongs in a horror maze is my lips, which seem to have bloomed fuller in the last month.

Although that might just be because *everything* has got fatter. My arse has 'bloomed fuller' too.

I creep out of the bathroom, the image of those children playing on my mind. What did they want? They must live in that big house. Do they usually spy on Katy? Isn't that against some sort of law?

I grab a blanket from the sofa and wrap it around myself, covering my swollen stomach as much as possible, like I always do. I take another look around the cabin and try to stop my nose from flying in the air like Maggie Smith in *Downton Abbey*.

How long am I going to stay here for? What is my actual—

'Hello?'

I jump as I see a shadow at the window, attempting to peer in through the drawn curtains. I grip onto the blanket, my eyes wide.

Who is that? That wasn't the voice of a child. That sounded like a very posh woman.

Oh my God, what am I going to *do*?

'Hello?' she calls again. 'It's Fiona, the . . . er . . . landlady. I need to speak to you.'

I feel a flutter of panic.

Shit. I didn't even think about the fact that Katy might get into trouble for me staying here. It's only for a week, isn't that allowed?

I step towards the door, making sure the blanket covers my entire body, and tentatively open the door.

Oh God, I haven't even brushed my teeth!

The woman – Fiona – who has practically bent over to peer through the keyhole, snaps her body up to her full height. She has porcelain skin and glossy caramel-coloured hair that is swept over her forehead in a loose fringe. She is wearing high-waist jeans and a yellow floral blouse. I notice behind her the children I spotted earlier.

'Hello,' I manage, trying to sound calm and as if this is all perfectly normal, and not as though I look like I've crawled out of the drainpipe.

She can't throw me out. I only want to be here for a few days. Surely no mother would throw out a pregnant woman. If she tries, I'll write to *Loose Women*. I'm sure they'll have something to say about it.

Fiona stares at me, failing to control the spiral of questions whizzing across her face.

'I'm Rachel,' I say quickly, 'Katy's twin sister. She said I could stay here for the week while she's away.'

I feel my cheeks tingle as the lie flies out of my mouth. Well, how is she to know that I didn't ask Katy's permission?

She opens and closes her mouth.

'You're Katy's sister?' she repeats. 'Gosh, you look just like her.' She finally smiles. 'I live in the main house. I'm sorry if my children frightened you. They're missing Katy already. I think they thought she might be back.'

She laughs and I try not to frown.

They miss Katy? How well does she know them?

'That's okay,' I say, smiling in the direction of the young girl, who gawps back at me. 'I'll keep myself to myself.'

Fiona pulls out her phone and scowls as her eyes skim over a message. I wish she'd leave so I can get dressed. I'm standing here without a bra on, for goodness' sake, and pregnancy nipples are not something to be taken lightly.

'Not to worry,' she says. 'The cabin is quite cute, isn't it?

Although living so close to your boss could be seen as hell for a lot of people!' She laughs again, throwing back her head as though she's dropped an absolute corker.

'Oh?' I say, looking around. 'Where does her boss live?'

Fiona looks at me as if I have two heads.

'There,' she says, gesturing behind her, 'that's my house.' She peels the girl from her leg. 'If you need anything, just let me know.'

She turns and herds the children back up the garden, holding an arm out behind her in a wave, and I stand in the doorway, trying to ignore the niggle of another one of Katy's lies being unveiled.

Why did she never tell me any of this?

★

I drop my splitting shopping bags onto the floor and jab the key into the lock as Katy's answerphone clicks into action. I know she'll still be mad about the email I sent, but I thought she'd at least answer for the chance to be self-righteous.

'Hi, Katy,' I say, 'it's me. I hope you're okay. I met Fiona earlier today, she seems nice. Why don't you give me a call when you get a second? I'm sure we have some stuff to talk about.'

I say the last bit without thinking and feel an instant fizz of anxiety burn through me. Katy wouldn't have worked out any of my lies since being in the house because I've been pretending all my secrets aren't real myself. Isaac wouldn't have told her. I doubt they've even seen each other; they've both been stubbornly pretending to hate each other ever since they broke up, and I'm sure neither of them will admit otherwise when nobody is around to force them.

'Anyway,' I add quickly, nudging the door open with my knee, 'call me when you get a second. Say hi to Bruno. Love you.'

I start unpacking the shopping, pulling out bottles of bleach, rubber gloves, antibacterial wipes and a lovely new diffuser as a peace offering. Everybody loves the smell of a nice room.

I'm just pulling the plastic off the gloves when I hear a small knock on the door. I feel my spine stiffen.

Oh God, what now?

I force a smile ready for Fiona, but when I open the door, I see the young girl standing there holding a can of tomatoes.

'Oh!' I say. 'Hello.'

'Is this yours?' she says, turning the tin between her hands.

'Yes,' I reply. 'Thank you.'

I reach to take it back, but she doesn't give it to me.

'Mummy says you're Katy's sister,' she says.

I look down at her. She has long hair that is spun into two French plaits, and is wearing floral jeans and an electric-pink T-shirt. Although her eyes are bright and angelic, she is looking at me as though she is about to flush my tomatoes down the toilet.

'Yes,' I say, 'I am.'

'You don't sound like her.'

I pause. That would be because Katy likes to pretend she isn't from Wales. She once accused me of hamming up my accent around her to make her feel bad. I've seen her Instagram stories where she's grabbing a coffee and walking along the South Bank at a brisk stroll, as though she's a born and bred Londoner.

'You look like her,' the girl adds. 'Well,' her wide eyes fall to my stomach, 'not exactly like her.'

I raise my eyebrows. At least that's one thing Katy isn't keeping from me. I'm the only secretly pregnant sister.

'I don't look anything like William,' the girl continues. 'He's only seven and I'm nine, so I'm older.'

I lean against the door frame. How long is this going to go on for? Can't she just give me back my tomatoes and go?

'Jasmine!'

I look up at the sound of Fiona's voice as she charges down the garden. She is now wearing a fitted suit dress with large, clumpy trainers, and carrying her heels in her hand. The boy, William, is skipping behind her, eating a large ice cream that teeters dangerously close to the back of her dress. Jasmine looks at her and quickly launches into a spiral of chatter.

'Mummy, I was just giving back her tomatoes, she dropped them. I was being helpful!'

'Well give them to her then!' Fiona says, rolling her eyes at me as if this is a private joke we're both in on.

I take the tomatoes off Jasmine and mutter a thank you.

'I'm so sorry,' Fiona says. 'You've been the talk of the house all day. They were desperate to meet you properly.'

I feel myself blush.

'But I told them to leave you alone,' she adds, shooting Jasmine a raised eyebrow.

'That's okay,' I say awkwardly. 'You look nice,' I offer as an attempt to steer away from the topic of me somehow being a main attraction.

'Oh.' Fiona looks down at herself, her propped sunglasses falling onto her face. 'Thank you,' she says, pushing them towards her nose. 'I've got a huge meeting. Katy is usually such an enormous help with everything, and my husband is on a work call, so I'm just trying to decide how to go with these two. I think we're all going to come to the office, aren't we?'

She smiles encouragingly down at Jasmine, who throws her head back in dismay. William, who was smiling happily, spots his sister's reaction and immediately copies.

'No!' Jasmine wails. 'I don't want to go to the office. It's so *boring!*'

I feel a jolt of alarm as William stamps his feet and I suddenly feel like they're about to riot.

'I want to stay here!' Jasmine pouts, crossing her arms across her chest. 'Why can't we stay here and play?'

William stomps to stand next to his sister and glares at his mum. Fiona, who has taken her sunglasses off, stares back at them. Standing close to her, I realise that her eyes are shadowed by dark circles and her collarbones jut out as she hunches forward.

'Because Daddy can't look after you,' she says, the bright quality in her voice fading away. 'I've told you that before.'

I see Jasmine's narrowed eyes shift, and for a moment I think she's going to give in. This only lasts a second; then, to my alarm, she snaps her head around to me.

'Why can't we play with Regina?'

I blink as Jasmine thrusts her skinny arm at me.

Who?

'Darling, her name is Rachel,' Fiona says, her smile returning as she shoots me an apologetic look.

'Rachel,' Jasmine says quickly. 'Why can't we play with Rachel?'

William turns away from Fiona, his big brown eyes blinking up at me. His mouth splits into a smile and I notice that he has two large top teeth, surrounded by a sea of tiny baby ones. He nods excitedly and I feel my face turn pink.

'Rachel is busy,' Fiona says, hoisting her bag onto her shoulder.

'We'll be good!' Jasmine cries, her feet firmly planted on the ground.

Very slowly, Fiona looks up at me. Her eyes are rounded in desperation, as though she's about to collapse at my feet. I feel a pang of guilt. This woman is allowing me to spend a week in her garden, and I could easily look after her children for an hour. We could just sit and watch a film.

'It's fine,' I hear myself say. 'I'm not up to much and I can keep an eye on them, if your husband is in the house,' I add. Meaning, if there is at least one responsible adult here I can scream for in case I accidentally break one of them.

She freezes, as if sudden movement might scare me away.

'Really?' she says. 'Are you sure? I completely get it if not. Maybe it's because you look so much like Katy, but I just feel like I can trust you, and like I said, my husband is in the house if anything happens.'

'Don't worry,' I say. 'I'm sure we'll be fine.'

CHAPTER ELEVEN

KATY

I jump as my phone vibrates next to me and Rachel's name lights up on the screen.

Finally! Signal!

Without reading her message, I jab her a frantic text back.

How the hell do you get your Wi-Fi to work?! I need it to work! It's important!

I hold my breath as the message slides off and then bounces happily back to me. I lurch my arm up into the air, desperately staring at the flickering bar of signal. How does Rachel survive like this? Was it this bad when I lived here?

I drop the phone to my side in defeat and curl my hand around my mouse, giving it another shake.

The internet has been down for hours. It gave me one spark of life this morning to show me Fiona's email and then promptly vanished into cyberspace. Every now and then, a flicker of connection appears and allows me to receive another panic-inducing email from one of my colleagues, but then is snatched away before I have the chance to reply. I've tried calling Fiona, but like she said, her phone is broken, which means she wouldn't have received my garbled message last night trying to explain who Rachel is, and now she'll think I'm ignoring her.

I mean, I might as well just cart myself off to HMRC and staple my P45 to my forehead.

Bruno nudges a ball against my feet and I kick it, wincing as he lunges after it and crashes into the table. He's finally accepted that I'll be staying here, or rather, he's worked out that I'm the only person available to throw the ball for him. Either way, it's stopped him from bloody barking at me every time I get up to go to the toilet. Which, by the way, is the last thing you need when you've already left it far too late and are on the verge of wetting yourself.

I needed to be online all day to try and clear up the mess I created at the charity ball. It's bad enough that I'm not there to defend myself in person – they'll all be gossiping about me in the office (fuelled, I'm sure, by Diane) – but now I haven't even been able to fight my corner digitally.

Bruno drops the ball back by my feet and I scowl at him.

'No,' I say, refreshing my screen again, 'I'm sorry, I can't take you out. I'm busy.'

How can Rachel cope with such bad internet? She's a PA at a big company, for God's sake, and for the majority of the time she works from home!

The laptop stares back at me, motionless, and I start to feel the urge to smash it on the floor.

I could call Rachel and ask her to put Fiona on, but there

is no way Rachel would hand the phone over without first asking me why I lied to her about living in what is essentially a garden shed. I can't have Rachel hearing from Fiona about what a catastrophic job I did at the auction, and what if Fiona is planning on firing me and confides in Rachel? And then Rachel coaches her on the best way to do it?

My face starts to prickle at the thought of it.

No.

Absolutely not.

I'd rather battle this dodgy internet.

I throw my head against the back of the sofa and let out a loud sigh. The twinkly light fitting sparkles down at me, a warm ivory light speckled across the perfect, cosy living room.

Something like this would never happen to Rachel. If she'd been in charge of planning the auction, everything would have gone brilliantly. That's the way life is for her: everything just seems to fall easily into place, every decision she's ever made has been the right one. I mean, look at her house. Look at her *life*. Married to her childhood sweetheart, living in a beautiful cottage with matching throws and thriving pot plants. Baking vegan goods from scratch as if it's no big deal whatsoever.

In an act of defiance, I ate one of the rogue Smarties last night to try and prove to myself that Rachel has also lied about being a vegan, but I couldn't tell the difference. It could have been vegan chocolate. They tasted pretty nice to me, but then all chocolate does. Also, I was pretty distracted by the tangled dog hair that I accidentally popped into my mouth with it. It was a low moment.

I pick the laptop up and thrust it above my head, scowling at the little bars in the corner, which blink at me stubbornly.

'Come on,' I say through gritted teeth, walking around the living room, 'just give me bloody Wi-Fi.'

With the laptop balanced on my forearm, I step towards the window and refresh my emails again. The latest message, from Diane, is still open on my screen, unanswered.

Hi Katy,

Hope you're having a nice break. Just to let you know I haven't broken a rib, just bruised it. Very sore, but doctor said I'll be okay.

Just reading it makes me feel as though my head might explode.

I mean, honestly, the audacity!

No 'sorry for ruining your auction by acting like a lunatic and smoking inside'; no 'sorry that I may have cost you your job'. Nothing!

I glance out of the window and my gaze falls on the Sailor's Ship. It's as though I've just spotted a mirage of the BT Tower.

Oh *yes*!

Of course, why didn't I think of this earlier? The pub will have Wi-Fi. All pubs do! And if the emails are dreadful – which they will be – then I can just get drunk without having to leave my chair. Perfect!

I shove my feet into my trainers and grab the keys. Bruno clocks what I'm doing instantly, and springs to my side, bouncing around and trying to manoeuvre himself as close to the door as possible in order to ensure that he is definitely coming with me.

I sigh.

'Bruno,' I say crossly, 'no. I'm working, remember? You can't come. I'll take you out later.'

He keeps his face pressed against the front door defiantly, and I try and shift myself round him, clutching my laptop in one hand. I manage to sidle past and slip through the door, Bruno barking loudly as I click it shut behind me.

As I push through the blue wooden gate at the end of the garden, I catch the eye of an old man sitting on a bench reading the paper. A bewildered look flicks across his face before a smile follows. I raise my hand at him in a wave, hugging my laptop close to my body as I charge towards the pub. The thick, salty wind rushes past me, taking my breath with it, and I hear the light squawk of a seagull, no doubt swooping low and dipping into the babbling sea.

A ribbon of smoke pipes from the pub's fat chimney, pushing out fumes of roast potatoes and steak-and-ale pie straight from the kitchen into the periwinkle-blue sky. The place looks the same as it always did; not that I'd expect it to change much in three years. It's made up of thick slabs of chalky bricks, and has a large sign that swings in the wind with an oily painting of two sailors chinking together tankards of ale over an old barrel with a fan of playing cards in each of their grubby hands. The thatched roof sits heavy on the top of the pub, like an old woman slouching under the weight of a beloved bonnet.

It was a rite of passage to work here for a summer as a teenager. Rachel and I did it together: she waited tables and I was on the bar. The same troupe of people arrived each day for their after-work pint or their Thursday darts and port club. It was familiar.

I shake the memory out of my mind. I never think about my childhood these days; I don't let myself. What's the point? It doesn't exist any more. The only real family I have now is my dad, and he's the one who messed our family up in the first place. It's been years since Rachel and I were the sisters who laughed together over spilt pints and sad-looking jacket potatoes behind the bar.

I scrunch up my face. God, I hate coming back here. It's like a form of torture, looking at every inch of the village and feeling my heart twitch as another happy memory flits into my mind. Then the pang of longing for what I had before, and finally the dull ache as I remember that it's all gone and it's not within my control to get it back. I could never force Rachel to forgive Dad, I couldn't convince Mum not to move away with her new family. I couldn't stop Grandma dying.

I shake my head furiously as my eyes start to sting.

I *hate* coming back here.

I reach the pub and climb the steps, a shiver tickling the back of my neck as the wind chases me inside. The barman looks up at me as I enter. He has thick, wiry eyebrows and is wearing a black T-shirt that stretches over his stomach. He smiles.

'Gosh,' he says, catching himself as he stares at me for a second too long, 'you look just like a girl in the village.'

My grip tightens around my laptop as an enormous fluffy poodle starts sniffing the backs of my legs.

'Rachel Dower?' I say. 'She's my twin sister. Can I use your Wi-Fi, please?'

The barman nods, gesturing to a small sign tacked on the wall with the login details. I feel a wave of relief.

I tap in the code and feel my heart race in my throat as a little coloured circle starts to spin on my screen. I just need to be able to log on and speak to Fiona and explain what's going on. Maybe I can video-call her or something. It would be much better to speak to her instead of email. I need to apologise about the ball, and Diane, and Rachel just showing up and—

'Oh hello!'

I jump as a cheerful voice coated in a thick Welsh accent trumpets in my ear. I look up and do a double-take at the woman before me, who is craning her neck to try and catch my eye. Although her hair is now dark and free of the blonde streaks she used to have as a teenager, I recognise the face of our old classmate immediately.

'It's Katy,' she beams, 'isn't it?'

My eyes flick between my computer and Ellie's smiling face.

'Yeah,' I say quickly. 'Hey, how are you?'

'Is Rachel here?' she says, looking around.

'No. She's in London.'

'I haven't seen her in months,' Ellie presses on, 'and normally she would never miss Brownies.'

Without quite meaning to, I shoot her a look of bemusement.

'She's the Tawny Owl,' Ellie says slowly, as though I'm very stupid. 'She usually helps every week.'

'Oh.' I shrug, squinting down at my laptop. 'I guess she's been busy.'

I angle my body towards the screen and shoot Ellie a smile over my shoulder, hoping she'll catch on that I'm here for work and can't chat.

'Oh,' she says, 'okay, and how are you? Have you really been living in London all this time?'

'Yes,' I say, jabbing the keyboard as the laptop threatens to freeze again.

'Oh!' she coos. 'How exciting. What brings you back here then?'

'Work.'

I know I'm being rude, but I can't help it. My eyes are stuck to the screen like magnets, and every time the Wi–Fi connection starts to spin, I feel as though I can barely breathe.

My eyes flick back to Ellie, and I notice her smile fade as she realises I'm finding my laptop more interesting than her.

'Right,' she says. 'Well, it was nice to see you.'

'You too,' I say automatically, flashing her a quick smile and trying to ignore the twinge of guilt as she walks back to her table.

'Hi.'

I snap my eyes up, feeling like a rabbit caught in headlights as Isaac appears next to me holding a pint.

'Hello,' I say shortly, staring back at the little circle of hope that's twirling around indecisively.

Come on, please connect. *Please.*

'You okay?' he says, leaning forward on the bar and making it clear he's not going anywhere. Great.

'Yes thanks,' I say tightly. 'You?'

'I'm fine,' he says, taking a sip of his beer. 'Just another day down at the farm. Did you get the eggs I left you?'

'Yes,' I say again, 'thank you.'

'They should be nice,' he says. 'I'm always quite proud of our eggs. I'm sure they're the reason Mrs Derby wins the best bake at the village fayre each year.'

I flick my eyes up. Adrenaline is thumping through my body, but as soon as I look at him, it washes away. I'd forgotten how permanently relaxed he is. I'd also forgotten how infuriating it is.

'Have you heard from Rachel?' he asks. 'Is she okay?'

I chew my lip as my laptop attempts to freeze.

'Kind of,' I say. 'She's fine. Her conference got moved to London, so she went to stay in my flat for the week.'

Without telling me, or even giving me twenty-four hours' notice. Hell, *one* hour of notice might have been nice!

Isaac takes another sip of his pint. 'So, what are you going to do with yourself this week? You've missed a lot since you've been away.'

'Work,' I say at once. 'I've got so much to do, I . . .' My voice trails off as a small box pops onto my screen.

Unable to connect.

No! Why isn't it working?

'Are you sure you're okay?'

My mad eyes swivel back up to Isaac and I feel my jaw slacken as I stare at him. My rage at the lack of internet suddenly latches onto his calm, happy-go-lucky demeanour, as if he is the sole reason I cannot access my emails.

'No,' I snap, jabbing my mouse back to the 'try again' button. 'My bloody internet won't work. Nothing works in this stupid village.' I start stabbing the password in again. 'I need the internet to do my job. We can't all just sit around feeding cows. It's *important*.'

I break off, my brain rattling.

Isaac's face tightens and he leans towards me, looking at my laptop screen.

'You've typed in the password wrong,' he says simply. 'You've put a capital F.'

I feel my face burn as the large F stares at me pointedly.

Oh.

'Right,' I mumble stupidly, 'thank you,' but he has already picked up his pint and left.

At long last my laptop springs into life, and any feelings of guilt I had at snapping at Isaac are replaced by hot, instant panic as emails topple onto my screen like digital dominoes.

Forty new messages.

CHAPTER TWELVE

RACHEL

I never wanted kids. I don't dislike children, I just don't feel like I understand them. I was never one of those women who desperately looked forward to being a mother. I had half accepted that one day I might have a baby with Danny if he wanted one, but only as a rite of passage. I never expected to have one on my own, but when the time came and I was presented with the decision – baby or no baby – I couldn't let it go.

I ease myself into a deckchair, one hand flopped lazily over my face as I count, making sure I can see where both the children are hiding at all times. William has sat down behind a large tree and Jasmine has wriggled under a bush.

That's quite clever, actually. I never would have looked there.

'Seven,' I shout, 'eight, nine . . .'

Fiona has been gone now for about an hour, and looking

after the children has consisted entirely of playing hide-and-seek in their massive garden. A game I suggested after Jasmine became obsessed with my bump and kept asking me questions that I didn't want to answer. I didn't even know the answers to half of them myself.

'Ten!' I call, moving my hand away from my face and savouring the final moment of lying in the sunshine in peace.

With great effort, I heave myself off the chair and place my hands on my hips, staring at the garden. The lawn is striped to perfection, as though it is freshly waxed each morning, and has little pockets of colour dotted throughout in the form of bright, crisp bushes. They must have a gardener. I can't imagine Fiona doing all of this, and I haven't seen her husband since I arrived. I don't even know if he really is in the house; for all I know he could be a wild figment of her imagination.

He could be the family pet.

I slowly walk over to the tree William is crouching behind. I see him suck in a great gulp of air as I approach, as if I might hear him breathing and give the game away. I walk deliberately away from the tree and hear him give a small yelp of astonishment that I'm heading in the wrong direction. I smile, and turn on the spot. He claps his hands to his face, his eyes wide in shock that I've found him, as if we haven't been playing this game for the past hour and he's continuously hidden in the same spot every single time.

'Found you.' I smile. 'Now let's find your sister.'

William scrambles up from the ground and charges towards the bushes.

'I know where she is!' he cries. 'I know!'

I pull my phone out of my pocket as he starts burrowing his

way into the bush. Katy hasn't called or emailed me back. She must still be angry.

'That's not fair!' Jasmine cries as she climbs out. 'William was peeking, he saw me hide!'

She looks up at me, scowling indignantly.

'Can we play again?' William turns to me, grinning.

I try not to raise my eyebrows at him.

Again? Seriously? How much fun can they get out of playing hide-and-seek? They should wait until they have to avoid exes in the supermarket; they'll be in for a treat.

'Let's have a break,' I say, sinking into the deckchair. 'Your mummy will be home soon.'

At least she'd better bloody be. How long does she expect me to look after her children for? I might be Katy's sister, but for all she knows I could be a serial killer.

My whole body aches as I loll in the deckchair like a stupid floppy whale that's just been scooped off the beach by a large crane.

'Where is Katy?' Jasmine asks, plopping herself by my feet.

'She's gone to stay at my house,' I say, resting my hand on my bump.

I could really do with a foot rub. Could I get the children to take a foot each? Or would that be an abuse of power?

Maybe I could turn it into a game.

'Why?'

I look down at Jasmine. She's shielding her eyes from the sun with her hand, her bright eyes scrunched up.

'Because I needed her to look after my dog.'

'Will she be back soon?' William asks, pulling up a fistful of grass and throwing it in the air like confetti.

Whoever the gardener is, I'm sure they'll be thrilled.

'Yeah.' I smile at him. 'She's only gone for a week.' I peer down at him as he sticks out his bottom lip. Clearly I've given the wrong answer. 'Does she look after you often?'

'Every day!' chimes in Jasmine. 'She always picks us up from school and helps us with our homework. She works for Mummy while we're at school.'

I stare at her.

Katy looks after the children every day? She told me she worked in the city, in a big swanky office. She's sent me pictures of her desk.

'Really?' I say. 'Has she done that for a while?'

Jasmine cocks her head. 'Er . . .' she says, 'she came here when I was six and William was four.'

'And how old are you now?' I ask.

Jasmine raises her eyebrows at me as though it is plainly obvious how old she is. 'Nine.'

I lean back in the chair.

Katy has been working as a nanny for three years? That's the entire time she's lived in London.

'Rachel!' William chirps, making me jump as he bounces onto his heels. 'Rachel, I can do a cartwheel. Can I show you?'

Oh God, what's the answer here? Are seven-year-olds supposed to cartwheel? Or has he basically asked if he can show me how to make a Jägerbomb?

Before I can answer, he has launched himself into the air. My whole body jerks forward as he tumbles to the ground, landing on his behind with a loud thump. Jasmine squeals with laughter and William blinks at me, and I can see the tears glistening in

123

his eyes. To my horror, I feel my left boob tingle, and panic darts through me.

Oh my God.

'It's okay!' I say shrilly, desperate to stop him from crying. 'You're okay! Come here!'

This happened once before, in some dreadful changing room last month. I was reluctantly shopping with Peggy for some new maternity clothes and a baby started screaming in the cubicle next to me. I was busy praying that my baby's cries would be more like a soft simper, as opposed to the help-I'm-being-violently-attacked yells I was hearing, when all of a sudden, my breasts *exploded*.

I mean, why does nobody ever warn you? How the hell are pregnant women supposed to go about their days when their breasts transform into water guns every time a child stubs their toe? Peggy laughed the whole thing off and bought me the hideous novelty *Bun in the Oven* T-shirt (which I was only trying on to please her), and said it was 'Mother Nature doing her job'.

Doing her job? Is that what my job is now? Following crying children around and offering my breasts wherever they may be needed?

I mean, does this happen to everyone? Did it happen to the Queen?

A tear breaks free onto William's cheek and I feel another jerk of panic.

I cannot have my nipples leak in front of these children. That is absolutely unacceptable.

'Don't cry!' I blurt. 'Hey, do you want to hear a joke?'

William's bottom lip stops trembling and Jasmine shuffles closer to me.

'Yes, we love jokes!' she cries.

William sinks onto the floor and blinks up at me expectantly.

Oh thank God, he's stopped crying. Now I just need to tell him a joke. God, what jokes do I know?

A man walks into a bar . . .

No, not that one.

What do you get if you cross a drunk man and a . . .

No, I *definitely* can't tell them that one.

Oh, I know!

'Okay, Jasmine.' I hold my hand out, palm open, 'what's green and invisible?'

She looks at my hand and then back up at me. 'I don't know.'

I raise my eyebrows at her expectantly, as if she should be able to see it. 'This apple.'

She looks back at my hand and then at William, who erupts into a chain of giggles.

It's worked! He's laughing!

'And William,' I turn to him, holding out my other hand, 'what's red and invisible?'

His eyes flick from my open palm back to my face.

'This tomato!'

This time, both of them collapse into giggles, before William jumps to his feet and holds out his own hand.

'What's purple and invisible?' he cries, sticking his chest out proudly. 'This dinosaur!'

Jasmine thrusts her open palm towards me.

'What's orange and invisible? This orange!'

They laugh manically at each other and I grin at them.

Hey, kids think I'm funny! Maybe that's the type of mum I'll be, the funny one. I'll dress up as a clown for children's birthday parties and tell jokes, and then my child will become a stand-up comedian and they'll say, 'I learnt everything I know from my mum.'

'I'm back!'

We all look up to see Fiona coming round the side of the house waving dramatically, like she's sending off a ship. She's holding three large carrier bags and has kicked off her high heels.

Oh, finally.

'Was it all right?' she asks apologetically, stepping onto the grass.

'Mum! Mum!' William practically shouts, shoving his hand in her face. 'What's yellow and invisible? Pikachu!'

Oh God, what have I started?

Fiona gives him an odd look and ruffles his hair. 'Lovely, darling.'

'It was great!' Jasmine cries, springing into the air. 'Can we play with Rachel every day?'

I feel a bolt of alarm.

Oh *no*. I don't want to spend the entire week skipping around with the children like Maria von Trapp.

'We'll see,' Fiona says, smiling at me as if she's just suggested she might give me a thousand pounds if I'm lucky. 'Now, look what I've got.' She holds the bags in the air and a thick smell fills the air. 'Fish and chips!'

The children squeal and leap up and down, dancing with each other as if this is the best news they've heard all day.

'Is Rachel having some too?' William asks, his eyes zooming back on me.

I open my mouth to protest, but to my alarm, Fiona answers for me.

'Of course!' she cries. 'I've bought enough for all of us, as a thank you for keeping you two entertained.'

The children cheer and race inside and Fiona smiles at me.

'I thought it would be a nice way to get to know you,' she says. 'Obviously if you have plans or want the night to yourself, then that's fine, but I'd love it if you'd join us.'

She flashes her white teeth at me and I freeze.

If Katy is angry with me now, she'll be positively furious if she finds out I turned down dinner with her boss.

I bite my lip.

I am starving, and thanks to spending my entire afternoon playing with the children, I haven't had time to cook anything and I do not trust that rogue ready meal in Katy's fridge.

What's one dinner?

'Sure,' I say, rocking myself out of the chair and back to standing. 'That would be lovely.'

★

William stretches across Jasmine, scrabbling to snatch the bottle of ketchup from the middle of the table.

'William!' she whines. 'Get off me!'

Fiona rolls her eyes and hands the bottle to William, who immediately splats a large blob of red sauce into the centre of his plate. Fiona unwraps the glistening paper and starts to serve up the food. She's about to hand me a plate when she freezes.

'Oh no!' she cries in dismay. 'I just remembered, you're vegan, aren't you? Katy told me. I guess you can have the mushy peas?'

My outstretched arm wavers, and I feel my stomach groan in disappointment.

Oh *no*. You simply cannot offer a pregnant woman fish and chips and then take them away at the last second in exchange for horrible mushy peas, the absolute worst part of any takeaway.

'Well,' I say meekly, 'I was a vegan, but—'

'What's a vegan?' Jasmine pipes up.

'It's where you don't have any meat or dairy,' Fiona says, ladling a generous portion of mushy peas onto a plate. I try not to gape at it in horror.

She puts the plate in front of me and I notice Jasmine looking at me, her brow furrowed.

'Mummy,' she says pointedly, lifting her chin in the air, 'I'm also a vegan.'

'No you are not,' snaps Fiona, shooting her a look. 'Now eat your dinner.'

I cannot survive on a plate of peas. I refuse.

'Actually,' I say quickly, feeling my cheeks immediately flare, 'I'm not a vegan any more. I'm more of a flexitarian.'

Jasmine frowns again. 'What's a flexitarian?'

Fiona blinks at me. 'So, you would like some fish?' she says slowly.

'I do try to be vegan,' I say earnestly, 'as much as I can, but I'm not strict with it.'

I break off, trying to fight the saliva pooling in my mouth as I stare at the fish and chips inches away from my plate.

Fiona shrugs and piles my plate with golden greasy batter and fat salty chips. I try not to whimper with relief.

William picks up his cutlery and starts smearing a chip in ketchup. I look around the table. Fiona's kitchen is spacious and bright, with wooden beams and a floor of mahogany tiles. As Jasmine and William dig in, I notice that there isn't a spare seat.

'Is your husband not eating?' I ask.

Fiona shakes her head, pulling out a bottle of white wine from the plastic bag.

'No,' she says, unscrewing the lid, 'he's busy working.'

'Daddy never eats with us,' Jasmine says.

'He did on my birthday!' William mumbles through a mouthful of chips.

Fiona holds the bottle towards me, and I shake my head.

'Sorry,' I say, 'pregnant.'

Gosh, I hope she's realised before now that I'm pregnant. I mean, I'm eight months gone!

She nods to herself in an 'of course' motion and glugs the near-transparent liquid into a large glass.

'So exciting that you're having a baby. Are you married?'

Her eyes flick down to my left hand, and I quickly swallow a chip, feeling my face tingle.

I haven't taken off my wedding ring. I don't know why. Danny has been gone for months.

'Yes,' I hear myself say. 'I've been married for two years. My husband works on cruise ships so is away a lot, but he's really excited.'

I pause, a hot feeling of shock shooting through me as I hear myself lie so freely. I stare down at my food, but as my words swim around my mind, my appetite is slowly replaced with the urge to vomit. What is wrong with me? Why can't I tell her the truth? She doesn't care, she doesn't even know Danny!

Fiona takes a swig of her wine, clearly unfazed by my answer.

'So,' I say, desperate to change the subject before any more lies fall out of my mouth, 'has Katy been here long?'

For a second I think Fiona is going to question why I don't

129

already know how long Katy has been in her job, but she stabs a chip with her fork and scrunches up her face as though trying to conjure up the memory.

'Two or three years,' she says. 'I needed an assistant. I run an events company called Hayes.'

Ah. So Katy does work for a company called Hayes. At least she hasn't been making that up.

'Katy applied, and she was so great.' Fiona leans over and wipes ketchup off William's cheek. 'At the interview, I asked where she was based and she said how she would need to relocate for the job. We'd just had the lodge built' – she lifts her wine glass towards the garden, where I can see the cabin glowing in the amber light of the lamp – 'because we were going to try and hire an au pair to help with the kids. It just felt perfect! It was only meant to be a temporary thing, but here we still are.'

She takes another sip of her wine, her eyes glazing over.

I put down my fork. I know I shouldn't pry. I should just ask Katy these questions myself, but now that I'm here, I can't stop myself.

'So,' I say, 'what exactly does she do for you? Does she work in the office?'

The word 'office' seems to break Fiona out of her trance, and she picks up another chip and dabs it in William's ketchup.

'Sometimes,' she says. 'She helps me with home life, the kids, my diary. She was involved with the last event I did, but that didn't go too well.'

She laughs loudly and Jasmine joins in.

'Mummy was really wet,' she says, grinning at me. 'She looked like she had gone swimming with all of her clothes on.'

Fiona smiles at me. 'There was an issue with the fire alarm.'

I try and smile back. Katy has always told me that she works in the office. None of this makes sense.

'But it's so exciting that Katy is going to be an auntie!' Fiona coos, leaning towards me. 'I bet she'll be fantastic. She's great with kids.'

Her words jolt me out of my thoughts with a cold shock.

'Yes,' I say quickly, 'though I haven't told her yet. I want it to be a surprise.'

I stare at her, trying to speak to her telepathically.

Please don't tell Katy I'm pregnant.

A look of confusion flits over her face, but she shrugs it away and takes another sip of wine.

'Oh,' she says, her eyes misting over again as she stares into the distance, 'how nice.'

Chapter Thirteen

Katy

I'm sitting on Rachel's sofa, my back poker straight as though I have a rod sewn into my skin. My hands, which have nearly frozen in their new claw position, hover over my laptop as my bloodshot eyes stare at the screen. They're dry and scratchy due to the lack of blinking I've done in the last day. Also, perhaps, the lack of sleep I had last night thanks to flickering paranoia of Fiona sending me a howler in the post and whimpering over my Cheerios like a commiserating Ron Weasley.

As soon as I had internet, I went through all forty emails that sprang onto my screen, hunting for some kind of clue that would seal my fate, but there was nothing. The only emails from Fiona, apart from her initial one that morning, were forwarded invoices and details of the auction winners. There was no mention of the disaster I'd caused, not to mention the assault of a colleague. It was like it never happened.

I scrunch up my eyes as they sear with pain, desperate for me to keep them closed for a second longer.

I tried to trick myself into believing that Fiona doesn't care and maybe it's no big deal. Perhaps this sort of thing happens all the time. Maybe it even made the whole event better and everyone is laughing about it, like it's a funny story that bonded the whole party together!

This fantasy lasted about four seconds.

Or she hasn't said anything because she wants to give me one last week of blind optimism before she fires me for being so completely incompetent. It was bad enough that I ruined the most important event of the entire year, but I also dumped my random sister on her property with no warning or apology.

My frozen hands twitch as a fizz of irritation shoots through me.

I still can't *believe* that Rachel moved into my house without my permission.

I've muted her calls and emails. She's tried to call me three times now, although she only left the one voicemail. I'll send her a message eventually, once I've worked out what I'm going to say.

Bruno yelps and I jump, the harsh sound shocking my body like a bolt of lightning. He has been firmly stropping because I still haven't taken him out on a walk. I pull myself to my feet and stomp towards the back door, kicking it open. Bruno zooms out and I quickly pull it shut, the wet air from outside speckling my face.

'There,' I say, dropping myself back on the sofa and staring at my screen again, 'go bark out there.'

I reread the email. I wrote it about an hour ago but I still haven't been able to send it. I actually composed it originally at

2 a.m., while I was lying in bed madly fantasising about every conversation going on in the office surrounding me and my failures.

Dear Fiona,

Hope you and the kids are okay.

Nice touch. Reminding her that I look after her bloody children all the time and they love me. If she fires me, they'll be devastated. Maybe I'll put Jasmine down as a character reference.

First of all, I am so sorry that my sister has arrived at the house. I had no idea she was going to do that.

Hmm. That suggests lack of control. I hit the delete key.

First of all, I am so sorry that my sister has arrived at the house. I was not expecting her to do that.

That's better. Stupid bloody Rachel.

She should keep herself to herself and not bother you or the children.

Code: she'd better keep herself to herself, and if she bothers you I will put butter in her lovely vegan face cream.

I would like to talk to you about the charity ball. How much did we raise in the end?

Ha. Very good way of subtly reminding Fiona that it was for charity after all and sacking me for a semi-harmless offence isn't very charitable.

Obviously it did not turn out the way I had hoped, due to unforeseen circumstances.

The unforeseen circumstances being Diane the raving maniac.

I hope you can see the hard work I put in . . .

I.e. that fucking big ice sculpture I ordered from Yorkshire. Do you have any idea how hard it is to find a courier who will transport an ice sculpture four hundred miles across the country?

. . . and may still consider me for the position of junior event coordinator in the office.

I bite my nail as I read the last sentence.

Fiona and I have spoken about me taking this job in passing, once. I finally plucked up the courage to bring up the fact that Caitlyn was leaving and I might like to be considered for the role, and Fiona shrugged (she was reading something on her phone) and said, 'Oh yeah, maybe.'

She didn't say no. She didn't leap out of her seat at the idea and marvel at why on earth she hadn't thought of it sooner, but she didn't say no. She said maybe.

Many thanks, Katy x

A humble offering of a kiss at the end, like a digital reminder that I once spent an entire evening making Jasmine's nativity costume when Fiona was in bed with the flu, so she really does owe me. Making an owl outfit from scratch is no easy feat.

I take a deep breath, my hand hovering over the keyboard. Before I can talk myself out of it, I hit send, holding my breath as I wait.

No internet connection!

I stare at my laptop, a great wave of fury bubbling under my skin.

Why won't this stupid piece of—

I grab my phone and jab at Rachel's name. The smooth ringtone starts rolling into my ears and I pace up and down the living room. I cannot believe she's had the nerve to leave me in this house without warning me that there is zero internet connection. I mean, does she have no respect for me at all? Does she not care how important my career is to me? Or that I have a life? What was she expecting me to do?

The phone clicks onto Rachel's answerphone and I throw my head back in annoyance.

Now she doesn't answer, when she's appeared more desperate to speak to me in the past two hours than she has done for the last two years.

A loud ripple of wind whooshes over the house and I scowl at the window as a black cloud spreads itself over the sun. I stomp towards the back door, my phone still pressed to my ear.

'Hi,' I say, 'it's me. Can you call me? It's impossible to get internet connection at the house and I have got to get online to do some work. I wish you had warned me about this. If I'd known I wouldn't be able to check my emails, I never would have come.'

I push the back door open and wait for Bruno to jump back inside the house.

'Also, I can't believe you never told me that Isaac's moved back in next door! Surely you knew how difficult I'd find it seeing him again, let alone being next door to him for an entire week.'

My heart races as I spill all my frustrations into Rachel's voicemail.

'I'm sure you've noticed that I bought the bike, but do you know what? I love it and I use it every day.'

I break off, suddenly aware that Bruno hasn't come inside. I scowl into the garden, trying to spot him.

Where is he?

'Please don't speak to Fiona while I'm away. It's a difficult time for me at work. I'm not sure if you've met her yet, but she is my boss,' I say, my voice stripped of any trace of anger as my eyes search for Bruno.

Why can't I see him? He usually runs inside as soon as I open the door.

'Anyway,' I say, a cold feeling of panic creeping through me, 'just call me back. I really need to get on the internet.'

I hang up, my arm dropping to my side.

'Bruno?' I call, leaning out of the back door. 'Bruno, come here!'

The echoing wind whisks my voice away and the garden blinks back at me, completely still. Rachel's garden is small and perfectly square. You can't get lost in it.

'Bruno!' I shout again, my voice more desperate. 'Bruno! You need to come inside!'

I step forward, my sock sinking into a square of damp mud. I wince, but I can't pull my eyes away from the garden, desperate to spot Bruno.

He's gone. He's not here. Where has he gone?

I pull my feet out of the mud and turn on my heel, running through the house. I grab my keys and slam the front door shut, and before I can even register my thoughts, I'm at Isaac's house, banging on the front door with my fist until he answers.

'It's Bruno,' I gabble as the door swings open, 'I think I've lost Bruno.'

★

Isaac looks at me as I zip Rachel's large anorak over my body and scowl. My God, this anorak is ugly. Why would she ever buy it? I know it's one of those super mountain gear brands and I'm sure she'd love to tell me all about how wonderful it is at keeping you dry and storing home-made granola bars, but couldn't she have got one that showed a bit of cleavage?

The coat hangs over my body and I look down at it. Does this really fit her? It's huge.

I squash my feet into wellington boots, strapping my Apple Watch firmly to my wrist. Isaac seems to have been born in outdoor gear, and is standing in the doorway in his ugly brown coat and his equally ugly bulky shoes. His curly hair is flopping in the wind and his bright eyes are scowling at me as though I'm the sun.

Not in a nice you-are-my-sunshine kind of way. More like a Christ-looking-at-you-is-like-having-my-eyes-singed-by-a-giant-ball-of-fire-and-you've-also-given-me-sunstroke way.

But he has agreed to help me, which is more than I was expecting. Perhaps more than I deserve, seeing that every time we've spoken since I arrived I've gone out of my way to make it obvious how little I want to speak to him.

Another blast of wind rattles the house and I wince. It's been about ten minutes since I thrashed Isaac's front door with every fibre of my being and then garbled my confession about what a terrible person I am. He just watched me, his face unchanging, and then picked up his coat and followed me out of the door. We haven't said a word to each other since. Really, I'm not sure I thought this through.

'You don't have to come,' I say quietly, trying to sound self-assured but unable to meet his eye. 'I'm sure I can find him.'

I slip the door keys into my pocket and we both walk out of the porch.

Bloody hell, it's freezing. When did it get so cold?

'You'll need my help,' Isaac says, looking towards the sea. 'I know the hills better than you do.'

I can't help but roll my eyes at the back of his head.

Oh please. What a pretentious answer. He's hardly Bear Grylls. He owns a gilet.

'Fine,' I say as I shut the gate behind us. 'I just want to find him. I don't know how he got out. Has he run away before?'

My eyes flit up to Isaac, desperate for him to reassure me and tell me that this happens all the time, but he doesn't even look at me. We start walking through the village towards a thin rusted staircase that climbs the height of the first cliff. I feel my stomach turn over.

'Do you really think he's up there?' I say. 'He wouldn't be able to climb those stairs by himself.'

Or would he? Let's be honest, I have grossly underestimated Bruno so far at every given opportunity.

'This is the walk Rachel takes him on every day,' Isaac says. 'It's what he's familiar with, and you can get to it through your back garden, which is where he escaped. I think he'll be around here somewhere.'

I squeeze my hands in my pockets and look over my shoulder, hoping that I might see Bruno bounding towards us and that he's just been hiding behind a flowerpot this whole time as a fun game. I feel a light splatter of rain dust my face and look up at the increasingly dark sky. Isaac flicks his hood up and carries on walking. I feel another twinge of guilt.

Isaac and I hardly finished on good terms. Until Sunday, the last time we saw each other was when we broke up.

'So,' I say, 'I thought you were living in Cardiff.'

I flinch. Why did that sound more like an accusation than a nice conversational question?

He keeps his eyes facing forward, his brow furrowed against the wind.

'I was,' he says. 'I moved back here a few years ago. I wanted to be with family. I like working on the farm.'

'Oh!' I say. 'Well, that makes sense. I can understand moving back here because you want to be with your family.'

For the first time, Isaac's eyes skirt towards me.

'What do you mean?' he asks.

'Well,' I say, 'I mean, you went to Cardiff. That's a city, it's a bit like London, isn't it? Full of life and everything, unlike here. Nobody in their right mind would want to live here unless they're retired, or like to pretend they're retired like Rachel does. There's nothing here. I think I'd die of boredom.'

I shoot him a smile, half expecting him to join in to complain about how boring life in Pembrokeshire is compared to Cardiff, but we fall back into silence.

'Well,' he says eventually, 'maybe I'll show you what we get up to in our boring lives,' he raises a sarcastic eyebrow, 'to stop us from dying of boredom.'

My face prickles.

'That's not what I meant.'

'I'll show you tomorrow if you like?' he says.

As I open my mouth to protest, I realise we've stopped walking.

'Here,' Isaac says as we reach the narrow staircase, 'ladies first.'

My eyes follow the ladder, which is pressed into the cliff face as if it has been carved into the rock. The wind, which has begun to swoop around us, sends splatters of rain into my face and I frown at Isaac, who is staring back at me expectantly.

'Could we drive?' I say. 'The weather seems to be getting worse.'

'No,' he says, 'and we should hurry up. We need to find Bruno before this storm hits.'

My eyes flit up. A heavy rumbling cloud has spread across the sky, drowning any flashes of blue. I pull the coat closer to my body and start to climb the ladder, horribly aware of how my wobbling arse will now be stuck in Isaac's face like a beacon of light for him to follow.

I must not have an involuntary asthma attack due to climbing these stairs and collapse in front of Isaac. I need to pretend that I climb stairs like these all the time and this is no big deal whatsoever. I will not give him the satisfaction of rescuing me again. I'd rather topple off the side of the cliff.

My legs begin to burn as I pull myself up. Streams of rain skid down the length of the rail and I feel my feet slip under the unsteady layering of steps. I glance over my shoulder at Isaac, who shoots me an impatient look, as if I'm walking slowly on purpose.

A bolt of lightning pierces the sky and my legs judder to a halt. Isaac knocks into me, and for a horrible moment I feel as though he might throw me over his shoulder if I don't move. The higher we climb, the harder the wind pummels against my ears, and although I know he's shouting something, I can barely hear him over the roaring gale.

'I just saw lightning!' I shout. 'We should turn back!'

'No!' Isaac yells. 'It's fine, we just need to keep moving!'

His firm body pushes gently against mine, and for a second I feel a small shock of heat shoot through my body. My sodden hand grips onto the icy railing and I continue to pull myself up the stairs.

Bloody Bruno, I'm going to kill him when I find him. I mean, what if he's not even up here and he's just having a lovely relaxing time in a sheltered nearby garden?

I squint my eyes upwards as my feet continue to climb. These steps feel as if they go on forever! I don't remember the climb being this hard when I was a teenager. There was a time when Rachel and I would run up them. With my free hand, I try to push back my hair, which is so wet it's begun to stick to my face like cling film.

I feel a small vibration on my wrist and look down, surprised that I have any feeling in my sodden hand at all. I realise my Apple Watch is flashing at me, and without quite meaning to, I stop walking again.

Oh my God, I have signal.

'What now?' Isaac shouts, his voice barely carried by the loud wind.

I must have climbed high enough to get signal! If I get to the top, I can finally send this email to Fiona.

'I've got signal!' I shout back, grinning over my shoulder. 'I finally have signal!'

I catch Isaac's eye and flinch. He's glowering at me.

'We need to keep moving!' he yells.

I am about to explain to him that of course I wasn't about to suggest that I stop here and start a new game of Candy Crush, but then realise that if I say another word, Isaac might throw me in the sea.

I furrow my brow as I scowl through the rain and spot a flash of green.

Okay, we're nearly at the top. It's only a few more steps.

With the fresh fuel of being able to connect to my emails pumping through me, I push my feet into the steps and pull myself upwards, trying to ignore the burning pain shooting up and down my legs.

'We're nearly there!' I yell, as I spot another dagger of lightning piercing the sky.

I hope Isaac knows what he's talking about and we're not about to get electrocuted.

The rain pummels against my skin and I suck in a gulp of earthy air, gasping as I reach the top. Great fields of green stretch out for miles, and the roaring sea slaps against the rocks below, dancing with the ferocious wind spinning through the sky. I turn to look at Isaac, who has climbed the final few steps and is standing behind me. For a second, he almost smiles at me. As I open my mouth to speak, my watch vibrates again.

Ah-ha! Signal!

'This way!' Isaac calls, marching past me like a Scout leader.

'Wait!' I shout back, tapping my watch.

Right. I definitely saved that email as a draft, so I just need to find it and then I can send it.

My watch buzzes continuously as all the emails I haven't been able to see over the past day spill onto the screen. I try and swipe them away quickly. I need to get to my drafts. The wind whips my hood off my head, but I keep focused on the watch.

I just need to send this one email.

'What are you doing?' Isaac shouts.

'I need to send an email!' I cry back, not daring to look at him as he throws his arms into the air in exasperation.

'What?' he yells. 'We need to find Bruno. Come on, this storm is getting worse!'

'Just give me a second!' I cry, frantically swiping all the notifications off the screen.

'No!' He marches back towards me. 'Katy, this is important.

Olivia Beirne

We need to find Bruno so that we can get back inside. It's not safe.'

He tries to take my hand away from the watch and I throw him off.

'This is important!' I cry. 'I need this for my work. It's—'

The words die in my mouth as the bar of signal keeping the watch alight vanishes. I feel a wave of dread.

No.

'Now look what you've done!' I yell, my eyes flying up to Isaac, who has already started walking down the path. 'I've lost my signal, you moved it!'

'Good!' he shouts over his shoulder. 'Come on!'

I glare at the back of his soaked curly head and storm after him.

'It's not good!' I yell. 'This is my job! I know it's never meant anything to you or Rachel, but it's— Oh!' My wrist vibrates again under another bar of signal. 'Isaac, wait! Wait! Just give me a second!'

Fat drops of rain splash onto the face of the watch and I try and rub them away, desperate to get onto my emails.

Come on. *Come on.*

I glance up and to my relief see Isaac storming back towards me. I don't care if he's angry, as long as he doesn't leave me here to be pecked to death by crows.

'Sorry,' I gabble, jabbing the watch, 'this will just take one minute— Oh *no*!'

The flicker of signal disappears again. Isaac turns on his heel and charges back down the path. I scurry behind him, but almost as soon as I begin to move, the watch vibrates again.

'Isaac!' I shout, my voice cracking in desperation. 'Sorry! Just give me a second, I need to send . . .'

I trail off and look up to see him standing right next to me, his face expressionless.

'Is it not working?' he says, and I almost jump at how calm his voice is.

'No!' I wail. 'I keep losing signal!'

A clap of thunder shakes the sky and I wince. Isaac's eyes flick up, then he holds out his hand.

'Give it to me,' he says. 'I'll fix it.'

He knows how to work it? Why didn't he say that earlier?

I hand him the watch quickly. He stuffs it into his pocket and starts to walk back down the path.

'I just need to get onto my emails,' I gabble desperately. 'I just need to email my boss, and then I can sort through the rest of them later.'

I frown as he ignores me, his eyes scouring the fields.

'Why aren't you doing anything?' I say. 'I thought you were fixing it.'

'We need to find Bruno,' he says, picking up his pace as another fork of lightning strikes in the distance. I feel a shock of anger.

Has he just confiscated my watch?

'I need to send an email!' I yell incredulously. 'You can't just take it! Give it back! Look!' I cry. 'I can see it lighting up in your pocket; that means it's got signal again! Just give it to me and I can send it! It will only take a second! Just give it to me!'

Isaac cuts off my screeches of desperation by pulling the watch out of his pocket.

'Don't move!' I yell. 'You'll lose the signal again! We just need to stay still for one minute, we just need to—'

But my words stick in my throat as he pulls back his arm

and launches my watch over the cliff. I watch in horror as it spins across the sky and is swallowed by the sea. He stares after it, his chest rising and falling heavily, and I feel hot anger ripple through me.

'What the hell are you doing?' I screech. 'What is the matter with you?'

'What is the matter with *you*?' he yells back, turning to face me. 'Your sister's dog is lost! You lost him! We need to find him before this storm gets worse and he gets stuck out here! How can you not care about anyone but yourself? He needs us! How can you be so blind to everything?'

I glare back at him, my ears ringing. Anger throbs through my body and I'm about to scream back when I see the shaggy, excitable shadow of Bruno bounding over the hills.

★

'Oh look.'

I stop walking as Isaac stretches his arm across me, gesturing to a rock, glistening in the rain. I squint, trying to work out what he's pointing at, then I spot it. A fat shimmering toad is sitting squat on the rock, its throat swelling rhythmically as though it's made from elastic. As I step closer, I feel my chest tighten.

'Your grandma loved toads, didn't she?' Isaac says, crouching down. 'I remember she cried when my cat once brought one in.'

The toad's bulbous eyes swivel towards me, and in the same beat it leaps into the bush. I never understood why Grandma loved toads so much, but she always made us stop and admire

146

them on walks. I find it strange now that some people are afraid of them.

'Yeah,' I say quietly as Isaac rises to his full height next to me, 'she did.'

I bury my face in the lip of my coat, trying to avoid his eyes.

I hate how much he knows about me. He even came to her funeral.

'I'm sorry about your watch.'

I feel an odd tingle in the pit of my stomach. Isaac's head is nestled into his coat; only his green eyes are peering out and locked forward.

I open and close my mouth, the many reactions to him literally throwing my watch over a cliff swirling in my mind, like they have been for the past hour.

I want to scream at him. It wasn't just my watch he broke, it was my chance to contact Fiona and try and make things right. With my laptop refusing to pick up any signal and Fiona's phone out of action, this might have been my only chance. I know I booked this week off work, but a week of silence is just a chance for Fiona to forget about me and any inkling she may have had that I could be a good junior events coordinator. I'll probably come back to find a new leggy employee, with glowing skin and streams of glossy hair, ready to go with her permanently relaxed expression and obsession with sparkling water.

But even though I'm angry, Isaac's words keep spinning through my mind and bringing a hollow feeling in my chest.

How can you not care about anyone but yourself?

Isaac and I always bickered, but we never really argued, not until we broke up. He always looked at me as though I was surrounded by a pool of golden light, but today his expression was almost one of disappointment. I didn't realise he was capable of looking at me like that.

'It's fine,' I mumble, staring down at Bruno as he tugs on his lead, pulling me towards the house. Isaac offered to hold him on the way home, but I refused. I wanted to prove that I wasn't completely useless.

The storm seemed to strip back its anger as we climbed down the cliff. The thunder rumbled lightly into more of a growl than a roar, and the flashes of lightning flickered in the distance, busy shocking other parts of Wales.

I pull my hood closer to my head, my hands feeling as if they might disintegrate. Sheets of rain continue to wash over us, as they have been from the second we set out.

I look up at Isaac as we reach my front gate, which is shaking slightly in the wind. Bruno whines and pushes his nose against it, but Isaac and I have stopped walking.

'Bye then,' I say quietly, barely making eye contact. 'Thanks for your help.'

Isaac gives me a half-smile.

'That's okay,' he says, shrugging his shoulders. 'I really am sorry about your watch,' he adds, forcing himself to meet my eyes. 'I shouldn't have done that.'

I feel my face grow hot.

'It's fine,' I say again, as Bruno nearly knocks me off balance by yanking on the lead.

'It's just,' Isaac pulls his eyes away from me, 'I sometimes don't . . . like I don't . . .' He trails off, pushing his boots into the mud.

I raise my eyebrows at him, waiting for him to finish.

'Okay,' I say eventually, kicking open the gate. 'Thanks again, Isaac.'

Chapter Fourteen

Rachel

I stare at the cleaning products, all neatly lined up in a row in order of size on the coffee table, standing proudly as if they're posing for a photo shoot. Katy's voicemail swirls round my head, like it has been since it came through this morning. I knew she'd be angry, but I hadn't expected her to be *that* angry.

I should have told her about the Wi-Fi. To be honest, I didn't think she'd have time for work; in my mind we'd either be spending the week together or she would have stormed out of the door the moment she unravelled all my lies.

I glance back down at my phone screen, the message to Katy still unread.

You need to sit on the old chair in my bedroom. Or turn the Wi-Fi on and off again. Ignore the orange light, it comes on for fifteen minutes, but after that it should work.

I slump my cheek into my hand as the baby shifts its position, then slide my hand onto my bump, my heart turning like it always does when I feel the baby move. None of my clothes fit me any more, not even the maternity bits I ordered online. I mean, am I that big? What do women do who are giving birth to twins? Or that woman in America who had octuplets? Was she just naked for her entire third trimester?

The only thing I've been able to squeeze myself into is an enormous maternity dress that is essentially a big sheet with a hole for my puffy face to pop through. So I will be living in this until I give birth, and if I wet myself before then (another fun factor they don't include on those yummy mummy baby films. I won't even go into what eight months of pregnancy does to your vagina, but let's just say mine currently looks like it's made out of puff pastry), I will wallow in my birthing pool until I go into labour like the enormous whale that I am.

Not that I have my birthing pool here, obviously. But I'm sure Fiona will have a spare paddling pool kicking about.

The one benefit of staying here is that I don't need to hide my bump. Fiona swallowed my lie that I'm happily married, and why shouldn't she?

I wasn't intending to tell anyone I was pregnant, not until I'd worked out what I was going to do. Although it's probably a good thing that Isaac barged his way into my house and Peggy caught me crying in the work loos, otherwise I wouldn't have told anyone until the baby was eleven years old.

Reluctantly Isaac swore himself to secrecy, not that he understood why. Nobody understands why I want to keep it a secret. I haven't even told Danny.

The bottle of bleach I've been staring at starts to mist up

before me, and I quickly wipe my eyes with the back of my hand.

My phone lights up next to me and I pick it up, feeling my stomach turn over as Katy's name flashes onto the screen. She's sent me a picture message.

Oh God, what now? Proof of me listening to her voicemail and ignoring her? A photo of her throwing all my white linen out of the window?

I open the message and see a photo of Bruno. He's curled up by Katy's feet, fast asleep with one of my cream blankets wrapped around him. A warm glow inflates in the pit of my stomach as I see that she has sent it with a heart emoji, and under the photo she's written, *Hope you're okay and the conference is going well.* I chew my lip. I'll tell her one day that the conference never existed.

As I close the message, the text from Isaac that came through this morning pops back onto my screen, glaring at me.

Hi, er . . . where are you? Aren't you supposed to be here to see Katy? Have you not told her anything? She's a total nightmare and I don't know how long I can stand her for. Please come back.

I smile at the message. Funny how they're both using me to vent their fury at being stuck next door to each other, and what a terrible situation they're in. Maybe it's because I'm the only one who knows how fine the line is for them between love and hate.

I lock my phone and push myself up to standing, scooping up a pile of Katy's washing and walking towards her machine.

I don't care if she gets annoyed; I'm going to clean her flat. It's bad enough that I have to climb up an actual ladder when I go to bed. I cannot stay in a flat that looks like it hosts a family of cockroaches.

As I stick the washing in the machine, adding fabric softener and feeling myself relax as the floral smell swirls around me, I hear a knock at the door.

I look over my shoulder and see Jasmine, her nose pressed to the window. I left their house last night almost as soon as I had finished eating, as the conversation was steering too close to my personal life. I did the polite thing, I accepted Fiona's generous offer of dinner. I even offered to help with the washing-up. I've paid my dues, and now I should be allowed to enjoy the rest of this week guilt-free and very much alone.

I pull open the door and Jasmine jumps onto the doormat, flashing her gap-toothed smile at me. She looks super cute in a tartan skirt and a white polo neck with a school crest embroidered on the chest. One of her socks has rolled down her ankle, and I notice a sticky red graze shimmering on her knee. She follows my gaze and grins.

'I fell over today,' she says proudly. 'We were playing stuck in the mud. Do you know how to play?' Her eyes suddenly widen at the idea, as though we could launch into another game.

An unflattering image pops into my mind of Jasmine trying to squeeze between my legs as I desperately try not to topple over like a tenpin skittle.

'Er,' I say, 'yes. But I can't play now, it might hurt the baby.'

I catch myself as I realise that this is the first time I've referred to the baby out loud, instead of murmuring 'I'm pregnant' like it was just something that was happening to me and was out of my control.

Jasmine looks at my stomach and scowls. I can almost see her little mind trying to work out how stuck in the mud might hurt a baby, when Fiona appears, half jogging down the garden.

William is running alongside her, his chubby arm in the air and a string of bubbles following him.

'Hi, Rachel,' Fiona says as she reaches me. She's clutching a stack of papers and is wearing an elegant shift dress with delicate strappy sandals.

'Sorry,' she says, shooting Jasmine a look. 'I told the children not to bother you. Rachel is busy, remember? She's not here to play with you.'

Jasmine scowls at her.

'School run?' I smile, as William starts spinning in circles to create a stream of bubbles.

Fiona rolls her eyes. 'Yes,' she says. 'Normally Katy and I do the school run together, and I go into the office in between. I work from home for the last few hours of the day, but my work is flexible, thankfully, and that's another reason why your sister is so brilliant.'

She smiles at me, and I feel a pang of guilt once again for the judgemental voicemails sitting on Katy's phone.

'Mummy!' Jasmine suddenly turns to Fiona and tugs on her arm. 'Show Rachel what we bought her!'

I frown.

'Oh!' Fiona laughs lightly. 'It's nothing. We just saw this and thought of you.'

'Where is it?' Jasmine says impatiently. 'I want to show her!'

'It's in the house, darling,' Fiona says, and with that Jasmine shoots up the garden like a ravenous bloodhound.

'You didn't have to buy me anything,' I say, feeling myself blush.

'It was Jasmine's idea,' Fiona says, kneeling down to help William with his bubbles. 'She's quite taken with you! Although

I'm not surprised. She adores Katy and you're practically identical. How's Katy getting on?'

'Fine,' I say automatically, feeling an odd tingle in the pit of my stomach at the reminder that I've barely spoken to my sister since she arrived in Wales and I'm pretty certain that she's actually doing terribly, thanks to me.

'Good!' Fiona says, pulling herself back to standing. 'She hasn't been replying to my emails, which is very unlike her, but I'm glad she's finally switching off. Ah!'

Jasmine skids to a halt next to Fiona and proudly sticks her hand out. A Waitrose vegan pasta dish for four stares up at me, and I smile.

'It's for all of us!' Jasmine chimes. 'Because I'm a vegan too.'

'Well,' Fiona says hastily, 'Rachel doesn't have to have dinner with us again, Jasmine. This meal is just for her.'

I look up and notice Fiona's face flushing.

'Is Daddy having dinner with us?' William asks, puffing out his cheeks to blow another bubble.

'No,' Fiona says, 'he'll be working late again tonight.'

'What are *we* having for dinner then?' Jasmine asks, still staring at the pasta dish in my hands.

'Spaghetti bolognese.'

'Is that vegan?'

I'm about to answer when Fiona gets there first.

'Yes, it is,' she says, shooting me a look. I try and hide my smile.

'I don't want that!' Jasmine says, screwing up her face. 'I want dinner with Rachel!'

Fiona's eyes narrow, and I almost want to laugh as Jasmine pulls an identical face back at her.

'It's okay,' I say quickly, 'we can all have it, I don't mind.'

Jasmine's face splits into a smile, and Fiona blinks at me.

'Really?' she says. 'Are you sure? I know you didn't plan a week in Chiswick just to spend it with us!'

She laughs a little too loudly and I feel a burning desire to reassure her, even though a week ago I didn't even know these people existed.

'No, really,' I say. 'It will be nice.'

Chapter Fifteen

Katy

I lean my weight on the kitchen counter as the coffee machine spins into life. White streams of light are flooding through the window, and I can see the orange glow of the sun peeking out over the hills like the fresh yolk of an egg. I didn't mean to get up this early – it's barely six – but I struggled to sleep. Again.

Bruno pokes his head around the kitchen door and tilts it at me. I don't know how he escaped from the back garden – although Isaac seemed to think there was an 'obvious hole' in the hedge – but I almost burst into tears when I saw him bounding across the field unharmed. I don't know if it was relief at not losing Rachel's dog or relief that he was okay.

'Hey.' I drop to my knees and hold out my hand towards him. He creeps forward until we are face to face, and then, before I can jump out of the way, flops his large body onto my legs. I wobble to the floor and Bruno sinks his weight into mine. Is he giving me a cuddle?

The coffee machine beeps impressively and I glance up towards its flashing light.

I rest my head against the kitchen cupboard and Bruno leans into me. Neatly framed photographs gaze down at me from the marble-white kitchen walls. I smile as my eyes scan them. Rachel has always loved photographs. When I asked for a set of paints for our thirteenth birthday, she begged for a camera, and she was forever dragging Grandma to Boots to get the photos printed so she could pin them up on the wall. She was always nagging me to pose, and secretly snapping away at me while I was painting. I pause at a photo of Danny and Rachel on their wedding day, their beaming faces plump and bright.

As I look closer, I notice shadows dotted across the wall. I didn't see them when I arrived, but now I realise that they are in the shape of missing frames. Did Rachel take some photos down?

I narrow my eyes, trying to work out who is missing. There are photos of Grandma, of me, even of Mum and Dad. There are lots of Bruno too, and as my eyes land on the final frame, my gut gives an uncomfortable squirm.

The only picture of Rachel and Danny is from their wedding day. That can't be right. But why would she take their photos down?

The coffee machine beeps again and Bruno turns his head to face me, his big eyes blinking at me.

'Sorry about yesterday,' I say, locking my arms around his neck. 'You really scared me, though. I promise I'll take you out for more walks from now on.'

157

He pushes his face closer to mine and I shrink backwards.

'Don't you dare lick me,' I say through tightly clamped lips. 'I know we're cuddling, but we're not there yet.'

I nudge Bruno off my lap and grab a coffee mug. For some reason, Rachel has kept all the mugs I made as a teenager. I don't know why; they don't match her Cath Kidston kitchen, the paint on the majority of them is faded, and one of the handles has fallen off. They look terrible.

I press another button on the machine, and a stream of coffee tinkles into the mug.

I haven't heard back from Rachel after that horrible voicemail I left her.

I feel a flash of guilt as snippets of my rant float back into my mind. Really, I shouldn't be allowed to leave voicemails. I should have just written her a letter; at least then by the time I found a stamp I could have cooled down and changed my mind. I sent her a happy photo of Bruno last night as a peace offering. Maybe if I call today she'll answer and we can have a real conversation.

I take a sip of my coffee, and jump as I hear a loud banging on the door. Bruno shoots out from under my feet, almost knocking me over, and yelps loudly as he bounds towards the window.

What? Who on earth is that?

I am about to flatten myself against the wall in an attempt to be out of sight when Isaac appears at the window. He stares right at me and I feel a burning flash of humiliation as I blink back at him, my hair screwed up above my head, spot cream crusted to my face and my old-lady pyjamas hanging off me.

Urgh, *again*? Does he pop by at the crack of dawn –

unannounced – every day? Is this just his thing? It's six in the bloody morning!

I freeze, feeling completely paralysed, as Bruno continues to bark, doing his classic trick of throwing his entire body against the window.

What am I supposed to do? Can I hide? Pretend this is just a figment of Isaac's imagination, or that I haven't seen him after all? Perhaps I could pretend I'm sleepwalking! Yes! I'll stick my arms out and glide back up the stairs and pretend none of this ever happened.

Although is it sleepwalkers who do that, or zombies?

Isaac knocks his knuckles on the window and raises his eyebrows at me, gesturing towards the front door.

Oh my God, he's not going to leave, is he? I can't see him now! I refuse!

Before I can stop myself, I shake my head in protest.

He can come back later when I'm good and ready, thank you very much!

To my annoyance, I see him laugh. He points again.

Oh for God's sake.

I stomp towards the door, quickly trying to pick the crusted spot cream off my face. Bruno bounces alongside me, thrilled that I'm giving in. Isaac seems to be his favourite person in the bloody world.

'Er, hi?' I say, trying to keep my eyes open as I step into a sudden beam of sunlight.

'Good morning to you too!' Isaac says brightly, and I fight the urge to throw my coffee over his chirpy face.

'It's six in the morning,' I whine. 'Why are you awake?'

The corners of his mouth turn up.

'I've been up since four,' he says. 'Did you forget our plan?'

He continues to smile, and I gawp back at him, suddenly unable to form any words whatsoever.

'We agreed yesterday,' he says conversationally. 'You wanted to see what life here was like in comparison to your exciting life in London.'

I wince as he repeats my words back to me.

Did I really say that?

'But if you've changed your mind, that's fine,' he continues. 'I wouldn't want you to do anything you can't handle, being a city girl and all. It might be too much.'

I open and close my mouth indignantly.

Is this why he's here? To try and prove a point about how out of touch I am?

'Don't be ridiculous,' I say indignantly, lifting my chin. 'I grew up here, just like you did.'

'Fine,' he says brightly. 'Well, we'll leave in ten minutes then, assuming this isn't your outfit for the day?'

I feel my face burn as he gestures to my fleece pyjamas.

'We said we'd meet up to*day*,' I say pointedly. 'This is not the day; this is morning.'

His mouth curls. 'The morning is part of the day.'

I open my mouth to argue, then stop myself.

Damn. He's right.

'If it's too early for you, I can come back later, or if you're not feeling up to it, we can take a rain check.'

I'm about to reply that *of course* it's too early for me and I need at least an hour to get ready, but my grip loosens on the door and for some reason I don't want to close it.

160

'No,' I say tightly, 'I just need to get dressed. Please,' I add, forcing a sugary layer to my voice, 'make yourself at home.'

I feel myself scrunch into a horrible false smile as Isaac steps inside, Bruno leading the way.

'Great,' he says, dropping onto the sofa. 'Do you want breakfast? I'll make it as a peace offering for your watch. You'll need some stamina for the day. I brought some more eggs.' He reaches into his bag and pulls out a small cardboard carton.

He needs to offer me a lot more than a lousy boiled egg for destroying my watch!

'No thank you,' I say, turning on my heel and stalking up the stairs. 'I hate eggs.'

And with that I flounce into my room and smother my face with every bit of make-up I can find in the quickest time possible. All the while trying to ignore my stomach howling at the idea of a delicious morning omelette.

I bloody love eggs.

*

I glare at Isaac as he hops over the fence like it's no big deal whatsoever.

Surely not. Surely Isaac hasn't arrived at my house at the crack of dawn, demanding I get dressed and dragging me out into the rain, just to trick me into helping out on his farm.

'Come on,' he says as he lands on the other side. 'You just need to straddle it.'

To my annoyance, I feel myself blush furiously. He definitely said that on purpose.

It took me almost half an hour to get ready. I had an absolute disaster trying to work out what to wear. It didn't help that I had no idea where we were going or what we were doing. I haven't seen him in years; God only knows what he gets up to these days.

The main fear fluttering around my mind was whether or not this was a date, seeing as Isaac never actually asked. If he had, I would have said no. Obviously. I do not want to be on a date with him. But still, in order to try and claw back some of my dignity after my earlier fleece pyjamas and morning breath, I spent at least ten minutes choosing my outfit. I ended up throwing on skinny jeans and my mustard, knitted jumper, so I can remind Isaac how great my boobs are (it's quite fitted) without being in danger of him telling me off for not wearing enough layers (like he did when I asked if I could wear a skirt).

I mean, thank God I didn't wear a skirt if this day is going to consist of light straddling.

'You okay?' he says as I swing my leg over the fence with ease, fighting the urge to punch the air in satisfaction.

Yeah. Stick that in your it-might-be-too-much-to-handle pipe, Isaac.

As I lift my chin to shoot him a look of triumph, I take a good look at the farm, and a warm sense of familiarity rolls through me. I spent my teenage years on this farm with Isaac.

'Do you still work here?' I ask, following him as we walk towards a barn. 'Is that why you came back?'

I gasp as a horse sticks its head out of a stall. It has a chestnut mane and long, curled eyelashes. Isaac stops walking and starts to pet it.

I feel my heart lift.

Are we going riding? I could forgive Isaac and his know-it-all attitude if he's taking me riding.

'Yeah,' he says, stroking the horse's long nose. 'My parents asked if I wanted to come back and help. I wanted to be with Felix too; he was going through a hard time at school.'

I frown. 'Felix?' I repeat, picturing Isaac's younger brother wearing a dinosaur T-shirt and giggling with a gap-toothed smile. 'Isn't he like, what, seven?'

Isaac grins at me. 'Thirteen.'

My mouth falls open. 'No!'

He laughs, feeding the horse an apple from his pocket. We fall back into silence, and a familiar simmering feeling starts to resurface.

'So,' I say, 'are we going riding?'

I reach out and touch the horse's mane.

'Why?' Isaac says, not taking his eyes off the animal. 'Do you fancy a ride?'

I feel a flash of heat surge through me. Isaac catches my eye and bursts into laughter.

'Oh come on!' he says, nudging me with his free arm. 'That was funny! You asked for it. Have you forgotten how to laugh since you've lived in London?'

'If you just want to piss about, then I'll leave,' I say haughtily, crossing my arms over my body. 'I have a lot of very important work to do.'

'Sorry,' Isaac says, trying to look apologetic and failing. 'It was only one joke.'

'And you said that other word earlier.'

'What word?'

'Straddle.'

Urgh. I've only been with him an hour and he's tricked me into saying the word *straddle*.

He laughs again.

'Right you are,' he says, giving the horse a final stroke and walking towards the farm. 'I'm showing you Welsh life today, that's all, just in case you've forgotten it.'

I roll my eyes at the back of his head.

'Of course I haven't forgotten it.'

'Good,' he says, shooting me a smile over his shoulder. 'Then this should be a breeze.'

CHAPTER SIXTEEN

RACHEL

I step back and proudly admire Katy's flat. I've scrubbed her kitchen (as well as any pregnant woman can scrub), I've dragged her wretched Henry hoover round and I've tidied and organised her washing. I feel a little zap of joy zoom through me as I admire my work.

I love having everything neat and in order. It makes me feel calm.

The cleanest thing in Katy's lodge is the Super Bike, which I've been secretly glowering at every thirty seconds. I don't know why I was shocked that she spent so much on a bike, considering as teenagers she once tricked Dad into buying her an 'essential' swimming costume for fifty pounds. She claimed our PE teacher had recommended it as the top swimsuit to wear in swimming lessons, whereas I knew it was in fact the top swimsuit to wear to get Isaac's attention when we all went paddleboarding.

I laugh at the memory. Dad was so mad when he found out. He was even angrier when Grandma accidentally-on-purpose threw out the receipt and insisted that we deserved nice things.

I jump out of my thoughts as my phone starts singing next to me. Peggy's name pops onto the screen and I smile.

'Hey!' I say, snapping off the rubber gloves. 'How are you?'

'Oh hello, love!' Peggy cries, her warm Welsh voice gleaming with surprise. She always seems totally shocked whenever I answer the phone. It's like she's never used a telephone before and just can't believe it's worked.

'Now listen,' she says, 'are you at home? Only there's a sale on at JoJo Maman Bébé and I'm going to pop in. Would you like to come?'

I try not to laugh at her weird attempt at a French accent.

'Oh, I'm not in,' I say without thinking, and then immediately want to kick myself.

Peggy has made no effort to hide the fact that she finds it utterly bizarre that I'm hiding my pregnancy from practically the entire world. She always spills into a lecture about how a baby is a gift and I should be thanking the Lord and praising Jesus, blah blah blah.

I think she's been watching too much *Call the Midwife*. She's not even religious!

'You're not in?' she repeats. 'Where are you, love – at the hospital?'

I chew on my nail.

Hmm. Usually I would have no issue spouting a harmless white lie to Peggy. But if there's one thing I've learnt, it's that she loves popping round without warning. If she thinks I'll be home later, then she'll raid the maternity section of New Look, then appear at the cottage with a Chinese, ready to do a fashion show.

'Er, no,' I say eventually. 'I'm actually in London.'

'London!' she shrieks, her voice piercing my eardrums as though I've told her I'm chilling out in the middle of the Sahara Desert.

Okay, I just need to play this down and pretend it's no big deal.

'Yup,' I say lightly. 'I just fancied a city break. I was going to go to Amsterdam, but I couldn't get flights.'

As soon as the words leave my mouth, I wish I could catch them and cram them back in.

'Darling, are you okay?' Peggy says in hushed tones. 'Are you really in London, or are you somewhere else? Are you in danger? If you are in danger, cough once.'

I roll my eyes. For goodness' sake. Scrap *Call the Midwife*; Peggy has clearly moved on to *Line of Duty*.

'Peggy, I haven't been kidnapped!' I say. 'I'm staying at my sister's place in London. I just wanted to get away.'

I can almost hear Peggy's brain manically trying to fathom why anyone would want to go on a mini break to London when you could go on a nice walk by the sea (her answer to everything).

'Oh right,' she says, 'so Katy's with you then, is she?'

Heat prickles up my neck. 'Yes. We thought it would be easier if I came to London instead.'

'Oh,' she says, 'well, that's nice. So how did Katy take the news? Are you having a lovely time together? Did you give her my present?'

I feel a wave of guilt. When I told Peggy that Katy was coming down to stay so that I could break the news, she got so excited that she bought her an *I'm going to be an auntie!* T-shirt.

I can't tell her that Katy isn't here. She'll never understand.

'Er, not yet,' I say. 'I'll give it to her later.'

'And was she excited?'

'Yup,' I say, crossing my fingers behind my back, 'she was thrilled.'

'Ah!' Peggy puffs in relief. 'I told you she would be. See, you were worrying about nothing, weren't you? And I bet she's moving back into the cottage too, isn't she?'

I open and close my mouth.

Okay, this is getting too much. I need to distract her.

'Actually, Peggy,' I say quickly, 'while you're shopping, could you possibly pick me up a . . .'

Shit. Think of something pregnancy-related. Something, anything!

My eyes fly madly around the lodge, desperate for something I can ask for, and land on William's tennis racket.

'. . . a baby tennis kit?'

My cheeks flame as the words fall out of my mouth.

God, I am a terrible person. Here's Peggy trying to help me like the guardian angel she is, and I—

'What the shag is that?'

Okay, maybe not an angel. An angel with a potty mouth. I'm sure they exist.

'Yup,' I babble, trying my best to sound convincing, 'I'd like the baby to start tennis right away. I read an article about it. That's how the Williams sisters got so good, and I actually had a dream last night that the baby became the youngest ever Wimbledon champion. I think it may be a premonition. It's really important that they start from birth.'

'From birth?' Peggy echoes, flabbergasted. 'Sweetheart, is baby tennis gear really a thing?'

Why did I say this? Why didn't I just ask her to get me a sodding babygro? I don't even like tennis!

'Yup,' I say again. 'They should have it at JoJo Maman Bébé. Obviously I'll transfer you the money.'

There is a silence down the phone and I practically hold my breath.

Please don't question me any more on the stupid tennis kit.

'Okay, love,' Peggy says, 'I'll do my best. It would be quite fun to go to Wimbledon one day, wouldn't it?'

I feel a wave of relief as we say goodbye and ring off. Okay, I'll just need to keep Peggy at bay for the next few days. She shouldn't ask any more questions about Katy, and by the time the baby arrives, she'll be so overcome with excitement that she'll forget all about it.

I flick the kettle on, pulling a decaf tea bag out of the cupboard and dropping it into a mug.

God, I miss caffeine.

I stayed with Fiona last night until much later than I'd intended to, and it was only when William started falling asleep in his pasta that we realised what the time was (much to the annoyance of Jasmine, who had been telling us all about her geography project where she has to make a globe).

The first night in their kitchen had felt forced, like it was obvious I had only agreed to be polite, but last night was different. The four of us sat around the table like it was completely normal, and for a moment I almost understood why Katy hasn't moved out into a flat. I felt as though I was part of a real family, eating dinner together, everyone chatting about their day. With Danny always working on cruise ships, I haven't had that since Katy and I were teenagers. Neither of us has.

I pick up my mug and manoeuvre myself onto the sofa. The baby shuffles around, and I feel a cold feeling spread through me as a new image creeps into my mind. It's just me and the baby, alone at the table. There's no happy chatter between a family, or visitors popping round for dinner. Katy sends the obligatory birthday card once a year and a stuffed animal, but that's it.

I shake the image out of my head.

Don't think about that. You have no idea how she's going to react. She might surprise you.

Maybe.

I pick up my phone and turn it in my hands. The last message from Katy, the photo of Bruno, smiles up at me. I never reacted to the voicemail she left me. She was right, again. I should have warned her about the dodgy connection and Isaac living next door. I was so wrapped up in my own problems that it didn't even cross my mind.

I click her name and hold the phone to my ear, gearing myself up to leave yet another voicemail. Ordinarily Katy and I never speak on the phone, mainly because neither of us ever answers. We swap the usual stories over email, or occasionally text message (mine are all rehearsed rubbish about my lovely week at work), and then tick the 'I'm a good, caring sister' box and carry on with our own lives, sending the odd email in between. I realised that was the best way to secure a response. Katy swears by her emails.

Sometimes I feel as though—

'Hello?'

My heart skips as Katy's voice springs into my ear. She answered? She never answers!

'Hi!' I say, feeling a bolt of adrenaline rush through me. I was not ready for this.

'How are you?' I say.

Although maybe she just answered so that she can shout at me down the phone.

'I'm okay!' she says. 'I'm sorry about that voicemail I left you.'

I pause.

'I'm sorry I didn't warn you about the internet. I did send you a message about how to get it to work,' I say quickly, 'but Fiona seems really nice. I don't think she'd be annoyed at you not working.'

I start to nibble my nails as I wait for Katy to respond.

'What do you mean?' she says. 'Have you spoken to her?'

Oh shit.

Is now the time to tell her that not only have I spoken to her, I've actually had dinner with her, twice?

'Er, yeah. A bit.'

I hear Katy huff down the phone.

'Does she seem angry?'

I frown. 'No,' I say. 'Why would she be angry?'

'Doesn't matter,' Katy says, the lightness in her voice gone. 'Look, I've got to go. I've got to sort out a goose.'

She's got to sort out a what?

The line goes dead, but I keep the phone to my ear, trying to squash the feeling that I've done something wrong, again.

I should have just sent her an email.

Chapter Seventeen

Katy

What Disney film is it where the princess is lightly scattering food for the animals? All the animals (who seem to have inexplicably long eyelashes) dance over to her and gently graze on the food, only stopping to chirp in time with a sweet harmony or shoot her a look of pure love.

Well whatever film it is, this goose is not in it.

The goose squawks loudly at me from across the pen, and I narrow my eyes, fighting the urge to make a run for it. Or throw my shoe at its stupid head.

It turns out that I completely wasted my energy earlier wondering whether or not this was a date. Who knows who I bothered flicking my eyeliner to perfection and applying subtle lip liner for, because it certainly isn't Isaac. It turns out he was just after some free labour. About ten minutes after we arrived, he started delegating chores for me to do, like some doleful old maid and then proceeded to swan off and leave me to it. Though not before smugly saying over his shoulder: 'You'll be fine, right?'

And now, an hour later, I have collected eggs, swept the courtyard (I mean, *really*) and am supposed to be feeding the chickens. That is if this goose doesn't kill me first.

I mean, yes. I spent a lot of time here as a teenager, but not doing *this*. We used to go horse riding or pet the piglets, and in spring sometimes we'd help feed the lambs with milk bottles. That was fine, lovely even. This is just manual labour.

I carefully drop another handful of seeds onto the ground, keeping my eyes firmly fixed on the goose, which keeps stretching its wings into the air like it's challenging me to a duel.

Where did it even come from? Geese aren't a farmyard animal, are they? Did Old MacDonald have a goose?

I stick my hand back into the bag of seeds, my mind still racing after my phone call with Rachel. She sounded different, a bit jittery and nervous where normally she's completely calm and in control. That can only mean one thing. Fiona must have said something to her about the disaster I caused at the auction, and confided in her about how she's going to have to let me go.

She was definitely hiding something.

'How's it going?'

I snap out of my thoughts as I hear Isaac behind me. He's leaning over the fence and smiling, that smug look back on his face. I try not to scowl at him.

I lift my chin. 'Fine!' I say, tossing another handful of feed into the pen.

The goose honks loudly.

'Good,' he says, hopping over the fence. He steps towards me and dips his hand into the bag. 'Sorry about that.' He gestures over his shoulder. 'I just needed to call one of our suppliers.' His smile is so genuine I almost feel my annoyance slip. 'So,' he says, 'what would you usually be doing now, if you were at home in London?'

I step over a splat of chicken poo.

Hmm. It's just gone 8 a.m. on a Wednesday, which means I'd be helping Jasmine and William get dressed before going on the school run with Fiona.

Not that I'll be admitting that.

'Oh,' I say, 'you know, I'd probably be having breakfast with some friends.'

Isaac shoots me a look. 'You go for breakfast before work?'

Ha. Perfect.

'Oh yeah,' I say, 'we do that all the time in London. Sometimes we even go to the Shard.'

I've never been to the Shard in my life, but good to throw it in there. It impresses virtually everyone.

'You go to the Shard, casually, before work on a Wednesday?' Isaac says slowly.

I feel my face pinch and turn away.

Hmm, okay. Maybe the Shard was a bit much. But you know, can't back down now.

'Oh yeah,' I say again. 'It's just a casual London thing, you know, just to have a latte and perhaps some—'

HONK!

Fuck.

I trip over my feet as the goose launches itself behind me, desperate to get at my bag of seed. I clutch the seed close to my body and turn my back, but the goose continues to squawk loudly and starts to jab me with its beak.

What is this animal's problem?

'Aargh!' I shriek, trying my best not to gallop around the pen like a terrified Shetland pony. 'What is it doing?'

'It's calling bullshit,' Isaac says as he leans back against the fence, not bothering to help me in any way with this wild animal that looks as if it's about to eat me.

'What?' I say, skirting away from the goose as best I can.

'Oh come on!' he laughs. 'Breakfast at the Shard on a Wednesday? Why won't you tell me what life is really like in London? Why are you so desperate to convince me that it's that much better than living here?'

I catch his eye, my grip loosening on the bag of seed. I feel my cheeks flare as his question cuts through my bravado.

'I told you what it's like,' I say, my voice wavering. 'You just can't imagine it because you've never been to London,' I add, fixing his steady eyes. 'You've barely left Wales, it's just not like you.'

'It's not like you either,' he says, raising his eyebrows at me. 'I may not know London, but I know you.'

I feel a flash of heat shoot through me and drop the bag to my waist indignantly. As I open my mouth to reply, the goose spots its opportunity and launches at my stomach. I scream and drop the bag, and suddenly all the birds are flapping around me, desperate to get the scattered seeds. Isaac jumps over the fence and grabs the bag off the floor. He goes to take my hand, but I snatch it away.

'Are you happy now?' I snap. 'You've proved your point. I don't belong here. I belong in London.'

He looks back at me, his chest rising and falling.

'That's not the point I was trying to make.'

*

Isaac hands me a steaming mug and I take it, giving him a limp smile as I do.

'I'm sorry about the goose,' he says, sitting on a bale of hay. 'I didn't think he'd actually attack you.' He looks at me and I notice the corners of his mouth turn up. 'He's usually just a bit aggy.'

'Are you laughing?' I say indignantly. 'That was traumatising for me! I thought I was going to be pecked to death by bloody poultry.'

A snigger pumps out of him this time, and to my annoyance, I start to laugh too. He shakes his head and sighs, lifting his tea to his lips. I feel my heart turn over as I recognise the fat clay mug cupped in his hands.

'That's one of my mugs,' I say, leaning forward to get a better look.

Grandma taught me how to make pottery when I was a teenager. Art flowed through her veins and out of her fingers like magic. There was always some large canvas propped up against the wall, splattered in paint or holding the smooth lines of her latest work. The mug Isaac is drinking from isn't one of my best – the clay is too thick and the handle is fat and wonky – but the paintwork is better than I remember it being. I can't believe he still has it.

He looks at it and smiles fondly. 'Oh yeah,' he says. 'This is my mug. I drink all my tea from it.'

He raises it in a cheers motion, and I notice a small painting of a horse at the bottom.

'Chestnut,' I say, as the name springs back into my mind. 'That was supposed to be your horse, that painting.' I squint at it, leaning forward to get a closer look. 'It's not very good, though.'

He turns the mug to face him. 'It's great. Looks just like her.'

I smile and take a sip of my own tea, which is perfectly sweet with three sugars. I didn't have to remind Isaac how I like my tea; he remembered.

'I'm sorry for what I said,' he says after a moment of silence. 'About you wanting to convince me about London. I'm sure your life there is great.'

I feel a stab of heat as doubt rolls over me.

Is my life great in London?

'Yeah,' I say, 'it is.'

We fall back into silence and I shuffle my feet against the concrete, trying to scrape the thick mud off the soles of my shoes.

'Do you want to see her?' Isaac says. 'Chestnut, I mean.'

I look up from my tea.

'Is she here?' I ask, looking around as if the horse is about to creep up behind me.

'Yeah,' he says. 'She didn't run off to flashy London.'

I flinch.

He hasn't let that go then.

He looks down at his tea and we fall back into an awkward silence.

'She's getting old now,' he says eventually, as though he's decided to answer my question properly, 'but she still loves going out for a ride, if you want to see her . . .'

His question trails off, sounding more like it came from a fourteen-year-old boy asking a girl to the cinema.

I haven't been horse riding since we broke up.

'Yeah,' I say, smiling at Isaac properly for the first time since I've been back, 'I'd love to.'

He grins and gets to his feet, downing the last dregs of his tea. I quickly do the same and follow him across the courtyard. There is a light drizzle of rain peppering the farm, but I don't really care. I take a deep breath, the salty sea air filling my lungs, and smile into the sky. Isaac gestures me round a corner and I pick up my pace to walk alongside him.

'Here she is,' he says as we reach the stable. 'You met Roberta earlier.'

I scrunch up my nose and Isaac laughs.

'Felix named her,' he says.

'Oh.' I smile.

Chestnut is standing at the back of the stable and lifts her head as we arrive.

'Hey, girl,' Isaac says gently, holding out his hand to say hello. 'Remember Kitkat? She used to come here a lot.'

I feel a light tickle in the pit of my stomach. Nobody has called me Kitkat in years. Although I don't know why anyone would; it was Isaac's nickname for me.

A large grin breaks out on my face as Chestnut walks towards us.

'Hey,' I say, reaching out and stroking her nose, 'hey, beautiful girl.'

We fall into silence as we both stroke her, laughing when she lets out a snort and shakes her mane.

'God,' I say, 'I hadn't realised how much I missed horses.'

'Riding them?' Isaac asks, his question this time free of any innuendo. Thank God.

'Everything about them,' I say. 'Riding them, being with them, looking after them. I haven't been around a horse since I left Wales.'

Chestnut pushes her face towards me, eager for more attention.

'Come on,' Isaac says, and begins to walk back across the courtyard.

'What?'

'Let's go for a ride!' he calls, grinning as he gestures me to follow him.

As I start to follow him, a large splat of rain hits the crown of my head.

'But it's raining!' I say, although I can't help but laugh.

Isaac reaches out to take my hand.

'Oh come on,' he grins. 'You don't really care about that, do you?'

This time I don't pull my hand away as I realise that he's right. I don't care at all.

CHAPTER EIGHTEEN

RACHEL

I clip the final sock onto Katy's washing line. Katy's new washing line, I should say; I ordered it for her off Amazon along with a real hoover (this was more for my benefit than hers) and a soup maker. I can even show her my favourite soup recipe next time I see her. Whenever that might be.

I re-peg a camisole to the line and try to ignore the flicker of fear in the pit of my stomach.

The novelty of running away to London in the dead of night to hide from my problems has worn off, and whether I like it or not, soon my problems will be flexing their muscles ready to carry me back home. Regardless of whether I've worked out how to deal with them.

I feel my phone vibrate in my back pocket and pull it out. Mum's name flashes up and I swipe open the message.

Sorry haven't called! In South of France with the children.

Several pictures pop onto the screen of Mum with her arms tightly wrapped around her second set of children, who are both under seven. Her new husband, Mark, is standing behind her, flashing a thumbs-up at the camera.

I get these types of messages about once a month, after she's let three calls roll into her voicemail and decided not to call me back. They are always quick, flashy apologies where she gives me a ten-second snapshot of how great her life is but never asks me about mine. The older I get, the harder I find it to remember if she was always like this or whether she just stopped caring after Dad had the affair.

I know Katy speaks to Dad all the time. He'd never ignore a call.

'Hi, Rachel!' Fiona calls, making her way down the garden, Jasmine and William both skipping by her side. 'I've just got off a call. Longest day ever. How was yours?'

She smiles as she reaches me, and I grin back at her.

'Oh!' she cries, closing her eyes and taking a deep breath. 'Something smells nice. Is that you?'

I look over my shoulder to where the slow cooker I found under the sink (my present to Katy two Christmases ago) is bubbling away happily with a curry.

'Yeah,' I say. 'I thought I'd dust off the slow cooker.'

'Delicious!' she coos, picking up a scrabbling William and resting him on her hip.

My heart squeezes as I watch the two of them. William wraps his chubby arms around Fiona's neck and pushes his cheek against hers.

Will I have a boy? Will that be me in a few years, blissfully happy with my child perched on my hip as though it's the most natural thing in the world, and not something I spent nine months pretending was just a weird dream?

William whispers in Fiona's ear and she laughs loudly, digging her fingers into his side and making him scream in delight.

How does she do that? How does she make it look so easy?

'Well,' she says, 'we'll leave you to it. Glad you're having a relaxing time.'

'Have you spoken to Katy today?' Jasmine demands as Fiona turns to walk back down the garden path.

I'm pulled back to reality by the question, and Katy's snappy voice down the phone rings through me.

'Er,' I say, 'yeah. She's okay, she's been playing with a goose today.'

'A goose!' William cries, throwing his arms in the air and almost knocking Fiona off balance. Jasmine peals with laughter, and I can't help but smile back, a warm feeling flooding me as we all laugh together.

'Come on, you two,' Fiona says. 'We need to leave poor Rachel alone. God knows what we'll have for dinner. I don't even know what food we've got in!' She shoots me a look over her shoulder, laughing gaily. The three of them begin to walk up the path, and before I can stop myself, I call after them, as if I'm the child they've forgotten to take with them.

'Wait,' I say. 'Why don't you have dinner with me? There's more than enough.'

The last sentence falls out of my mouth in a rushed gabble and I feel my cheeks pinch, my body leaning towards them as if we're all attached by a piece of string.

Fiona opens her mouth to answer, but Jasmine gets there first.

'Yes!' she cries, punching her arm in the air. 'William, we're having dinner with Rachel *again*!'

William scrambles out of Fiona's arms and they both start a happy dance on the grass. Fiona peers at me.

'Are you sure?' she says slowly. 'We don't want to put you out, and we've bothered you a lot on this trip.'

I look back at her, a Catherine wheel of anxiety spiralling through me at the thought of Katy finding out how much time I've been spending with her boss, doing exactly the thing she told me not to do. But then a stronger feeling takes over.

I don't want to be by myself. These past few days have made me feel more part of a family than I have done in years.

'Really,' I say earnestly, 'I've loved it.'

CHAPTER NINETEEN

KATY

'Here we are,' Isaac grins, stepping back to allow me to climb the steps that lead up to the Sailor's Ship. My legs ache from riding as I make my way up, and a fresh slice of sunshine peeks through the clouds. Oh *now* it stops raining, after we've got royally soaked galloping across fields and are about to sit inside a lovely warm pub.

Isaac let me ride Chestnut while he took a larger, younger horse out. For a moment, I was worried I'd forgotten how to ride and had flashing visions of being bucked off and landing splat in a puddle of manure. But as soon as I climbed on, electricity shot through me, snatching away any simmering anxiety, and as I galloped through the fields, I felt happier than I'd felt in years. I felt completely free.

I catch sight of my reflection in the glass of the pub door and try to suppress a shudder. The only issue with this is that I forgot what riding in near-torrential rain would do to my hair/ face, and now I look like Worzel Gummidge.

I tuck my hair behind my ears in a desperate attempt to keep it tame.

Could I sneak home and have a quick shower?

'So!' Isaac chirps. 'What do you fancy?'

Isaac laughed a lot when we were out riding; we both did. I don't even know what we were laughing about, but it was as though we caught each other's eye and realised how ridiculous it was that we were pretending to still be angry at each other. In that moment, we couldn't help but drop the forced scowls we'd been throwing back and forth for days. We just laughed instead.

In a friendly way, obviously. Nothing more. I'm sure I'd have the same feeling if I went riding with Fiona. Assuming, that is, that she hadn't started the ride by firing me and I wasn't galloping after her in mad desperation for her to reconsider.

I lean over the bar to peer down at the drinks fridge, ducking beneath the low, mahogany beams that glisten under the dim lights and resting my elbows on one of the towelling beer mats that are spread across the bar, of brightly coloured animals holding up frothy pints.

'I don't know,' I say quietly, trying to spot a drink I'd recognise.

I hardly ever drink in London. I don't really get the chance. Occasionally Fiona and I share a bottle of wine on a Friday night, and about once a month I summon up enough courage to attend the Friday-night drinks with the team from Hayes, where I obediently drink whatever everybody else is drinking in a lame attempt to fit in. But I can hardly order a porn star martini here.

I think if I said the words porn star in front of the old barman, he might collapse.

The inside of the pub seems smaller than I remember it, with a wonky tiled floor and framed photos of ships hanging on the cracked walls. A light smell of ale fills the place, just like it always did, except for on Sundays, when the thick smell of roast beef was strong enough to swallow the entire village. Each chair is a different shape and size, and every table is covered in rings, a tribute to the many pints that have been happily guzzled by the locals. I catch Isaac tipping an imaginary hat to a windswept couple perched on squishy sofas by the fire, and feel warmth spread through me. I'd forgotten what it feels like to know everybody in the local pub. It feels like coming home.

'Cider?' Isaac offers. 'You like cider, right?'

I look back at him. The rain has made his curly hair madder than ever, and his cheeks are tinged pink from the brisk wind, but his cheekbones still demand attention, sticking out of his face proudly.

Before I can stop myself, I'm grinning at him again as my heart lifts.

I don't have to pretend to be anything but myself with him. He doesn't care. I could ask for my drink to be served in a wellington boot and he wouldn't bat an eye.

'Sure,' I say.

The barman hands us two pints filled to the brim with a yellowish-brown liquid. Isaac nods his thanks, then gestures for me to follow him. I glance back at the barman anxiously.

'Don't we have to pay?'

Isaac shakes his head and places our pints down on a copper-brown table that tips slightly under the struggle of having slightly uneven legs. I sit in the chair opposite, feeling myself sink into it as though the arms are curling around my body and giving me a hug.

'He'll stick it on a tab,' he adds, noting my worried face. 'So,' he says, picking up his pint and gesturing for me to do the same, 'cheers then.'

'What are we toasting?' I ask, holding up my glass.

He grins. 'You having your Welsh accent back.'

I try and shoot him an indignant look, but fail.

'I never lost my accent,' I say, taking a sip of the cider. A sweet apple taste floods the inside of my mouth, and I feel a blanket of warmth spread over my damp body as the bubbles pop down my throat.

How did he know exactly what I needed?

'So,' I say, resting the glass on the arm of the chair, 'you're one of the regulars now?'

He frowns at me and I cock my head towards a group of middle-aged men sitting at the bar and jostling each other affectionately.

He laughs and I feel a frisson of excitement. I love it when I make Isaac laugh.

'I guess so,' he says. 'Look.' He moves his eyes back to the bar. 'Recognise anyone?'

I swivel in my seat and spot a skinny lad holding a tray of chips. He has a mop of curly hair and is muttering apologies to the drinkers as he sidles through them. His face, which is stark white and dotted with pimples, is creased into an awkward expression, and his fringe flops over his eyes, clearly desperate to cover as much of his embarrassed face as possible.

My mouth falls open and I turn back to Isaac. 'Is that Felix?'

'Yup. He's supposed to only work in the back as a pot washer, but occasionally he helps out as a waiter. I'll get him to come and say hello in a bit.'

'He won't remember me,' I say.

'Of course he will!' Isaac says at once. 'You spent years in our house. You were part of our family!'

I feel a small stab of heat in the pit of my stomach, and Isaac takes a sip of his cider, ever so slightly avoiding my eye. We fall into silence and I pick up my glass again.

'So,' Isaac says eventually, 'have you spoken to Rachel recently?'

I feel a jolt behind my belly button as guilt immediately springs through me. We haven't spoken about Rachel properly since I've been back.

'Er,' I say, 'a bit. Why?'

He shrugs. 'Just wondering.'

He shifts back in his seat and looks down at his phone. To my alarm, I feel the burning need to defend myself.

'We aren't really that close any more,' I say. 'You know, since I moved away. We're very different, too. She was way more into the happily-ever-after thing with Danny, which is great, I'm happy for her. But she's not very good at understanding that not everyone is able to be perfect, you know?'

I catch myself before I add the rest of my explanation:

She also ditched me last minute when we were supposed to be moving to London together and has totally cut off our dad, even though it breaks his heart. We never even have a real conversation any more. She seems totally happy with her life and so I guess I'm totally happy with mine. It's just how it is.

I can't say all that to him. He'd never understand.

I stare at him, suddenly aware of how desperate I am for his

188

validation that I'm not a bad person. He shrugs at me, his expression one of indifference, and I feel myself wilt ever so slightly. I take another glug of cider and pull out my own phone, pushing the feeling back down inside.

'I don't like coming back here,' I mutter, my face hot. I suddenly feel as though the walls are closing in around me.

Isaac looks up. 'Why?'

'I don't have nice memories,' I say, scratching the back of my neck. 'They're tainted.'

He stares at me, and for a moment I feel that he might challenge me.

'Well make some new ones then,' he says, raising his pint glass to me.

At the sight of his smile, I feel the tightness coiling around my chest fall away, and despite myself, I smile back at him.

'So who are you making mugs for these days?' he asks.

I turn my glass between my hands.

I couldn't make pottery in London; the girls at Hayes think I'm weird enough as it is.

'I'm not,' I say. 'I haven't made anything in years.'

'How come?'

I shrug. 'Just haven't.'

He opens his mouth to reply but then sits up, his eyes fixed over my shoulder.

'Felix, come here.'

I turn my head as Felix stumbles over. The tray, now empty of chips, is swinging between his fingers and he blushes intensely as soon as he sees me. For a second I think he's going to run away.

'This is Katy,' Isaac says. 'Remember Katy?'

Felix dares himself to glance at me for a split second and then immediately looks back at his brother.

'Yes.'

'Well, say hello then.'

'Er,' he mumbles, 'hello, Katy.'

'Hi,' I say back.

Good Lord, this is awkward! Does he hate me? Has Isaac secretly got a dartboard in their house that they all throw knives at every Friday?

'You've grown!' I blurt, desperate to say something normal, and then immediately want to kick myself for being so obviously patronising.

Of course he's grown, you moron, you haven't seen him in years.

What am I going to do next? Start reeling off dreadful anecdotes about what life was like when I was his age?

'How's work, mate?' Isaac says, smoothing over my odd comment like I'm their batty eighty-year-old great-aunt.

'Fine,' Felix says, leaning on a nearby table. 'I'm only meant to be here for another ten minutes, but it's pretty busy.'

'You'd better get back to it then!' Isaac grins, holding his pint towards Felix and pointing to the bar. Felix rolls his eyes and slinks back across the pub, disappearing behind a set of swing doors.

'He's so cute,' I say. 'I can't believe he's thirteen.'

'Yeah,' Isaac says, still looking over my shoulder to where Felix has just left. 'He's so shy, he can't talk to girls at all.'

I smile into my pint.

Okay, good. Maybe he doesn't hate me.

'Unlike me.' He gives a mock sigh. 'I was always such a hit with the girls at school.'

I snort. 'You were not! You could only speak to me via notes for years!'

He shrugs. 'And yet,' he grins, 'here you still are.'

I feel an odd flutter in the pit of my stomach that I quickly try and squash.

'I'm trying to help Felix with his confidence,' he says. 'That's why we got him this job.'

'That's nice.'

He tips the dregs of his cider down his throat. 'It's what you do for family, isn't it? Look out for each other.'

He meets my eyes and I feel my face flush. He gestures at my glass and I tip the remainder into my mouth and nod.

'Oh, and for the record,' he says, picking up both glasses and standing up, 'I don't think Rachel's life is as perfect as you might think.'

He saunters towards the bar and I frown.

What is that supposed to mean?

CHAPTER TWENTY

RACHEL

'This one!' William throws his arms into the air and scrabbles at the bookcase, his little pot belly sticking out under his Thomas the Tank Engine pyjama top as he stands on tiptoes.

'No!' Jasmine whines, throwing herself onto her bed. 'I hate that story.'

'Well, it's William's turn to choose,' Fiona says, reaching forward and pulling the book from the shelf. William jumps on the balls of his feet as she hands it to him and leaps into his own bed. Fiona turns back to look at Jasmine, who has let out a huge groan. 'You can read to yourself if you want.'

Jasmine picks up a book from her bedside table and opens it defiantly, shooting her mother a look as though daring her to challenge her.

I smile and sink onto a chair in the corner of the room. The children begged me to stay for a story after dinner. Fiona tried to politely make excuses for me, but I surprised myself by saying yes, not because I felt it would be rude not to, but because it sounded like fun.

'You'll be doing this soon,' she says, smiling at me over the book that William is now reading aloud. 'Do you know what you're having?'

I'm about to answer 'a baby' when I realise that she's talking about the gender.

Obviously you're having a baby. What else would you give birth to? A duck?

I tuck my hands under my thighs.

I haven't found out anything about the baby, other than that it's healthy. The nurse asked if I wanted to know the sex, but I said no. I didn't want to know too much. I was scared.

After the scan, I went to a shop and bought a yellow babygro, and when I got it home and laid it out in front of me, all I felt was an overwhelming sense of fear. How was I supposed to take care of something so small? How was I supposed to know what to do?

I never felt as though I'd be a bad mum, but in that moment I couldn't squash the screaming realisation that I had no idea how to be a good one. So I tucked the babygro under my pillow and have been taking a little peek at it each night.

'No,' I say, my mouth dry. 'It's a surprise.'

I let out a gasp as the baby gives a kick, and Jasmine drops her book.

'What is it?' Fiona says quickly. 'Are you okay?'

I clasp my hands onto my bump and give a shaky laugh.

'Sorry,' I say. 'It just kicked. The baby, I mean.'

At this, Jasmine scrambles out of bed and runs towards me.

'Can I feel?' she cries, sticking out her hands as she reaches me. 'Mummy?' She whips her head round to give Fiona a desperate look. 'Can I feel Rachel's tummy?'

Fiona laughs as William carries on reading.

'Ask Rachel!' she says.

Jasmine turns her eyes back to me, her skinny arms still held out in front of her. I pause, trying to fight the urge to bark 'No!' and run away.

'Sure,' I say, 'although it might not—'

My words are lost as Jasmine plants her hands excitedly on my stomach.

'It might not kick again,' I say. 'I don't know what made it do that.'

'Try talking to the baby, Jasmine,' Fiona says. 'That's what we used to do to William, remember?'

Jasmine nods intently, fixing her eyes on the bump as though she's trying to communicate telepathically.

'Hello, baby,' she says, her voice giddy with excitement. 'My name is Jasmine, we're going to be friends and maybe I'll show you— Oh!' She squeals, her eyes wide as the baby gives another kick. 'It kicked!' she cries, turning to face Fiona and William. 'The baby kicked, I felt it!'

At this, William leaps out of bed and charges towards me. I laugh as he sticks his hands straight on my stomach, and Fiona tuts loudly.

'William!' she scolds. 'You need to ask Rachel first!'

'I don't mind.' I smile. 'I think the baby was talking back to you, Jasmine.'

Jasmine nods and leans closer to my bump.

'Hello, baby. William is also here now, he's my brother.'

194

'Hello!' cries William loudly.

'We only met your mummy a few days ago, but we think she's going to be the best mummy in the world. Except for our mummy,' she adds quickly, shooting Fiona a big smile over her shoulder.

I stare down at Jasmine's blonde head, a lump forming in my throat.

'Come on,' Fiona says, bundling the children away from me. 'That's enough excitement for one night. Rachel and the baby will still be here tomorrow.'

Jasmine and William climb back into their beds and I quickly attempt to blink the tears away. I get to my feet and follow Fiona to the door.

'Right,' she says as she waits in the doorway, 'say goodnight to Rachel.'

'Goodnight, Rachel!' Jasmine and William chime in unison.

'Goodnight, baby!' William shouts, making Jasmine collapse back into giggles.

I laugh too, holding my hand up in a wave.

'Goodnight, guys.'

★

'Wine?'

Without quite meaning to, I shoot Fiona a look. She rolls her eyes at herself.

'Sorry,' she says, 'of course. I keep forgetting you're not Katy. You're so similar.'

I take off my glasses and clean them with my sleeve as Fiona takes out a bottle of wine from the fridge.

'I'm fine with my tea,' I say, holding up the cup Fiona made me before the kids went to bed, 'but thank you.'

She sits in the chair opposite me and splashes wine into her glass. 'I only ever have one glass,' she says, as though I've questioned her, 'so I'm always ready to drive if, God forbid, anything happens.'

'Doesn't your husband drive?' I ask as my eyes flick up to the large clock hanging on the wall.

It's almost nine at night. Where is he?

'Yes,' she says, taking a sip, 'but it's easier if I know I can do it.'

We fall into silence and I take a mouthful of my tepid tea. Fiona pulls a face at her wine glass.

'Oh,' she says, 'that's very sweet.' She turns the bottle round so she can read the label. 'I think this is one I bought for Katy.'

I feel a flash of loyalty at Katy's name. She sounded so tense earlier, more so than usual.

I really didn't mean to cause her stress by asking her to house-sit. It didn't cross my mind that she might actually need to spend time working.

'I think Katy's going mad that the Wi-Fi's so bad in Wales,' I say. 'She loves working for you.'

Fiona lifts her eyes to meet mine, a look of disbelief on her face.

'Really?' she says. 'I'm half expecting her to leave and go off to do something more exciting.'

'She's very loyal.'

'Oh, I know.' She takes another sip of wine and winces. 'She's an angel. She arrived in my life like an angel, actually.'

I turn my mug in my hands.

That's a weird thing to say.

'Really?'

Fiona nods. 'I couldn't believe it when she turned up for the interview. You know when you just meet someone and get an instant good feeling about them? I've got some rotters in my life, but Katy's one of the good ones. She really is part of the family.'

My heart twitches.

Part of the family.

'She's too good for us, though!' She laughs. 'I tell her that every day. I say, Katy, you're too good for us!'

'She told me that she helped you with an event,' I say. 'She was so excited.'

Fiona leans back in her seat, and I can almost see my words skim over her head. 'I don't know where I'd be without her. She came just at the right time, when everything was about to fall to shit.'

As I open my mouth to reply, she looks at me as though snapping out of a trance.

'God, Rachel, I'm so sorry,' she says. 'Would you like another cup of tea?'

Chapter Twenty-One

Katy

I lean back against Rachel's sofa, my head spinning slightly as the taste of sweet cider lingers in the back of my throat. We stayed at the pub until it closed, drinking pint after pint until my head started to swim. By the end of the night, I'd forgotten all about my smeared eyeliner and frizzy hair. When I was with Isaac, it felt as though none of that mattered.

The familiar zap of longing pings through my stomach and I feel an instant shock of fear, like I have done pretty much every day this week.

I can't have feelings for Isaac. I'm going back to London in three days, and we broke up for a reason. Although the more time I spend with him, the harder I'm finding it to remember what that reason was.

I take a deep breath, pulling my eyes open and looking at the cream walls dotted with picture frames. Rachel really has made the cottage perfect; it's like stepping into a Laura Ashley brochure. But as I stare at the walls, my eyes linger once again on the gaps where photos have been taken down. It's so obvious now; how did I not realise it the moment I arrived?

Isaac's voice plays in my head as I stare at Rachel's happy eyes beaming down at me from the single framed photograph of her and Danny.

I don't think Rachel's life is as perfect as you might think.

I frown, trying to work out what he meant. He swept to the bar as soon as he said it, and when I tried to question him further, he changed the subject. For a second I thought he almost blushed, as though he'd slipped up and was keen to move on, but he just said that he'd meant nothing by it.

I flop my arms over my head, arching back against the plumped pillows.

But if he meant nothing by it, why did he say it? And how does he know more about my sister than I do? I mean, she's my twin! I know we don't see each other very often and we rarely speak properly any more, but we're still sisters.

I feel a knot of worry in the pit of my stomach and I chew my lip. How can Rachel's life not be perfect? I'm experiencing it right now. Her house is spotless and filled with expensive, beautiful things. There was even a cherry cake waiting for me when I arrived on Sunday. She married the love of her life, her job pays brilliantly; she got everything she ever wanted.

As I take in the cottage, smiling at each of Rachel's neatly placed things, I sit up slightly. Where is Danny in this house? I know he's away a lot, but it doesn't even look like a man lives here any more.

My eyes land on another photo of Rachel, but this time I'm

in the photo with her. It was taken the summer before I left to go to university. We're both laughing, standing on the top of a hill and brandishing our arms in the air as rain clings to our coats. We're covered in mud and gripping fiercely onto each other.

She didn't used to be so perfect. As I look around, I realise that photo is the only sign that Rachel is a real, flawed person. Her house is more like a museum. Suddenly it dawns on me that maybe that's the point.

I pick up my phone and quickly unlock it. It's almost midnight, but I somehow know that Rachel is awake, and for the first time in years, I need to hear how she is. I need to check that she really is okay.

I dial her number and wait.

CHAPTER TWENTY-TWO

RACHEL

I jab the key into the lock and click the door open. I don't know what time it is. Fiona and I ended up sitting up talking for hours. Her husband never came home, or if he did, he didn't bother us.

I haven't seen him once since I arrived.

As I start to walk towards the kitchen, a beam of light flashes from the settee. I step towards it, frowning as I realise that my phone is ringing.

Who is calling me at this time?

I pick up the phone and my stomach lurches as Katy's name stares up at me from the screen. Out of nowhere, a feeling of guilt for spending the evening with Fiona washes over me – the only thing Katy asked me not to do.

Well, not the only thing she asked me not to do, considering I'm literally standing in her home. But, you know, the most recent.

For a second, I think about letting the call tick over to voice-mail. I could easily be asleep. But why is she calling me at this time? What if something's wrong? The only person she really knows in the village is Isaac, and God only knows if they're getting on.

I swipe the call and hold the phone to my ear.

'Hello?'

'Oh!' Katy's voice spills into my ear. 'You're awake.'

'Yeah,' I say, wrapping my arm around my stomach as if Katy can see me through the phone. 'Are you okay?'

'Yeah,' she says quickly, 'I'm fine. Are you okay?'

'Yeah,' I reply, as I sit down on the sofa, my back stiff.

'Good.'

We drift into silence and I grip the phone to my ear, my hand damp.

'So,' Katy says, 'have you seen Fiona today?'

The guilt twitching inside my throat spikes.

'Yeah,' I say. 'Have you managed to get on the internet yet?'

'No,' she says. 'I didn't really work today. I did manage to get a connection at the pub, but it's not very good.'

'The Ship?' I say. 'Have you been at the Ship?'

I hear her laugh. 'Yeah, a bit.'

'Well,' I say, 'you could always give me a message to pass on to Fiona.'

'No, that's okay.' Katy cuts across me. 'I have emailed her, but she hasn't replied, that's all. I just wanted to check she's okay.'

'Oh,' I say, 'yeah. She's fine.'

We fall back into silence. I open my mouth to try and speak, but nothing comes out.

Is this why she called me in the middle of the night, to ask questions about Fiona? Is she that anxious about her job?

'Rachel,' she breaks the silence, 'are you okay?'

'Yeah,' I say automatically, 'I'm fine. Are—'

'No,' Katy says, 'are you really okay?'

I freeze, my mouth dry as the opportunity I've been waiting for opens out in front of me.

Tell her. Tell her you're not fine. Tell her about Danny. Tell her about the baby. Ask for her help. Tell her how alone you feel. Tell her everything.

The thought oozes through my mind and I hold the phone to my ear, feeling paralysed.

'Yeah,' I say eventually, hearing myself speak in a calm, upbeat voice, 'I'm fine. What about you?'

Although it's small, I hear Katy sigh.

'Yeah,' she says, 'I'm fine too.'

The silence creeps in around us once again and the guilt of another lie that I've freely told my sister screams through my body.

Why can't you just tell her?

'Well,' Katy says, 'I'd better go to bed, it's late.'

I feel a stab of desperation.

Don't go. Don't hang up.

'Sure,' I say, 'and I'll speak to Fiona if you want. Check she got your email.'

'Sure,' Katy says, her voice now sounding tired, 'whatever.'

Am I ever going to be able to tell her?

The line goes dead and I drop my arm to my lap, my heart hammering in my throat as the silence of the flat hangs around me and the familiar, unbearable fear of being alone sinks into my skin. Before I can stop myself, I pick up the phone again and jab a quick, desperate text to the one family member I haven't tried to speak to.

I send a message to my dad.

★

When I wake up the next morning my head is hammering and my mouth feels like sandpaper. I properly cried last night; not the odd tear that I brush away before anyone can see, but real crying. I let it all out. I must have fallen asleep eventually, and as I turn my phone over, I see that it's 10.05. I guess I've got over my pregnancy insomnia.

I swallow, trying to fight the feeling that I might be sick. I need to eat something, even if I feel like I'm being eaten alive by anxiety; the baby needs feeding.

Before I can talk myself out of it, I swing my legs round and shuffle down the ladder.

Katy knows something. She always asks me how I am, but not like that. She sounded like she really wanted to know. She can't know I'm pregnant or she would have said, but she knows something isn't right.

Why couldn't I just tell her? Maybe Peggy and Isaac are right: Katy might be thrilled to be an auntie and be looking for a reason to move back to Wales. She might be having a great time there; she might want us to be real sisters again.

Even as these thoughts swirl through my mind, my chest starts to tighten, but before I can unpick my fears even further, I hear my phone vibrate.

I haven't heard back from Dad. Truthfully, I'm not even sure if the number I have for him works any more. Every now and then I get a message from him saying his number has changed, but I can't remember if I ever bothered to save it. I didn't want to speak to him. It would serve me right if he now didn't want to speak to me.

I pick up my phone and Peggy's name flashes on the screen with a text message.

Hello love! Know you're not in, but I've got all these bits I bought so am going to drop them round on my way to work. I'll give your plants a water too, as I know how demanding your orchid is! Lots of love!! Xx

I grab my phone and dial her number, clamping the phone desperately to my ear.

And now I really feel like I'm going to be sick.

Chapter Twenty-Three

Katy

I sink into the bath, beaming with delight as the fat bubbles gleam under the champagne light of Rachel's bathroom. Now I can understand her obsession with lotions and potions; this is *paradise*. Is this what she does every morning? Maybe I should start the day with a luxurious bubble bath! Perhaps that's the secret to happiness.

I also snuck her weird boyfriend pillow into my bed last night and slept with my legs hooked around it, and let me tell you, I've never experienced comfort like it! How could I have judged her for her collection of pillows and lotions when this is what the reality is? She lives like a queen!

She'll be having a terrible time in my lodge, where I only have one pillow that isn't lumpy and the only shower gel I own is that intense mint-flavoured one that I got half price that gives you thrush if you use it too generously.

Gosh, Rachel gives me the most relaxing sleep of my life and I give her a yeast infection. She would never let me live that one down.

I take a sip of my tea and shut my eyes, her jumpy voice replaying in my mind.

There is definitely something going on with her that she isn't telling me. We don't speak on the phone often, but when we do, she always sounds calm and serene. She trills about Danny and the cottage and her fabulous job, and I harp on about the glamorous life of a successful cosmopolitan events exec, and then we hang up. I've never heard her so tense before.

I also can't shake the feeling that something is odd about the missing pictures. Why would she take them down? Rachel loves photos and—

I jolt out of my thoughts as I hear the door slam downstairs. Without quite meaning to, I slop the remainder of my tea into the bath, then scowl down at the water. Great, now I'm essentially sitting in a teapot.

I scowl. Was that just the wind? Did I leave the back door open? Or—

'Well hello there, Bruno! How are you, my darling boy?'

I jerk up to sitting as a Welsh voice sings through the house.

Who the hell is *that*?

As carefully as I can, I climb out of the bath and wrap a towel around myself.

A burglar? It can't be! How many burglars know Bruno and refer to him as their 'darling boy'? Rachel doesn't have a cleaner, does she? Surely she would have warned me if someone was going to pop round and let themselves in?

I shove my pyjamas back on and stick my head out of the bathroom door, my head spinning.

'Now, let's see how that orchid is doing, shall we?'

I open my mouth to shout out, and then close it again as I suddenly have the overwhelming urge to hide under the bed.

This is ridiculous! This is *my cottage*. I mean, yes, Rachel lives here, but it is technically half mine too, and there is a stranger in it. I can't just hide. I must confront them!

With a fresh surge of determination, I wrap my dressing gown round my body and creep down the stairs, instinctively grabbing my can of deodorant as I go. You know, just in case she's a psychopath and I have to spritz her in the eyes. I freeze as a mobile starts to ring.

'Oh, speak of the devil,' the woman trills as the phone is silenced. 'Hello, love! Yes, I just got in.'

She trails off and I peek through the banister at the back of her auburn head. She's wearing a paisley dress and large dangly earrings. She doesn't look like a serial killer.

But then that's what they'd *want* you to think.

'Okay, calm down,' she says softly into her phone. 'What are you talking about?'

My fingers tense around the can of deodorant.

Who is she on the phone to? An accomplice? Trying to talk her out of the crime? Getting cold feet?

I hear her sigh.

'I really think you're worrying about nothing, love.'

I creep down another stair, determination rising through me.

They are *not* worrying about nothing, because I will call the police quicker than James Bond! Not that he ever called the police, actually, but if he did, I'm sure it would be pretty fast.

'Okay, okay,' she says. 'I'll go, and don't worry, I won't say anything. Maybe go back to bed and get some rest. Bye, love.'

My eyes widen.

She's going? The accomplice talked her out of it?

She rubs her forehead with her thumb and forefinger, and then before I have a chance to move, she turns on the spot and screams at the sight of me. Her high-pitched squawk triggers a terrified shriek of my own, and for some reason I let out a manic spritz of the deodorant into the air. The woman clutches her chest and stares at me, her gaze running over my body, and I feel my face flush. Now that I can see her kind eyes and the carrier bags at her feet, she doesn't look like a serial killer. She looks like Mrs Tiggywinkle.

'Who are you?' I blurt, my heart racing in my chest as I lower the deodorant can. She looks dubiously at me.

'I'm Peggy,' she says. 'I'm a friend of Rachel's. I'm so sorry, I didn't realise you were staying here. You must be Katy. Gosh,' she smiles, 'you really are identical, aren't you?'

Her warm voice wraps around me like a hug, and I feel a wave of guilt.

God, imagine if I had blinded this poor woman with Dove Rose Infusion?

'Yeah,' I say, 'I'm Katy, hi.'

Her eyes linger on me, and for a second it looks like she might burst into tears.

Oh God, did I really frighten her?

'I'm sorry I scared you,' I say quickly. 'I just heard someone downstairs and . . .' I trail off stupidly, not wanting to admit that

I'd revved myself up for doing a tuck-and-roll through the living room and enveloping her in a curtain like a bewildered seaweed wrap.

'No,' she waves her hand in front of her face, 'it's fine. I'm sorry I let myself in.' She laughs. 'Rachel is used to me by now.'

We fall into silence and I shuffle my feet awkwardly.

'So,' I say eventually, 'is there something you needed?' I gesture down to the carrier bags, and she jumps slightly.

'Oh!' she says. 'No. I just came to water the plants, but if you're here, then I'm sure it's all being taken care of.'

She smiles at me and I nod.

Must remember to water the plants.

We drift back into silence and I shuffle my feet, feeling like an actor who has forgotten their lines.

'Er, would you like a cup of tea?' I offer awkwardly.

Obviously she'll say no, but it feels rude not to offer her something and I—

'Oh, I'm gasping for a tea!' she coos, turning and bustling into the kitchen.

I blink after her, tugging on the cord of my dressing gown.

'I'll just go and get changed,' I call after her. 'Sorry, I wasn't expecting—'

'So Rachel tells me you live in *London*?'

Peggy reappears, her eyes glittering as though I've cartwheeled straight from a speakeasy with an elongated cigarette holder and white silk gloves.

'Yeah,' I say, trying not to blush as she glows back at me.

She looks so happy to see me, and she's never even met me before.

'I work in events,' I add.

She drops onto the sofa and pats the space next to her. I shuffle over, trying to control my hot face as I plonk myself down in my fleece pyjamas.

I've had more people see me in these stupid pyjamas in the past few days than I have in the two years I've bloody owned them.

'How do you know Rachel?' I ask.

'We work together!' Peggy says happily. 'I'm the office manager, so I take care of everything really. Me and Rachel just clicked! She reminds me so much of my daughter, Tabitha. She's just had a baby, you know, but I don't see much of her. She lives far away.'

She pauses for breath, and I'm about to reply when the kettle clicks and Peggy springs back up, making another cooing sound.

'How do you take your tea, love?' she calls from the kitchen. 'Same as Rachel? Just milk?'

'I . . . Wait!' I cry, leaping to my feet before I can stop myself.

Finally I can get to the bottom of this one.

'Milk?' I repeat. 'Isn't Rachel a vegan?'

The rogue Smarties, the stash of sausage rolls in the freezer, the stockpiling of Mr Kipling . . .

Peggy grips the carton of milk in her hand, her wide eyes blinking at me as though I'm holding a glaring light over her head.

'I don't think so, love,' she says eventually, searching my face for the correct answer. 'Are you a vegan?'

I want to laugh.

Have we both been lying to each other about being vegan?

'No,' I say, taking the milk off her and putting it back in the fridge. 'I'm not vegetarian either,' I add.

Peggy hands me my tea and we both walk back into the sitting room.

'Why did you think she was a vegan?'

I feel my face redden.

Hmm, because lying to each other is actually quite normal for us?

I shrug, picking up a biscuit and ramming it in my tea. 'Oh,' I say lightly, 'just thought she was.'

Peggy nods, holding her cup to her pink lips.

'Have you spoken much to Rachel recently?' she asks.

Yes, but she barely speaks to me without being on autopilot.

'Yeah!' I say at once. 'We spoke last night.'

Peggy picks up a biscuit, and I realise that her cheeks have started to mirror mine.

'Good,' she says. 'She's lucky she has a sister she can talk to.'

I open my mouth to reply, but the words can't quite make it out.

She's not lucky; she has a sister she doesn't want to talk to, and I need to work out why that is.

★

Bruno bounces around my feet, hardly able to believe his luck that I'm willingly taking him out for a walk, even though we've done it every day since he ran away.

'Calm down,' I laugh, kneeling down to clip the lead onto his collar. As soon as I get close, he plants his rough wet tongue on my cheek and I scrunch up my face.

'Bleurgh!' I cry, although I'm still smiling. 'Bruno, *no*. Not the face!'

I get to my feet and zip up Rachel's coat, catching sight of myself in the large wall mirror.

My skin is speckled with freckles, something I usually hide at all costs. But now they beam out of my face with pride and I suddenly feel quite attached to them. My hair, which has had a constant spring since being swept up in the Welsh sea air, is glistening with light streaks of blonde stolen from the sun. I smile at myself. I look different, but not in a bad way. The stress line that's normally creased across my forehead has vanished. I look happy.

'Right.' I turn back to Bruno, who is staring up at me imploringly. 'Shall we go, boy? Shall we go on an adventure?'

My voice slides up at the end, and he tugs on his lead. I stagger behind him, the grin staying firmly on my face as he pulls me towards the front door.

'Give me a second!' I laugh, stuffing some dog biscuits in my coat pocket. I pull open the door and gasp as Bruno yanks me forward, straight into Isaac.

'Oh!' I cry. 'Hey.'

For the first time since I arrived in Wales, he's not head to toe in farm gear. Instead he's wearing jeans and a maroon fitted jumper that hugs his arms. He smiles at me and my heart turns over.

Stop that, heart. You do not have feelings for Isaac. We're just friends now.

'Going on a walk?' he says, rubbing Bruno's ears.

'Yeah,' I say. 'I think I remember one me and Rachel used to go on when we were teenagers, but if I get a bit lost, I'm sure Bruno can bring us back home.'

I grin down at Bruno, who is sitting by my feet panting up at me. At the mention of Rachel, I feel a small pang of worry.

The moment Peggy left, my mind started to spin with thoughts about what Rachel was hiding, but only one option seemed plausible.

'Oh,' I say, 'I spoke to Rachel last night.'

Isaac frowns at me. 'Last night?' he repeats. 'We didn't leave the pub until like, half eleven!'

I grin. 'Yeah,' I say. 'I'm surprised she picked up. Do, er, do you know how long Danny has been away?'

The question that has been pulling at my mind since I hung up last night spills out of my mouth, and I feel my cheeks pinch as I ask it. I should know the answer to this; I shouldn't have to ask Isaac. She's my sister.

Isaac looks back down at Bruno. 'No,' he says, 'I'm not sure. A while, though. How come?'

I ignore his question and plough on. 'And do you know whether she did anything for her birthday?' I say. 'Our birthday, I mean. It was earlier this month.'

'I know when your birthday is.' Isaac grins at me. 'March the first.'

I smile. Something else he remembers about me.

'No,' he says, 'I don't think so. She hasn't been out much recently.'

I look at my feet, and the small balloon of worry that has been growing in the pit of my stomach expands.

Right. There is something wrong. Why didn't anybody celebrate Rachel's birthday with her? Where are her friends? More importantly, where is Danny?

'Okay,' I say, 'thank you. Right.' I shake the lead and Bruno springs back up. 'Come on then, buddy.' I go to walk down the path, and then turn back to face Isaac. 'Do you want to walk with us?'

He smiles, and to my annoyance, I feel my heart flip again.

'That's okay,' he says. 'I've got stuff to be getting on with. I just wanted to see what your plans are for today. I've got a surprise for you.'

I place my hand on my hip and raise my eyebrows. 'Does this involve another goose?'

He laughs. 'I'll pop round at about four.'

'Sure,' I say. 'See you then.'

He walks past me and gets into his car. As he pulls off, Bruno barks.

'Don't you get any ideas,' I say quietly. 'We're just friends now.'

Although as I look down at Bruno's blank face, I'm not sure whether I'm saying that to him or to myself.

*

A wave of heat wafts in front of my face as I pull open the oven door and carefully clasp my towel-covered hands around the cake, which trembles slightly in my nervous grip. Without quite meaning to, I drop it onto the counter with a clatter and stare down at it, a feeling of pride tickling the back of my throat.

Well, it certainly looks like a cake, and it smells *great*.

I peer down at it, half expecting it to combust.

I didn't mean to eat the entire cake Rachel left me. I mean, Christ, I've only been here four days! After I got back from my walk, I made myself another coffee (I really must buy one of those machines for the lodge. After a week of coffee that tastes like silk, I simply cannot go back to plain old Nescafé), then went to the cake tin to cut myself a modest slice to nibble on, only to find a pathetic crumb looking back up at me. And unless

Rachel has a family of mice living here (very unlikely) or Bruno has been cutting himself the odd slice without me realising (even more unlikely), I must have eaten it all.

I can't have Rachel return home to find that I've drunk all her posh coffee, finished her fancy bubble bath (by *accident*, I should add) and guzzled all her baked goods. I mean, Christ. I'm like Goldilocks on her period.

So I decided to re-create Grandma's recipe so I can leave it as a peace offering. A peace offering also acting as a decoy from the fact that I spilt hot chocolate on one of her posh cushions, which is now hidden under a lovely throw.

I drop back into the kitchen chair as I scoop another spoonful of delicious chilli into my mouth. I don't know why I was scouring the cottage for clues of whether Rachel was really a vegan, when all I had to do is open her freezer and find all of our favourite meals. Let me tell you, if I was struggling being a vegan before (and by struggling I mean, I have been 'having a day off' for the past five million days), then seeing Rachel's home-cooked meals stacked up and ready to go would have broken me. I've been eating like a queen! Bolognese, chilli, curry . . . it's been fantastic. I've eaten nearly everything, which Rachel will be pleased about. She takes great pride in her cooking.

Bruno skirts out from under my feet as I hear a knock on the door, and my eyes flick to the wall clock: four o'clock. Isaac is bang on time. Not that he would have any excuse to be late, seeing as his journey literally takes seven seconds. But still, nice to know he's eager.

I smooth my hair down and pull open the door, stepping back to let him in. He grins at me, giving Bruno a ruffle of the ears.

'Oh,' he says, 'something smells good.'

Before I can stop myself, I puff out my chest.

'Yes,' I say lightly, 'I just baked a cake.'

God, no wonder Rachel does this sort of thing all the time. I feel so *smug*.

'You can't have any, though,' I add as Isaac peers at the steaming cake tin. 'It's for Rachel, when she comes home.' I raise my eyebrows. 'Really, I followed a recipe and everything.'

'I'm impressed,' he says, pushing off his shoes. 'I thought Rachel was the family baker.'

'We can both be good at baking,' I say, picking up a gingham towel and throwing it over the cake like Bree Van de Kamp in *Desperate Housewives*.

Wow, look at me go! Next thing you know I'll be commenting on soggy bottoms and moist sponges and pronouncing layers as *laaaairs*.

'Very nice,' he says. 'So what did . . .' He trails off as his eyes move to my empty chilli bowl.

'Where did you get that?' he asks.

'Rachel made it!' I say happily. 'Her freezer was filled with food, and she told me to help myself to anything. Isn't that nice?'

Isaac doesn't stop looking at the chilli, and I can see his brow twitching.

'So,' he says slowly, 'have you eaten everything in the freezer?'

I feel small patches appear on my cheeks.

'Not in one go,' I say, plucking the bowl from the table and stacking it in the dishwasher. 'Why do you care?'

He shakes his head. 'I don't,' he says, and when I turn round, his smile is back.

He is so weird.

'So,' I say, sinking into Rachel's plump armchair, 'what's this big surprise?'

'Ah,' he says, sitting down and unzipping his rucksack, 'I've got you a present.'

'Oh?'

He sticks both hands into the depths of the rucksack and drops a large plastic bag on the coffee table with a loud thud. I stare down at it blankly. He catches my expression and laughs.

'Open it,' he says. 'You'll like it.'

He pushes it towards me and I lean forward, shooting him looks of confusion until I pull the bag open and my eyes land on an enormous lump of clay. My jaw drops.

'I thought it was really sad that you don't make anything any more,' he says, 'so I spoke to some people in the village about where to buy clay and thought I'd get you some.'

He pauses, waiting for me to say something. But I'm transfixed.

'I know how much you used to love making stuff,' he continues. 'Remember that dream we had where you'd open your own pottery shop? Rachel would make the cakes and the coffee and I'd provide eggs and milk from the farm.' He runs his fingers through his hair. 'I know you've got different dreams now, but I just thought this might be fun.'

Finally I force myself to look up at him, and as I do, I feel a tear spill out of my eye. I brush it away quickly.

I haven't made anything since Grandma died. I made excuses about how I never had the time or it wasn't a cool thing to do in London, but really it was just something else I pushed down inside of me.

Isaac jolts, his smile vanishing.

'Oh my God,' he says. 'I'm so sorry, Katy. I didn't mean to upset you. I know it's something you used to do with your grandma and . . .' He trails off and I wipe my cheeks with my sleeve.

'Sorry.' I laugh awkwardly. 'It just brings back so many memories being here. We haven't scattered her ashes either, and I think a part of me feels like I've never said a proper goodbye to her.'

I take a deep breath as I hear myself say the words aloud. It's the first time I've admitted that to anyone.

Isaac looks at me helplessly and I shake my shoulders, pushing the tears away.

'Sorry.' I take a deep breath. 'This is so thoughtful, I love it. I just wasn't expecting it, that's all.'

'Well,' he shrugs modestly, 'it was meant to be a surprise.'

I grin at him and he laughs, relief washing over his face. He moves closer and grabs the lump of clay.

'I didn't buy it just so we could stare at it,' he says. 'Let's make something. I can be your student. Do you still have the wheel?'

I look at him, my heart thumping in my chest as his eyes spark at me.

'Yeah,' I say. 'It's in the shed.'

★

I push the door of the shed with my shoulder, trying to ignore the nerves that are dancing around my body with such force they may as well be doing the Macarena.

I had no intention of going in the shed while I was here. I was actually having quite a nice time pretending it didn't exist, or that it was just a shed filled with old gardening equipment and rusty old bikes like everybody else's. But our shed was much more special than that. Dad made it into a home studio for me and Grandma when I was about twelve, and we'd sit in here for hours making pottery. Rachel would join us occasionally, but only when we had breaks to drink juice or eat lunch. Most of the time it was just the two of us.

I couldn't see the point of going inside now, though. I knew Grandma wouldn't be there, and I wasn't going to be making any pottery, so why would I?

I did keep an eye on it through the kitchen window, though, and sometimes I—

'God, did someone die in here?'

I snap out of my thoughts and glare at Isaac, who has tucked his face into his T-shirt in disgust.

'*Isaac!*'

'Sorry,' he says. 'It just smells so bad.'

I glare at him. 'You are such a princess,' I snap. 'It's not about the smell. It's about the pottery.'

I step into the shed defiantly and try not to gag as a thick, damp smell sticks to the back of my throat.

Okay, perhaps it does smell terrible in here.

'Let me grab some candles,' Isaac says, ducking back towards the house, 'or some air freshener or something.'

I nod absent-mindedly and look around, putting the basin of water I'm carrying down. My wheel is still there, covered in a thick layer of dust, and next to it is my chair. Grandma and I would take it in turns to make something, while the other would watch and chat. We always said that one day we'd get another wheel so that we could work at the same time. But as she got older, Grandma found it harder to control the clay.

'Okay.' Isaac reappears, his arms filled with candles and cans of air freshener. 'I think this will do it.'

I try and scowl at him, but as soon as I catch his concerned expression, I can't help laughing.

'Honestly,' I say, taking some candles from him and placing them around the shed, 'and you say I'm uptight? You're supposed to be the farm boy.'

He hands me a lighter, and I flick the orange tongue towards the wicks.

'Don't use the air freshener!' I say quickly as he gives a can a shake. 'It's really flammable. The candles will be fine.'

He looks down at the can and shrugs.

'Okay,' he agrees, 'candles are more romantic anyway.'

I feel a jolt of electricity shoot through me as I light the final candle, trying to hide my blushing face.

'Right,' I say, turning to face him, 'what do you want to make?'

He blinks at me. 'I thought you were making it?'

I grin. 'You wanted a lesson, didn't you? We can make it together. Come on.' I pull the chair out and nod my head towards it. 'Sit.'

Isaac places the cans on the floor and sinks into the seat. I heave the lump of clay from the bag and drop it onto the wheel.

'What's easy to make?' he asks. 'A bowl?'

I cock my head, moving the basin of water to the ledge next to the wheel.

'Sure,' I say, crouching down next to him. As I dip my hands in water and lay them on the clay, I feel a rush of heat spread through my body.

I haven't done this in years. Why haven't I done this in years?

I look up at Isaac and try not to laugh as he gawps back at me.

'Okay,' I say, 'so you need to get your hands wet.'

I gesture to the water. He dips his hands in dubiously. As he places them back on the clay, I feel my stomach turn over.

I need to try and ignore the fact that we're taking part in an activity that has literally been proven to lead to sex. There was a whole film about it, for goodness' sake.

'What next?'

I focus my eyes back on the clay, trying to control my roaring cheeks.

'Do you see that pedal by your foot?'

He moves his foot onto the pedal, and I almost fall over as the clay spins into my hands.

'Wait!' I laugh. 'You need to do it gently at first, then you can speed up.'

My face burns as Isaac leans into the wheel.

Oh God, why does everything sound so bloody sexual?

'Okay,' he says, 'I'm ready.'

I try and shoot him a cool smile, but as my eyes catch his, I feel as though I've been electrocuted.

Bloody hell, I've got to calm down or I'll pass out with hysteria, like a poor damsel in distress.

'Okay,' I say. I place my hands on the opposite side of the clay to Isaac's and brace myself for it to come to life. As soon as the wheel starts to move, my hands move with it. I don't even have to think about what I need to do for this to work. I just know.

'We're shaping the clay first,' I say, my voice hoarse as I carefully move my hands, 'then we'll make it into a bowl.'

The clay spills over my hands and I dip them back into the water. Isaac does the same, and our fingers touch. For a second, we just stare at each other, before he grabs my face, kissing me firmly on the mouth. I sink into him, the wheel slowing to a halt as he moves towards me.

The candles really are more romantic.

Chapter Twenty-Four

Rachel

I hover at the front door, taking in the murky red paint and the brass number that shines under the flickering hallway light. My hands, which have been clenched into fists since I arrived, are hanging by my sides, tense and useless. I was so fuelled with an urge to speak to my dad that I sent the messages without much thought. The silence in the cabin had seeped into every corner, and I felt like I was sinking. Grandma has gone, Mum never calls, and I can't seem to tell Katy the truth about *anything* for fear of her not giving me the reaction I need. Dad is the only one left.

But now I'm here, I feel like I'm drowning all over again.

I lift my clenched fist, my other hand instinctively reaching for my stomach. Before I can talk myself out of it, I rap on the door, making a quick staccato sound, and stand back. Within seconds, it swings open. At the sight of him, I almost burst.

He's got rounder since I last saw him, and his hair is flecked with grey, but his electric-blue eyes shine at me the way they always did. As I stand in front of him, I realise that the pain I was so afraid of is nowhere to be seen, and when he smiles at me, all the anger I felt at him for what he did to Mum leaves my body and the tears break free and fall onto my cheeks. At this, Dad steps out of the flat and puts his strong, safe arms around me in the way only a dad can, and in that moment, for the first time since Danny left, I feel like everything might be okay.

★

Two wobbly mugs are placed on the table, next to a plate of biscuits. Shining jammy dodgers, fat bourbons and gooey chocolate cookies lie side by side, and as I stare at them, my mouth fills with saliva.

'Here you are then,' Dad says, handing me tea in one of Katy's mugs.

I cup my hands around it, smiling at her teenage handiwork. 'Thanks,' I say, 'this is perfect.'

I jump as a loud, outraged yelp echoes through the flat from under the door of Dad's bedroom. He locked Betsy in there after I nearly tripped over her as she danced around my feet.

Dad shuffles into the wooden chair at the head of the table and smiles at me.

'Sorry,' he laughs, wiping the corners of his eyes, 'I just can't stop looking at you. You're so grown up.'

I smile awkwardly, feeling my cheeks flush as I look down at my tea.

There are so many elephants in this room, we might as well be at the circus.

'Yeah,' I say, 'I mean, there are some obvious changes . . .'

I gesture down to my bump.

'Bet you didn't know you were about to be a grandad.'

I hear myself laugh awkwardly, as though I've admitted that I'm arriving with a big, ugly secret. The realisation shocks me and I grip my hand onto my bump.

I'm not ashamed of you.

'I know!' Dad laughs. 'I can't believe it! It's fantastic! I bet Danny is so excited. Is he back from his latest cruise yet?'

His words hang in the air and I stare down at my tea, my hands gripped so tightly around the mug that they start to burn. Dad's smile droops.

'Rachel?' he says, trying to catch my eye. 'What is it?'

I lift my head to look at him, but when I try to speak, my mouth feels as though it's full of sand. Slowly Dad's expression changes and he nods.

'Ah,' he says, 'I see. I'm sorry, love.'

'It's not his,' I manage. 'He doesn't even know.'

The shame burns through me as I hear the words spoken aloud, and my clammy hands peel away from the mug.

'Who does know?'

'Nobody.'

Dad raises his eyebrows. 'Nobody?' he repeats. 'Why not?'

'I'm scared I can't do it,' I mumble. 'I'm scared I'll be a bad mum. I—'

'Hey.' I jump as Dad's voice cuts through me, thick with his Welsh accent as he leans forward and grips my hand. 'You will be a great mum.'

I try and control my tears, which are now streaming down my face.

'Even though I'm bringing this baby into a broken family?' I say quietly, finally voicing one of my deepest fears, which rumbles in the pit of my stomach as I hear it out loud.

For a second Dad doesn't speak, but his grip stays firm on mine.

'Just because a family doesn't look how you thought it might doesn't make it broken.'

I pull my gaze up to meet his, my stomach turning over as his bright eyes stare fiercely into mine. Guilt rolls through me as I look into his kind face, and I realise how much I have needed this. How much I have needed my dad.

'I'm so sorry I never returned your calls.'

He gives my hand a firm squeeze and winks at me.

'You're here now,' he says. 'That's what matters.'

★

Great bubbles of red liquid stretch and pop in the saucepan, and I turn my wooden spoon, gently stirring the sauce. Stacks of new Tupperware sit next to me, all shiny and new, not stained red like mine are.

As I stir the pot, a lightness spreads through my body. Ever since I left Dad's, the fear I've been carrying around hasn't felt so heavy. I ended up staying for hours, sitting at his kitchen table and chatting.

Whilst I was there, I took a good look around. His Welsh rugby scarf was still tacked to his bedroom wall, and Katy's pottery sat proudly on almost every surface. There were more signs of Katy in his flat than there are in the lodge: photos of them at the cinema, out for dinner, waving Welsh flags and watching the rugby World Cup on his cream sofa. As I looked at Katy's beaming face, I felt an ice-cold rush through me. All she wanted was for me to forgive Dad and allow us to be a family, but I refused. I didn't even want to know. I didn't care how much it hurt my dad or how much she needed me. And now I'm terrified she'll do the same to me.

I jump back as the sauce splats at me, and turn the heat down. Tomorrow my time in London is up and I go back to Wales. Whether I like it or not, and no matter how much I bury my head in the sand, this baby is coming. I can't keep it from Katy for much longer. Dad promised me he wouldn't say a word, but in a few weeks I won't be able to pretend it isn't real. A living, breathing human is hard to keep secret.

I turn my phone in my hand as Peggy's latest message shines up at me.

Met the famous Katy! She seems nice. Don't worry, I didn't talk to her about anything. Although I think you should. She's just like you.

I chew my lip as another message pops onto the screen.

Also, have you had a chance to try any of those vaginal stretches? I found this fab diagram online, I'll ping it over now.

Good God, the last thing I want is Peggy sending a diagram of vaginal stretches to my work email account. How will I explain that to IT when I'm called in for receiving inappropriate content?

There is a knock at the door and I turn to see Fiona's shadow. I wave at her to come in, turning down the heat under the sauce.

'Hi, Rachel.' She smiles. 'Oh, something smells nice!'

She gawps at the stacks of Tupperware and I feel my chest stretch with pride.

'Thanks,' I say. 'I just decided to fill Katy's freezer with some bits. I like cooking.'

'I can see.' She perches on the arm of the sofa. 'Have you heard much from Katy? Is she enjoying Wales?'

My heart twinges, and the guilt flutters again.

'Yes,' I say, 'although I think she's found it hard not working. I think she's been a bit anxious about it.'

I glance at Fiona to try and catch her reaction, but she's busy examining her hands, frowning at a smudge of something on her pillar-box-red nails. She starts to rub it off.

'Oh?' she says absent-mindedly.

'Yeah,' I say. 'Did you see an email from her? I don't know what it was about, but she mentioned—'

'Yes.' Fiona cuts me off, her voice now cold and businesslike. 'I did receive it, Rachel. I will take a look at it.'

I close my mouth. She's made it clear that I'm not to ask any more questions. A damp heat prickles up my neck and my hands grip onto my sides as I suddenly feel as though I've just made things worse.

'Great,' I say, trying to keep my voice bright, 'thank you. She'll be back late tomorrow anyway,' I add.

Fiona flicks her eyes up at me. 'Is it tomorrow you're going?'

I nod. 'Tomorrow morning.'

'Oh, well let's have a farewell dinner then!' she cries, the warm, hospitable Fiona back. 'I'm sure Jasmine and William will want to say goodbye. Unless you wanted to go out?' She stands up. 'Actually see London outside of Chiswick? We could go to the theatre!'

229

I try not to laugh as she flings her arms in the air and then almost instantly drops them back down.

'Oh no.' Her face falls. 'It's Jasmine's school play tonight. Oh, I can't believe we're busy. I'm never busy.'

She runs her fingers through her hair, looking genuinely annoyed, and for some reason I feel a wave of disappointment.

'Honestly, it's fine,' I say. 'You've done so much for me already. I wouldn't expect—'

'I know!' she cries, clapping her hands and making me jump. 'Let's have an early dinner at four. The show doesn't start until six. How's that?'

I blink. She really wants to see me that badly?

'Oh,' I say, 'sure. That sounds lovely.'

The bright smile Fiona often wears springs back onto her face and she turns and totters out of the lodge.

'See you then!' she sings. 'I'll pop out and buy some goodies. Did you know they do vegan ice cream now?' she adds, sticking her head back in and raising her eyebrows. I laugh and nod as she looks at me as though this information is worth a round of applause.

'Sounds great,' I say. 'See you then.'

CHAPTER TWENTY-FIVE

KATY

I laugh as Bruno gallops ahead of me, pummelling his legs into the ground and charging through the fields at full force. It's as though he's never been on a walk in his life, although this is one I took out of Rachel's manual as being in his 'top three favourites'. I rolled my eyes when she first sent me the list (like, come on, he's a dog!). But watching him leap across the fields and dance with the swaying stalks of grass, she may have a point.

He stops running and stares at me, panting heavily, waiting for me to follow.

'I'm here!' I say, another laugh spilling out of me. 'I'm coming. I'm just not as fast as you are.'

Bruno takes this as fact and bounds off again through the fields.

I'm also not as relaxed. Me and Isaac practically pulled an

all-nighter in that shed, and it wasn't until the final candle flickered out that we realised that maybe we should go inside.

I tuck my hands in my coat pockets.

I shouldn't have slept with him. I knew that the moment it happened, but a large part of me didn't care. As soon as he arrived with the clay, the feelings I've been trying to fight took over, and for the first time since I arrived in Wales, I allowed myself just to love him. To be honest, I'm not sure I ever stopped; I just knew that I shouldn't. I'm not staying in Wales, and long-distance relationships don't work. One person ends up giving up on the other; look at me and Rachel.

We haven't spoken about it. He left early to go to the farm and I managed to steal a few hours' sleep before Bruno's desperate barking snapped me awake.

The sun is bright and slices through the clouds, making me squint, but there is a cool nip to the air. I take a deep breath, pushing the fresh air deep into my lungs, and shut my eyes, turning my face up to the sun. I feel my shoulders drop as I glance down at my phone, free of any messages from Rachel. Ever since our last conversation, I have felt a horrible niggle in the pit of my stomach that something isn't quite right.

My brain has been working overtime since I hung up the phone to her on Wednesday, desperately trying to piece together memories over the years like a mad detective. When was the last time I saw her in person? When was the last time I saw Danny? When was the last time we did a video call, instead of an email or text? Did she sound happy? How did she look?

It never occurred to me that she might be alone here, even though I knew Danny worked away for the majority of the year. I was the one who moved to a scary new city all by myself. I was the one who left my family, friends and boyfriend behind. I was the one who should be lonely, not her.

But a louder voice pierces through my mind.

Why would she take down the photos of Danny?

I dig my hands deeper in my coat pockets.

Have they split? Is that what she's been hiding? Has he left her?

I rub my forehead with the back of my hand as Bruno speeds towards me, checking I'm still following him. Poor thing, I probably scared him half to death when I lost him. I can't lose him this time; I'd never get back home.

I squint into the sun as Bruno leaps up at two figures in the distance. As they step closer, I recognise one of them immediately as Ellie, and feel a twinge of guilt. Last time I saw her, I was trying to log on to that stupid Wi-Fi and I was hardly conversationalist of the year. Actually, I think I was downright rude.

I push a large smile onto my face as I reach them, Bruno skirting between us like he's introducing everyone.

'Hi, Ellie,' I say, holding my hand above my eyes to block out the sun.

'Oh,' Ellie says. 'Hi, Katy, I thought you were Rachel when I saw Bruno. This is Sadie.' She turns to the girl next to her, who has bright pink hair and a nose ring. 'Katy is Rachel Dower's sister.'

Sadie pulls a face of recognition and smiles at me.

'Is Rachel with you?' Ellie says hopefully.

'No,' I reply, 'she's still in London.'

'Is she all right?' Sadie asks. 'We haven't seen her in ages.'

My stomach flips over.

I have no idea.

'Yeah,' I say brightly. 'Did you know it was her birthday a

few weeks ago?' I move my eyes back to Ellie, who stares back at me, her face indignant.

'Of course!' she says. 'We all messaged her to try and arrange something, but she didn't reply.'

'Well,' Sadie interjects, 'she sort of did. She just brushed us off.'

Another piece of the puzzle slides into my mind and I bite my lip.

Why would she do that? I know Rachel can be shy, but she's not antisocial. She loves her friends.

I pull my phone out of my pocket.

'Can I take your numbers?' I ask, passing the phone to Ellie, who looks at it dubiously. 'I want to plan something.'

As I take the phone back, a message appears on the screen. It's from Isaac.

Are you free tonight? I'd like to make you dinner. I can cook now, you know. See, another surprise you'll love.

★

I look at myself in the mirror for the fourteenth time and squirm with embarrassment at my reflection. I gave myself two hours; that's how long it takes me to get ready for a day in the office with Fiona or a big work event. Normally I'll spend at least an hour straightening my naturally wavy hair within an inch of its life. Then I'll smother my face in thick pale foundation to mask my freckles, like I'm drowning them in cream. I'll spend about twenty minutes carefully drawing my eyebrows in place to ensure that they are perfectly symmetrical, and then I'll apply a set of pointy fake eyelashes, in the hope that nobody will notice that they're not the eyelash extensions all the other girls wear but I can't quite afford.

But today, I didn't feel like flattening my hair or hiding my freckles. I even found myself liking them, and so getting ready only involved a flick of mascara and a swipe of pale lipstick. I haven't gone out like that since I moved to London.

The outfit took much longer to construct. I hadn't packed any date outfits; why on earth would I? If I'd suspected that Isaac would be lurking next door, I would have manhandled the train driver and driven us all back to London.

So I've gone for skinny jeans and a fitted lacy top. I think I look okay.

Bruno lets out a yelp and I jump, clutching my hand to my chest.

I will never get used to him doing that.

I turn to look at him sitting on the sofa staring at me.

'What do you think?' I say, trying to squash the nerves fluttering in the pit of my stomach. 'Do I look okay?'

I raise my eyebrows as Bruno blinks back at me, silent.

Oh, so *now* he doesn't bark.

'Useless,' I mutter, grabbing my handbag. I make my way to the front door and grab the keys off the hook. Bruno scrabbles after me, but I shoot him a look.

'We've spoken about this,' I say. 'You can't come with me everywhere. I'll be back later.'

Why on earth am I talking to this dog like he can understand me? Is this what Rachel does? It's like having a child.

I click the front door shut and start walking down the garden path.

I shouldn't be going on this date. I should have said no.

Nothing good will come of it. I'm leaving tomorrow and going back to London. But as soon as Isaac asked me, a stronger feeling took over and the voice inside me screaming to do the sensible thing was silenced. I wanted to say yes. I wanted to spend more time with him. So that's what I'm going to do.

He pulls open the door and I feel my heart turn over as he smiles at me. He's wearing a checked shirt and jeans, and as he leans in for a hug, I get a whiff of his manly aftershave.

'You look nice,' he says, looking me right in the eyes. I can't help it; the grin I was trying to keep at bay splits across my face and I beam at him.

'Thank you,' I say, stepping inside his house.

'So,' he says, as I push off my shoes, 'I hope you don't mind, but I thought I'd cook us fish. I went down to the fishmonger's this morning.'

He hands me a glass of wine and I take it, resisting the temptation to neck it in one gulp in the hope of silencing my jittering nerves.

He lifts his own glass and we chink them together.

★

I place my knife and fork down, allowing my body to sink back into my chair as my stomach stretches in appreciation.

Isaac places a final piece of sea bream into his mouth and I smile at him.

'That was delicious,' I say, my voice slow and relaxed. 'I haven't had sea bream in years.'

He frowns at me. 'Why not?'

'I just never eat it in London. Fish is better by the sea.'

He nods in agreement as he swallows his mouthful.

'I've got something for you,' he says, reaching behind him and pulling out a box.

'Another present?' I laugh. 'You can't keep buying me things.'

He smiles and hands me a box. 'This is more of an IOU.'

I take it from him.

'What have you bought me?' I ask.

He shrugs. 'Well open it and you'll find out.'

I slowly unfold the gold paper that is wrapped around the box and gasp as an Apple Watch box peers up at me.

He bought me an Apple Watch?

'Isaac,' I breathe, 'I can't accept this; these are really expensive.'

I feel a stab of worry as I look back up at him. I know how much they cost. Fiona gave me hers when she got a new one for Christmas. I'd never be able to afford one brand new.

'Well I should have thought about that before I threw yours into the sea.' He grins as he gets to his feet, taking our plates with him. I look down at the box and smile.

'You can even hack into my internet if you want,' he says. 'I know how obsessed you are with emails.'

I roll my eyes in his direction but waste no time in setting up the watch and tapping in Isaac's Wi–Fi password.

'Rachel would be so mad if she knew I'd done that,' he laughs from the kitchen. 'You know how much work she does to keep our beaches clean, and there I am openly lobbing stuff into the sea.'

For a second I forget about the watch. I turn in my seat to face him.

'Isaac,' I say, 'can I talk to you about something?'

He reappears from the kitchen and sits down next to me.

'Sure,' he says lightly.

I pause, the statement spinning around my mind like it has been all day.

'I don't think Rachel is very happy,' I say.

I glance up at him, expecting him to frown or at least look shocked by my statement, but his face doesn't move.

'I think she's lonely,' I continue. 'I think Danny might have been away for a while.'

I pause. I've decided not to ask him outright if Danny and Rachel have split. If she hasn't told me, then I'm not sure she will have told anyone.

'I don't think I've been a very good sister to her,' I add.

This time I don't dare look at him, and my face burns as I say the words out loud. A part of me is hoping he might defend me and try and shut the conversation down, but he just listens. I am half grateful.

'So I want to do something for her,' I say, 'to show her how much people care about her, and maybe, like, perk her up.'

My eyes flit up to Isaac. He looks back at me, waiting.

Why isn't he saying anything?

'I'm going to throw her a surprise birthday party,' I say, the wave of excitement I felt when I first thought of the idea rising through me. 'In her house. I want to invite her friends and that Peggy woman I met the other day, and you and I'll be there too, and I don't know,' I shrug, 'I think it would be nice.'

I fold my hands into each other, and as I beam at Isaac, a look of panic flashes across his face.

'Really?' he says. 'I don't know if she'd like that.'

I feel a stab of annoyance.

I know I haven't seen her in a while, but she is my sister and I think I know her better than he does.

'She will,' I say confidently. 'I'll make it perfect for her.'

'And when do you think you'll throw this party?'

'Early next week,' I say. 'I think Tuesday – that's my day off. I'll come back from London for it. I'll wait for her to take Bruno out and then I'll get everyone in her house. I'll just keep hold of her spare key for a few more days.'

At this, Isaac's expression changes. I can almost see a thousand thoughts running across his face.

'You're going back to London, then?'

I pause, feeling my smile twitch.

'Of course I am,' I say, trying to keep my voice light. 'My whole life is there.'

'I'm not.'

A dart of fear stabs my chest, but I will myself to keep smiling.

No. He's trying to talk about it. Why is he trying to talk about it? Can't we just sit in blissful ignorance for a few more hours?

'Well that's why we're not a couple,' I say. 'You know, it's been fun seeing you again these last few days, but—'

I break off as Isaac grabs my hands.

'Katy,' he says, 'don't try and tell me that these last few days have just been a bit of fun. It was more than that. Or it was for me.'

He stares down at my hands and I feel my neck prickle.

I want to tell him how it was for me too. I want to be honest. I want to just stop lying to him, but as I meet his eyes, I feel my chest tighten. I can't do it. How can I admit to him that these past few days with him have been the happiest I've had in years? That I've never felt anything even close to this since we broke up? He'd try and persuade me to move back here, and I can't do that. I have no purpose in Wales any more. I don't belong here.

'Well it was just fun for me!' I hear myself laugh. 'Come on, Isaac. We're adults now.' I pull my hands away.

'I don't believe you.' He shakes his head. 'I love you, Katy. I thought I'd got over you, but seeing you again made me realise I never stopped loving you. I know you feel it too. You can't walk away from this.'

I stare back, unable to say anything. Then Isaac moves his head towards me and kisses me. His lips are soft, and I stay rigid for a second before allowing myself to sink into the kiss. I take a breath as he grips his hands onto my head and kisses me harder, and the feelings I have been fighting since I saw him again break free and rush over my body. Suddenly I feel my wrist vibrate. Without quite meaning to, I pull away.

'Sorry,' I say breathlessly, gesturing to the watch.

Isaac hovers, his face scrunched into a scowl.

As I go to turn the watch off, Fiona's name flashes on the screen and I feel my stomach drop.

'It's my boss,' I say quietly, my eyes flying over the email. 'She wants me back in London asap.'

CHAPTER TWENTY-SIX

RACHEL

I smooth down my top as I walk down the garden path towards Fiona's impressive home. William and Jasmine's bedroom light is on, and I can see Fiona sitting in the kitchen next to William. I feel a warm glow. This house feels more like a home than mine has for the past two years. Grandma took the last flicker of life with her when she died. I didn't realise how much I loved being part of a family until I slotted myself into Fiona's. My chest aches at the thought of leaving tomorrow and returning to my cold, empty cottage. Alone, again.

I feel the baby squirm around and place my hand on my bump.

Well, I won't be alone for much longer.

As I lift my hand to knock on the French doors that lead into the kitchen, William spots me and springs to his feet, abandoning the picture he was colouring in. I smile as he tugs on the door and throws his arms around me, his blonde head resting on my bump and his little arms only reaching me.

'Rachel!' he cries, letting me go. 'Look, look, I've been drawing you.'

He tugs me towards the table and Fiona smiles at me as Jasmine thunders down the stairs. She is head to toe in white and has half a set of cat's whiskers painted on her face.

'Rachel!' she says, interrupting William, who is trying to show me his drawing. 'Mummy said that you're leaving tomorrow and we have to say goodbye to you!'

She looks at me indignantly, as though what Fiona has told her is a downright lie and she's expecting me to unveil the truth.

'Don't be so rude,' Fiona scolds. 'How about, hello, Rachel how are you? Would you like a cup of tea or a biscuit?' She rolls her eyes at me and small patches of pink form on Jasmine's cheeks.

'It's my school play today,' she gabbles. 'Mummy, Daddy and William are all coming to watch me. I'm playing a cat.'

'You look great,' I smile.

'Look,' William says again, tugging on my sleeve as I sink down onto a bench. 'Look what I drew today.'

He pushes the picture in front of me and I feel as though he's thrown a bucket of ice water in my face.

It's a drawing of a stick woman with glasses and lots of dark hair. She's holding something in her arms and standing in front of a purple house next to a male stick figure. At the top, large wonky letters spell out:

RACHEL AND HER BABY

I swallow, a lump forming in my throat as I realise that a seven-year-old has a better grasp of my reality than I do.

'That's you,' William says proudly, pointing a finger at the stick woman, 'and that's your baby.'

'Do you really live in a purple house?' Jasmine says, her eyes wide as she stares at the drawing. 'Mummy said you did.'

'No,' Fiona says, getting to her feet and flicking the kettle on. 'I said it might be nice for Rachel to live in a purple house, as it's her favourite colour.'

'How do you know that?' I say.

'You wear purple every day!' Jasmine squeals. 'I noticed because it's my favourite colour too.'

She sticks her chest out boldly and William shoves the drawing closer to my face.

'Do you like it, Rachel?' he says, trying to push Jasmine out of the way. 'That's your husband,' he adds, jabbing his finger at the stick man.

I look down at the drawing, my heart thudding.

'What's his name?' Jasmine asks.

'Danny,' I say, my mouth dry.

'Right.' Fiona claps her hands together. 'Let's make Rachel a tea, shall we? Jasmine, have you given her your present?'

Jasmine jumps as if Fiona has given her a small electric shock and turns on the spot to bolt up the stairs. Fiona places a steaming mug in front of me and rests her head in her hands before quickly jabbing something into her phone.

'Don't do this to me,' she mutters under her breath.

I smile and look down at William, who is still holding his drawing out to me expectantly. I give him a squeeze.

'Thank you,' I say, trying to control the lump swelling in my throat. 'I will cherish this drawing forever. I'll put it on my fridge.'

'Oh!' Fiona coos, her head snapping up from her phone as she ruffles William's hair. 'On the fridge! That's a prime spot, isn't it, William?'

She winks at him and then jumps as her phone vibrates aggressively across the table. She snatches it up and charges out of the kitchen. William's large eyes follow her for a second as her loud, furious mutters fade, and I quickly pick up his drawing.

'I would love to live in a purple house,' I say, smiling at him as he moves his gaze away from the kitchen door. 'I think that would be great. What colour house would you like to live in?'

He cocks his head to one side and looks up, as though every colour he knows is flying above his head.

'I don't know,' he says. 'I like so many colours.'

'How about a rainbow house?'

He grins. 'Yeah!' he cries. 'A big rainbow house with a slide!'

I laugh as Jasmine crashes back into the room, her little hands squashed into fists, which she springs open to reveal two beaded bracelets.

'I made us friendship bracelets,' she says, 'so you won't forget me.'

I look down at the bracelets, one made with fat pink beads and the other mirroring it in purple. I hold out my hand and she pushes the purple bracelet onto my wrist and shoves the pink one on her own, grinning at our matching jewellery.

'Don't you worry about that,' I say, staring down at the bracelets, 'I will never forget you.'

Jasmine sticks her chest out proudly as Fiona reappears, her body slouched over like a balloon with no air. Her phone is now hanging by her side and her face is sullen. She sinks into a chair and takes hold of Jasmine's hands, turning her towards her.

'Mummy, look!' Jasmine cries. 'Rachel likes the bracelet!'

'That's wonderful, darling.'

I try to catch Fiona's eye to ask if she's okay, but she keeps staring at Jasmine.

'Jasmine, sweetheart,' she says quietly, 'I've got some bad news, I'm afraid.'

Jasmine stares back at her, eyes wide and expectant.

'Daddy has to work late again,' Fiona says, her voice tired. 'He can't come to the school play.'

I feel my chest ache for a moment, and when I hear Jasmine burst into tears, it feels as though my heart has snapped clean in two. I notice William hovering behind his sister and I smile at him. At this, he steps towards me and rests his head on my bump.

'But he promised,' Jasmine cries, fat tears spilling down her round cheeks. 'He said he wanted to see my costume. He said he'd put it in his diary.'

Fiona looks back at Jasmine, and for a second it seems as if she's about to cry, too.

'We'll send him a picture, and I'll film it so that we can all watch it together,' Fiona says, wiping the tears off Jasmine's face.

'Rachel, are you coming?'

William lifts his head from my bump and blinks up at me, and I notice that Jasmine has stopped crying and is looking at me too, waiting for my answer. I quickly steal a glance at Fiona, expecting her to shake her head apologetically, but she just looks back at me.

'Well if you'd like me to come, Jasmine,' I say, 'I'd love to.'

Chapter Twenty-Seven

Katy

I lean on the side of Isaac's bath, my heart ringing in my ears as I read the message for the third time.

Hi, I know this is a bit weird, but Fiona has asked me to go watch Jasmine in the school play and I can't say no. Hope that's okay.

I feel a shock of nerves flit through me as I picture the two of them drinking wine together and chatting about life.

I knew she'd end up speaking to Fiona. Even if Rachel listened to my every word (which she never does), Fiona would have found her. She joked about not being able to survive without me, so I knew that as soon as she spotted a cardboard cut-out of myself sitting in my cabin, she'd see it as a replacement for the week. An even better version, in fact. Rachel wouldn't bore her by reminding her of meetings she needs to attend and contracts she needs to sign. Rachel didn't screw up the most important event for her company. If anything, she'd be the perfect upgrade.

But I didn't expect it to go this far. I thought maybe they'd share one dinner, and then Rachel would make her excuses. Not end up going to Jasmine's school play. I mean, what is she doing? Does Fiona know what's wrong with her? Has Rachel confided in her?

I sigh.

Rachel's message was a welcome distraction from Fiona's email. I switched the watch off and told Isaac I didn't want to talk about going back to London, but I could tell by the look in his eyes that he wasn't about to let it go. He'd just asked me to stay in Wales with him, and I hadn't replied. I hadn't said yes.

I bring Fiona's email up again, and my heart turns over.

Hi Katy, sorry for not replying sooner. I think we need to talk about a few things. Looking forward to seeing you tomorrow. I need you back ASAP!

I read it again, a feeling of dread filling my body.

I think we need to talk about a few things.

What things? What does that mean? That could mean anything. Is she going to offer me the job in the office, or fire me? All I know is that I need to get back to London. I can't believe I took my eye off the ball and allowed myself to get swept up in Isaac and all those bloody relaxing walks. Why wasn't I checking my emails? I was on the cusp of a promotion, the job I've wanted for years! What was I thinking?

I've been in the bathroom for about ten minutes now, not that I think Isaac will particularly notice. He'll be pretending to wash up.

My phone vibrates next to me and I look down at a text message from Ellie.

Hi Katy, lovely to see you earlier. Surprise party for Rachel sounds like a great idea! I can do Tuesday evening. I'll bring some of the other girls, they all miss Rachel too! Let me know what time x

For a second, I almost forget about the looming email from Fiona and smile at the phone. I don't care what Isaac says, there is something not right with Rachel. I'm not sure I can fix it, but maybe this party will make it a little bit better.

I pull myself to standing and catch sight of myself in the mirror. The carefree face of three hours ago has gone, and the frown line across my forehead has returned. I stare at it, my chest pounding.

When did that come back?

Chapter Twenty-Eight

Rachel

I shuffle in the tiny plastic chair, wincing as I hear it groan under my weight.

Why oh *why* have they put the children's chairs out for us to sit on? What adult is the same weight as an eight-year-old? Don't they have any normal-sized chairs in this school? All I'll have to do is sneeze and it will snap in half, leaving me scrabbling on the floor like an upturned beetle.

'I can't see,' William moans, craning his head from left to right. Fiona hoists him onto her lap and rolls her eyes at me.

'Thank you so much for doing this,' she says. 'We were about to have a proper meltdown.'

I shift again as the baby jabs its elbow into my ribs. Fiona catches my expression and smiles sympathetically.

'God, I'm sorry,' she says, 'dragging you to this when you're so pregnant. All you should be doing is lying down and having people bring you chocolate.'

I laugh, placing my hands over the bump to try and calm the baby down.

'It's fine,' I say. 'I just might cry while watching it. I'm so hormonal, anything seems to set me off. I cried watching *Cash in the Attic* the other day.'

William screws up his face. 'My granny watches that.'

I laugh. 'Exactly.'

'Well if you need to step out, that's totally fine.'

Hmph. Like I'll be able to get out of this chair by myself.

I take out my phone. Katy hasn't texted me back, not that I'm surprised. I've practically ignored all her requests since I arrived, but me going to a precious family event with her boss is probably enough to make her head explode.

I'll try and call her tomorrow to explain.

My chest tightens as I remember I'm going home tomorrow. I have to tell her the truth soon; I'm running out of time.

'Ah!' Fiona says, as the lights go down and the light murmur from the audience dies away. William straightens his back, pulling himself as tall as he can in order to see. As the teacher finishes the introduction and the children troop on stage, my eyes scan the rows until I spot Jasmine. She's on the far left of the stage, her shoulders pushed back and her eyes fixed defiantly on the audience. As the piano tinkles and the children start singing, I feel my throat swell. I glance across at Fiona, embarrassed at myself for crying when they've only just started, and notice that her face is already wet.

★

Fiona clicks the handbrake up and looks into the rear-view mirror. She smiles at me and I follow her gaze. Both William and Jasmine are fast asleep, their heads lolling from side to side like abandoned puppets.

'We were only driving for fifteen minutes,' Fiona says.

I smile. 'Must be all the excitement.'

She nods. 'And all the drama.'

The play lasted about forty minutes, and seemed to be an odd version of *Puss in Boots*, which explained why Jasmine was dressed as a cat. The hall was jam-packed with beaming parents (one of whom climbed onstage with a little boy who almost cried after forgetting his lines), and the roof nearly flew off when the curtain came down.

Fiona leans her head against the headrest and closes her eyes.

'You're happily married, aren't you?' she says.

Her words are like a slap in the face, and I freeze.

Why is she asking me that? What does she mean?

'I was too once,' she continues, keeping her eyes closed.

I blink at her.

'He pulls this shit all the time,' she says quietly.

'It is bad that he has to work such long hours,' I offer.

Fiona laughs.

'He's not working,' she says. 'He's having an affair.'

What?

'He's been having an affair for years,' she says lightly, finally opening her eyes and fixing her stony gaze forward. 'Way before Katy arrived. I don't know who with. Multiple women I expect.'

I stare at her, my heart humming in my ears.

My dad cheated on my mum, right before he left. Their marriage was already in pieces, but that was the final blow.

I don't want to have this conversation with her; I barely know her. I want to change the subject. This isn't my business. But I feel myself pulled towards her. I can't look away.

'Does he know you know?' I say.

She shrugs. 'Who knows? Probably not, or he'd expect me to leave him and take the kids.'

'Well why don't you?' I say, my voice stronger. 'You're an amazing mum, Fiona, you're all the kids need. You could do it.'

A small laugh pumps out of her and she pulls her sagging eyes up to meet mine.

'I wish I was as sure as you.'

CHAPTER TWENTY-NINE

KATY

I fling open my suitcase and start to fold my clothes as neatly as possible. I've been awake since six. I didn't set an alarm, but my eyes pinged open as soon as the yellow sunlight crept into my room. I grabbed my phone immediately, hoping for a message from Rachel reassuring me that everything was okay and giving me some sort of update as to why she couldn't say no to crashing a private family event with my boss.

I scowl at my phone, which is still smiling up at me, motion-less.

My train doesn't leave until midday. Once I realised Rachel wasn't going to make contact with me, I started cleaning the house and restoring it to its naturally perfect state. I even managed to resist trying the fantastic cherry cake I made, which is sitting proudly on the kitchen table, ready and waiting for Rachel.

I try and smile as I fold my clothes, but a chill rinses over me as Isaac's face pushes into my mind. I left his house shortly after I got the message from Rachel. A part of me told him I was going home early to see if he'd react and ask me to stay, but he didn't. He barely said anything.

I shouldn't have gone on a date with him. I knew it was a bad idea. We only work when we're together, and I need to go back to London. That's all there is to it. I mean, really, aside from Rachel and Danny, how many people actually end up with their childhood sweethearts? And let's be honest, I'm not even one hundred per cent sure that they're even still together.

As I sigh and run my fingers through my hair, my phone flashes. I grab it and see a message from Ellie.

Hi! So excited for the party. I've spoken to the other girls and they are up for it too. Let me know if you want me to bring anything. Will be so good to see Rachel again, we can't wait x

I stare down at the text.

I know something is wrong with Rachel. I can feel it, but whatever it is, she won't tell me. I'm not expecting her to tell me at the party, but I'm hoping she might realise that things aren't as bad as she thinks they are. I'm hoping she'll realise she can still trust me and decide to let me in.

Bruno yelps from downstairs and I jump as I hear a knock on the front door. My stomach squeezes as I put down a pile of socks and run down the stairs. I knew Isaac would stop by at some point this morning, but I was hoping it would be after I left.

I pull open the door and feel my stomach turn over. He's back to how he looked on the first day I arrived. His face is scrunched up and his shoulders are hunched over, as though he's creating a barrier that I can't get through. His eyes dart around, making sure to look absolutely anywhere that doesn't involve making eye contact with me, and he's back in those horrible brown boots.

He's still mad. I knew he would be.

'Hi,' I say, reaching down and grabbing Bruno as he threatens to bound outside.

'Hi.'

I'm about to ask him how he is, but I clamp my lips together as I feel a rush of irritation storm through me.

If he wants to knock on my door without warning, then he can make the small talk. I never said to him that I was going to stay in Wales; he should know how important my job is to me. How can he expect me to give everything up for him? Who does he think he is?

I feel my chin lift as I wait for him to speak. He continues to shuffle in his boots.

'Have you heard from Rachel?'

I raise my eyebrows. That can't be the question he's come round to ask me.

'Not today,' I say coolly. 'Have you?'

'No.'

'Right.'

We sink back into silence and a gust of wind whips past us.

Is he not going to say anything else? Why is he here? What does he want?

'Right,' I say again. 'Well, I need to pack. I leave in just under an hour, so . . .'

I lean on the door and pretend I'm about to shut it, and finally Isaac's green eyes snap up to mine. I feel a jolt of electricity shoot through me and will my face to remain still.

'So you're going then?' he says, his voice cold.

'Yes,' I say, matching his tone. 'I need to get back to work.'

He shrugs. 'Fine.' He looks away again. 'I was a bit drunk last night. I shouldn't have said that stuff to you about staying here. I didn't mean it.'

My stomach drops.

He's taking back what he said?

'Right,' I say, trying to keep my voice steady as my heart thumps in my chest. 'Well, good.'

He shoves his hands in his pockets. 'I still don't think you should throw that party for Rachel,' he says childishly.

I feel a zap of annoyance.

Why does he think he knows Rachel so much better than I do?

'Well I don't care what you think,' I snap. 'Now I really need to pack. I'll see you at the party, assuming you'll come.'

'Look,' Isaac shuffles his feet awkwardly, 'this isn't about us. I really think Rachel wouldn't want a party right now. I just think—'

'Coo-ee!'

My scowl shifts from Isaac as I spot Peggy bundling down the path holding a large Tupperware box. A long emerald pashmina is twisted round her neck and fluttering in the wind, and her kind eyes are framed in glittery eyeliner.

Does she always dress like this?

Actually, I'm glad she's here. I need to invite her to the party.

'Hi, Peggy,' I say, forcing myself to smile. 'How are you?'

She beams at us both. 'Sorry to drop in again!' she says, ignoring my question, 'but I was baking shortbread this morning and made too much, so I thought you might like some for the journey home.' Her eyes twinkle at me. 'Or I thought we could have some now over a cuppa and get to know each other a bit better,' she adds, looking over my shoulder as though planning to sneak past me.

I try to hide my confusion. Why does she want to get to know me?

'Oh, that's so kind,' I say, after realising I've been silent for a few seconds, 'but I've got a train to catch. But,' I add pointedly, shooting Isaac a look, 'hopefully I'll see you on Tuesday. I'm throwing Rachel a surprise birthday party, as she didn't have much of a celebration on our actual birthday.'

Peggy opens her mouth to speak, but Isaac gets there first.

'And I was saying to Katy that perhaps Rachel wouldn't like a surprise party now?' He raises her eyebrows at Peggy and I glare at him.

Who is he to try and ruin my idea by getting Peggy on his side?

Peggy looks from me to Isaac, and then suddenly a wide smile springs onto her face.

'I think that's a wonderful idea, love!' she trills. 'I think Rachel will love it, and it will give the two of you a chance to catch up and have a good talk.'

And then, bizarrely, she leans forward and gives my wrist a squeeze.

That was weird.

'Well, I won't keep you if you've got a train to catch,' Peggy says, handing me the Tupperware. 'I'll see you on Tuesday!'

I go to shoot Isaac a look of triumph, but to my alarm, his shoulders are slumped forward.

Is he really that anti the party?

'It'll be at four p.m. at the cottage,' I say, trying to ignore the weird feeling in the pit of my stomach. 'See you then.'

Peggy waves and clacks back towards her car. As she leaves, I look back at Isaac, whose chin is now pressed into his chest as though he's trying to hide himself.

'Will you come?' I say.

He leans down and rubs Bruno's ears, his face still creased in a deep frown.

'Sure,' he says, his voice flat. 'Bye then. Enjoy London.'

'Bye,' I manage, but it comes out as barely more than a whisper as Isaac turns on his heel and disappears. The door clicks shut and Bruno lets out a whine, and as I look down at him, I notice my eyes are filled with tears.

'For God's sake,' I mutter, wiping the tears away and marching back up the stairs.

I can't cry over Isaac. There is no point.

Back in my bedroom, I start throwing clothes into the suitcase, no longer bothering to carefully fold anything.

I've moved on. I've made a better life for myself in London, a happier life. I moved from Wales for a reason. I hate it here. All being here does is remind me of everything I've lost. My parents, my childhood, my grandma.

As Grandma's kind face moves into my mind, the tears I've been fighting push their way to the surface and my heart starts to ache. I never understood the phrase 'heartbroken' until she died, but it literally felt as though my heart was torn clean in two.

My can of deodorant rolls off the bed onto the floor. I reach down to pick it up and catch my breath as my eyes land on a small container. Slowly I reach forward and pull it out from under the bed.

House Swap

As I hold it in my hands, I suddenly feel as if I'm going to collapse.

I know what this is. It's the urn I've been searching for – that Rachel and I have been searching for – for the last two years. It's the urn Rachel has always claimed Mum has kept, even though we wanted to scatter the ashes together. Even though it was Grandma's dying wish to be scattered on the cliff above the village.

But she's had it, all this time Rachel's had it.

My hands tighten around the urn and fat tears splatter down my face as I stare down at the name engraved on the side.

Violet Carpenter

It's Grandma's ashes.

CHAPTER THIRTY

RACHEL

I look around Katy's cabin, which is moving up and down slightly as I bob on Jasmine's space hopper. There was no way I'd manage to carry my pregnancy ball to London by myself, so I shoved it in the loft along with everything else before I left. Jasmine loved the idea of me borrowing her hopper instead.

My train leaves in ninety minutes, and although this is just a little lodge that Katy isn't even in, I don't want to go. I feel closer to her here than I have done since she moved away. I feel as though as soon as I leave we'll go back to our static, false relationship.

I draw a large heart on a pink Post-it note, Katy's favourite colour, and stick it on the fridge. The lodge looks almost unrecognisable. I've filled her freezer, cleaned the place from top to bottom and left little Post-it notes with positive messages for her to find. I hate the idea of work being so stressful for her in the last week thanks to me, so at least she can come back to a clean, calming home.

I clamber to my feet, holding my coat around me, as I catch sight of myself in Katy's floor-length mirror.

My bump is now swelling out of me, arching my back and making me lollop about like Mr Blobby. I can't believe how enormous I've become. I dread to think how big this baby is. If I allow myself to think about childbirth for too long, I feel as if my vagina might close up in fright.

I pick up my suitcase and wheel it out of the lodge, taking one last look before I close the door behind me. Thank God the place was such a tip when I arrived; cleaning and cooking ended up being the perfect distraction. If I hadn't had those things to do, I would have gone mad.

I rap my knuckles on the French doors that lead into Fiona's kitchen. Jasmine springs up and pulls the door open, her face bursting with glee.

'You're still here!' she cries, launching her arms around my middle. 'I thought you'd gone!'

'I am going,' I say, giving her a squeeze. 'I just wanted to say goodbye to you all.'

Fiona leans against the door frame and pulls Jasmine closer to her. Today, her face looks sunken and the usual bright, spontaneous light that shines isn't there.

'It's been lovely to meet you, Rachel,' she says, her voice calm and steady.

I feel my stomach turn over. She must regret telling me everything last night.

'Thank you for letting me stay,' I say. 'I've had a lovely time.'

'You're wearing my bracelet!' Jasmine chimes, grabbing hold of my hand and yanking it towards her.

'Yeah,' I say, smiling down at her, 'of course.'

'Would you like a lift to the station?'

'No,' I say, 'thank you. My taxi should be here any second. I'd better go and wait for it.'

I give a little wave to William, who is clinging to Fiona's leg, and then pull my suitcase over the gravel, wishing I could go back to laughing with Fiona and the children over dinner like we were a big family.

Is this the Fiona Katy sees? Cold and distant? Is this why her flat was in such a state when I arrived and she was so obsessed with connecting to the internet so she could log onto her emails?

I climb into the back of the taxi and mumble a hello to the driver. The next ten minutes slide by as I stare out of the window trying to silence the thoughts flying through my mind. Eventually my phone snaps me back to reality with one short, sharp buzz:

I know about Grandma's ashes. I don't know what's going on with you lately, but I know you're a liar.

My blood turns cold as I read the last line.

I clearly don't know anything about you, and I don't want to.

CHAPTER THIRTY-ONE

KATY

I press my face against the window of the taxi, pushing tears from my face as they continue to fall. I didn't have much family before I left London, and now I'm returning, I feel as though I have virtually none at all.

Our grandma was the light in our family. She moved into our home when we were about eight. For years I never knew why, and just assumed that she wanted to be with us all the time and couldn't bear to live away from us, but as I got older, I realised it was to shield our ears from the shouting coming from our parents. In the end, she almost raised us. She took us to school and helped us with our homework; she taught Rachel how to bake and bought me my first set of paints. She was the beating heart that held us all together, and when she died, I felt as though she took a part of me with her.

We knew she was going to die months before she did, although we denied it. She wasn't well, and had recently turned ninety. I always said how she had to make it to one hundred, to get a letter from the Queen if nothing else! She laughed at this. She did try to tell me that this was the end, but I wouldn't listen. One of the last things she said to Rachel and me was how she wanted to be scattered on the cliff facing our house, so she could always look over us and join us on our walks. Every day that went by when those ashes weren't scattered, I felt a weight of guilt pull me down that we weren't doing what she'd asked. But we couldn't; our mum wanted to hold onto the ashes.

Or, as it turns out, Rachel wanted to.

The lump in my throat thickens as I turn my phone over in my hand and open the message I sent her, which glistens up at me through the mask of tears. A hot blend of guilt and anger rolls up me as I read the message again.

I shouldn't have sent that to her, I shouldn't have said that I don't want to know her any more, but I couldn't stop myself, and as I stare down at the message and blink at the two blue ticks, I can't bring myself to take it back.

Grandma was *ours*; she was the only part of our family that we both agreed on and loved equally. How could Rachel keep her from me like this?

I've spent the past few days trying to work out what Rachel is hiding from me, but now I wish I had never bothered. She clearly doesn't want to let me into her life, or be any more than sisters who send each other birthday cards and exchange small talk over Christmas. Why should I try and force us to be anything else if that's not what she wants? I can't make her let me in.

The taxi crunches over the gravel as we pull onto Fiona's driveway and my heart starts thudding a different rhythm.

House Swap

Fiona's email to me wasn't anything significant. She didn't give anything away about whether she was going to offer me a promotion or fire me; she just asked that I see her when I'm back as she'd like to speak to me. I didn't dare ask why; I just responded to say I'd be home tomorrow and I'd see her bright and early in the morning.

If she fires me, I don't know where I'll go. I can hardly go back to Wales. Not now.

I thank the driver and climb out of the taxi, swinging my bag over my shoulder as I duck into the rain. The only light glowing in Fiona's house is in her bedroom, and as I start to wonder whether she's seen me, she flings the window open and scowls at me through the rain. I hold up a hand to wave and see her face drop. Fiona has always been terrible at hiding her emotions.

Oh God, she doesn't look happy to see me. She's not going to fire me now, in the middle of the night, is she?

I stand under the porch of the lodge to shelter from the rain, and spot the kitchen light in Fiona's house flick on. She flings the back door open and runs through the garden, her slippers squelching in the mud. I try not to laugh as she stumbles through the rain towards me.

What is she doing?

'Katy!' she cries as she reaches me, pushing her wet hair out of her face.

'Hi,' I say. 'How are you?'

I want to add: and why have you just run towards me in the middle of the night when it's chucking it down with rain?

'Oh yes, I'm fine,' she says, brushing my question away. 'Have you heard from Rachel? Did she get back okay?'

265

I feel heat bristle the back of my neck at Rachel's name.

'Probably,' I say. 'I haven't heard from her.'

'Oh.'

'I'm not sure I will either,' I add, trying not sound bitter but failing miserably. 'We're not that close.'

I click open the front door and push it open. As I step inside, my breath is snatched away from me. The cabin is almost unrecognisable. The surfaces are gleaming, my clothes are hung up proudly and my pillows are fat and plumped. I drop my bag, almost oblivious to Fiona following me inside, and walk towards the fridge, picking up a bright pink Post-it note. The flat is covered in them, all stuck in random places. There is a fat heart drawn on this one with the words *You can do anything* written underneath it.

'That's a shame,' Fiona says, making me jump as I realise she's right next to me. 'I'd love to have a sister like her.'

She walks back out of the flat and I peel another Post-it note off the toaster. As I read it, I feel like I might cry.

You will always be my sister.

As I clutch the note tightly in my hand, the thick anger gripping onto my insides wilts and a stronger feeling takes over. I stare down at the words, determination spinning through my body.

I'm not giving up on her.

She's my sister.

CHAPTER THIRTY-TWO

RACHEL

I clasp my fingers around my steaming mug, wincing as the heat sears through my hands, but I don't let go. I slot another piece of Katy's cherry cake into my mouth. It's dry, with an intense rubber quality, and all the cherries have sunk to the bottom like stones, but I'm eating it anyway. I can't believe she made it. Katy never bakes. If it wasn't so terrible, I'd have thought she'd bought it and was trying to pass it off as her own.

I take off my glasses, shutting my heavy eyes, which sting slightly as the tears prick behind my tired eyelids. When I reopen them, I'm looking at the photo of me and Danny on our wedding day. The only photo of us left in the cottage.

I look so happy in that photo; I couldn't bear to take it down. It felt like I was saying goodbye to that part of me forever. For some reason, keeping it there felt like a glimmer of hope that one day I would be that happy again.

Bruno rests his chin on my lap, his tail whacking against the floor as he wags it expectantly. He nearly broke the window when I arrived home with the force he threw his body at it. He didn't look thin or fidgety at all; it seems Katy took great care of him. To my surprise, she's actually taken good care of everything. When I got back last night, I found the house almost exactly as I'd left it. She had hoovered, made her bed and put fresh flowers on the table that look as though they've come from Isaac's farm, which makes me think they got along after all.

I take a deep breath as fear rolls over me.

There was no point replying to Katy's message. I had no defence. It's exactly what she thinks. I kept the ashes after Grandma's funeral and never told her. I lied to her when she asked about scattering them and said that our mum had them. I'm not sure when I was going to tell her the truth. If I'm honest, I'm not sure I ever was.

The front door rattles and Bruno races towards it, barking loudly as somebody knocks. I pull myself to my feet, a small groan escaping my lips as I hold onto my stomach as though I need to support my bump in my arms at all times. I didn't think it was possible to be this pregnant, and I've still got two weeks to go! I mean, I know I'm carrying another human being, but this is just ridiculous.

I reach the front door and see Isaac's shadow. I feel a small wave of relief as I open the door and Bruno pushes past me to greet him properly, but the relief evaporates as soon as I clock his expression. He's scowling. Isaac never scowls at me.

'Hey,' I say, stepping back to allow him to come in out of the rain. 'You okay?'

His eyes flit over my body in alarm, and for a second I think he's going to turn on his heel and run back down the garden path, but he doesn't.

'Have you got bigger?' he says, dumbfounded.

I feel my cheeks flare as he steps inside.

Well, how's that for a hello?

'I am pregnant,' I say tersely, pushing the door shut after him. 'Do you want a tea?' I ask, as he stands awkwardly in the living room.

'No,' he says. 'Yes. No.' He runs his fingers through his hair and looks out of the window. 'No, sorry. I can't. I need to go soon.'

I ease myself into the armchair, hoping Isaac will copy me and sit down, but he doesn't.

What is he doing? I frown. He's been in this house hundreds of times and now he's acting like a random guest.

'Right,' I say, 'what's up?'

'Have you heard from Katy?' he says quickly, as though he's been holding the words in his mouth like a swarm of bees.

I feel a shock of heat.

'No,' I lie. 'Have you?'

'No.'

We fall into silence and I raise my eyebrows at him expect-antly, waiting for him to tell me what he wants. He stuffs his hands into his pockets, his eyes flicking around the room anxiously. I try not to gawp at him.

What is the matter with him?

'So you didn't tell her? I thought you were going to tell her, I thought that was the point of everything.'

He waves his arm across the living room and my hands twist into each other.

'Do you know how hard it was to keep it from her?' he carries on. 'She knows something is going on with you. She asked me more than once.'

'I freaked out,' I say in a small voice.

'She was a total nightmare, you know,' he says, the words spitting out of him, 'but she's not as bad as you think she is. She doesn't deserve to be lied to.'

My eyes snap up to him.

'She lied to me too,' I say sharply. 'She told me she had this amazing, glamorous life, but—'

'Oh come on,' Isaac almost laughs as he begins to pace around the living room, 'we all knew that her spiel about her great life in London was bullshit.'

'I'm not the only one who's been lying to her,' I say, my face hot. 'Did you tell her how you feel? How you've been miserable ever since she left?'

He stops pacing and finally meets my eyes. The tension in his face slides away and he looks at me hopelessly.

'Yeah, I did,' he says, sinking down onto the arm of the sofa, 'and she didn't care. She ran away, back to London. She didn't want to know.'

I stare at him, a lump in my throat.

So she walked away from Isaac.

'That's what I think she'll do to me too,' I say quietly, my voice thick.

He shakes her head. 'You should trust her. She wouldn't do that.'

'Why not?' I say. 'I did it to her. I stopped speaking to our dad even though she begged me not to. I left her to go to London by herself when I'd promised I would go with her. She doesn't owe me anything. I've been a terrible sister to her.'

We fall into silence and Isaac leans back into the sofa. Bruno pushes his face towards Isaac's knee. I brush the tears quickly out of my eyes.

'She's your twin, though,' he says eventually. 'You don't walk away from family, not when it matters.'

I stare down at my hands, which are twisted together like a damp cloth.

Walking away when it matters is exactly what my family has always done. My parents walked away from each other when they were supposed to be in love. Mum walked away from her daughters when she found a new family. Katy and I walked away from each other when Grandma died.

'I think it's gone too far this time,' I say in a small voice. 'I don't think we can come back from this.'

'But you haven't told her yet!' Isaac says, exasperated. 'How can you know when you haven't even—'

'Not that.' I shake my head. 'I did something worse than that. I lied about Grandma's ashes.' As I speak, the fat tears I've been battling fall down my face and I don't bother wiping them away. 'I always told Katy that our mum had them and wouldn't let us scatter them, but Katy found them. I've had them this whole time.'

I keep my eyes fixed on my hands, but I can see from the corner of my eye that Isaac is gaping at me. He knows better than anyone how much Katy loved our grandma; he knows what this would do to her. I've always known too, but it didn't stop me.

'Why did you lie?' he says.

I open my mouth to answer, but any defence I have is too flimsy to explain. When our parents left, Grandma was all we

271

had. We always said we didn't mind; she was our favourite anyway. Our parents never felt like real parents, they didn't really act like them. When Grandma died, Katy had left and Danny was off on another cruise ship, and I couldn't bear to let someone else go. I had the power to keep her with me, so I took it.

'Look,' Isaac says, leaning towards me, 'you need to give Katy the chance to be there for you. You're making the decision for her.'

I let out a small sob as guilt swarms through me. At this, Bruno turns his head and pads towards me, resting his head on my bump and flicking his large eyes up to look at me.

'I'm scared she'll reject me,' I say weakly, heat burning at my skin as I speak my fear aloud. 'I'm scared she'll go back to London and she won't want to have a relationship with me.'

Isaac sighs. As he opens his mouth to speak, he clocks the cherry cake sitting on the kitchen table.

'Hey,' he says, a small smile flitting onto his face, 'what do you think of the cake?'

CHAPTER THIRTY-THREE

KATY

I stare at my reflection in the mirror, trying to ignore the fact that my heart has been racing in my chest since I arrived back. I glance at the coffee table, where last night I collected up all the Post-it notes I could find and read them until my eyes screamed for me to close them and fall asleep.

Rachel had filled the notes with love, hope and positive messages and stuck them all over the lodge. While I was looking for them, I also found that she had filled my freezer with food. As I sat and read each note, I felt my heart begin to swell until it ached too much to read any more. I haven't had anyone look after me in years, and Rachel was doing it from miles away. How can she be so far away from me and still know exactly what I need?

But as I thought all of this, the loudest thought stretched into my mind until it was the only one I could hear.

273

How does Rachel know so clearly what I need and I have no idea what I can do to help her? I still can't understand why she hid the ashes from me, but I also know I can't leave her while something is going on. Even if I have to force her to let me in.

I sigh and straighten my blouse. I can't think about that now. I need to speak to Fiona. I'll have to try and crack Rachel later.

When I got ready this morning, I started my usual hair and make-up routine, but as I looked at my wild dark curls, I suddenly found that I didn't want to. I look more like me with my curly hair and my freckles.

I pluck my keys from the coffee table and click the door shut behind me. I seem to have packed the rain with me when I left Wales, and I skirt across the garden as quickly as I can and gently tap on the French doors. I feel a surge of warmth spread through me as William scrambles up to get to the door before Jasmine, and tugs it open with glee.

'Katy's back!' he shouts right in my face, before turning to look at Fiona, who is reading paperwork at the kitchen table. Jasmine grabs my hand and tugs me inside and I quickly push my shoes off my feet.

'Hi,' I smile, 'how are you guys?'

'Hello, darling.' Fiona smiles at me over the top of her reading glasses. 'Nice to have you back.'

'Katy, Katy!' Jasmine cries, gripping my arm. 'We met your sister! She looks just like you!'

'Except . . .' William says, and he fills his cheeks with air and stretches out his arms as wide as they'll go.

My mouth falls open. Has Rachel put on weight? That's very unlike her; she's always been obsessed with diet and exercise.

She's the type of person who does park runs every Saturday and enters half-marathons for fun.

'William!' Fiona snaps, and William drops his arms back to his sides and turns pink.

'She let us touch her tummy too,' he gabbles, and at this Fiona slams down her paperwork and William and Jasmine jump.

'Right, upstairs, you two!' she says crossly. 'Go and brush your teeth, we need to leave soon. Go on, go!'

William and Jasmine skirt upstairs and I sink into a chair.

Gosh, how embarrassing for Rachel. It's not like William and Jasmine have never seen someone with a bit of belly before, surely? Why would they think it's so exciting to touch it?

'Did you have a nice time in Wales?' Fiona says lightly, her eyes moving back to the stack of papers in front of her.

'I tried to work,' I say quickly, 'but the connection was terrible. It was hard to get onto my emails or anything.'

I stick my damp hands under my thighs as my heart rate picks up and the tense feeling I shed whilst I was in Wales creeps back through my body. Fiona cocks her head and cracks open a highlighter.

'That's okay.'

'And obviously I'm sorry about what happened with the fire alarm,' I blurt. 'I thought the auction was going pretty well until that happened and I did try to manage it as best I could.'

I break off, staring at Fiona imploringly as she continues to highlight the document.

Please say something. Please, just fire me or tell me that everything is okay. Anything.

She doesn't look up and I feel myself wilt.

Why isn't she saying anything?

275

'Because,' I continue, unable to stop myself from filling the silence, 'I was really hoping you might consider me for Caitlin's position in the office. I feel that—'

'Ready!'

Jasmine charges back into the kitchen, closely followed by William, who is baring his teeth at us like a small lion. Finally Fiona snaps out of her trance with the paperwork and looks at her children.

'Right,' she claps her hands together, 'shoes, please, come on!'

The children race back out of the kitchen towards the front door and Fiona smiles at me.

'Sorry, Katy,' she says. 'I've been trying to get my head around this contract.'

She blinks up at me and I stare back at her stupidly.

Was she listening to me at all?

'Mum!' Jasmine's voice echoes up the hallway. 'Mum! Where is my book bag?'

'Oh for goodness' sake.' Fiona rolls her eyes at me and gets to her feet. 'It's great to have you back, Katy. We've really missed you.' She pats my shoulder, and before I can stop myself, I jump to my feet.

'Sorry,' I blurt, 'I just really wanted to speak to you about my job.'

She turns to face me, and for a second I can't read her expression at all.

'That's really what you want?' she says. 'To stay here and work for me?'

I stare back at her, her question causing a tingle of panic to rise through me.

Of course it's what I want; it's the only thing I've wanted for years.

Isn't it?

'Yes,' I say, my voice wavering.

Fiona stares back at me, a look almost of disbelief on her face.

'Okay,' she shrugs, holding up a coat for William to slot his arms into, 'it's yours. If that's what you want.'

She says the words slowly, and the glee that has been trying to burst through me is suddenly somehow masked in fear, as though it's being dragged down by thick tar.

I fix my gaze on her, the look of indifference I've been trying to master for the past three years finally falling onto my face with ease.

'Yes,' I say, 'it is.'

★

I wave to Jasmine and William out of the car window as they run indoors, shepherded by their teachers, who herd the children together like highly experienced Border Collies. The rain pummels down on the bonnet of the car and I lean into the heated seat, my mind racing.

It's happened. It's finally happened. Finally I am going to be a junior events executive. I'll go into the office every day and have my own desk; I'll even bring in my own mug like everybody else does. I'll be able to tell everyone that I've made it in London as a successful woman working on events full-time, which is pretty much what I've been telling them for the past few years, but this time it will be true.

I take a deep breath and try to silence the nerves that have been fluttering under my skin since my conversation with Fiona back at the house.

My phone vibrates in my hands and I turn it over. Ellie's name flashes on the screen.

Hi Katy, are we still on for tomorrow? I think Sophie is going to make a cake! I know Rachel's birthday was a few weeks ago, but thought it would be nice. Let me know what time you want us there x

I read the text again.

When I found Grandma's ashes, I was ready to text Ellie and Isaac and cancel Rachel's party straight away, and I had every intention of doing it as soon as I arrived back at the cabin, but then I found the notes and everything Rachel had done for me in the past week, and the familiar feeling I've been carrying for the last few days resurfaced. There is something not right with Rachel, and I need to find out what it is. She's my twin; I need to make sure she's okay.

I jump as Fiona wrenches the car door open and tumbles inside, gasping as she is finally sheltered from the rain. I look at her and try not to laugh. Her perfectly blow-dried hair looks as if someone has thrown a bucket of water over the top, and her silk blouse is sticking to her body like it's made of cling film.

'Urgh,' she groans, snapping the mirror down in front of her face and scowling at her reflection. 'What is the point of spending triple the amount on make-up if it's just going to fall off your face at the first sight of rain?'

She tries to wipe away the smears of black that have gathered under her eyes, and I switch my phone to silent.

'Thank you so much for this job offer,' I say. 'I'm so excited.'

She tries to flash me a smile, but as soon as she lays eyes on me, her expression is immediately stolen by a frown.

'You deserve it,' she says tonelessly, rubbing under her eyes desperately. 'Listen,' she adds, 'I won't need you to start for another week or so; we'll have to sort out some paperwork. Why don't you extend your holiday and go back to Wales? You never take your annual leave anyway.'

I try to keep my mouth from dropping open as she says this so casually, after making such a fuss about me taking time off in the first place.

'Really?' I say. 'Are you sure?'

She flicks the mirror back up and turns the key in the ignition, and for a moment I feel as though she's trying to avoid my eyes.

'Yes,' she says, 'and actually I need to go home to get changed now, thanks to that bloody teacher who wanted to talk to me about Jasmine in the pouring rain, so I'll drop you back too. You may as well go back this evening.'

I look down at my phone. The surprise party for Rachel is tomorrow.

'Okay,' I say slowly, 'so when do you want me back?'

'Oh,' she says, waving her hand in the air as we pull away, 'sometime next week. Whenever.'

'Right,' I say, chewing my lip as I reopen Ellie's message. 'Okay. Thanks.'

Chapter Thirty-Four

Rachel

I stare at my stomach, which is sticking up through the water like a desolate island. My bath is tepid, as it always has to be when you're pregnant, and far from the steaming bubble bath I was craving, but if I close my eyes and dip my head under the surface, the sound of water rushing around my ears almost rinses my brain of the fear that is constantly thumping through me. Just for a second.

Katy had an absolute field day in my house. She used all my bubble bath and at least half of my lotion (my anti-stretch-mark one and everything! Like she even *needs* it!). Also, I'm pretty sure she used my pregnancy pillow, or at the very least tried it out, which almost makes me laugh out loud. What on earth did she think it was?

I rest my hand on my bump as the baby wriggles round.

'What will it be like when you're here?' I say quietly. 'Will you be like Jasmine or William? Do you think I will be as good at it as Fiona is?'

A lump swells in my throat as the baby kicks. I'm unsure as to whether it's a 'yes' or a 'no', but it's nice to know that someone is listening. I pull my eyes open as I hear Bruno bark from downstairs, and curse under my breath. He only barks for two reasons: if he needs a wee or if there is someone at the door. Neither of those reasons will go away in a hurry.

As carefully as I can, I climb out of the bath and drape the extra-large dressing gown around my body. I glance down at my phone, secretly hoping Katy may have texted me, but it stares back up at me motionless. I haven't heard from her since she found Grandma's ashes; not that I'm really expecting to, but I had half hoped that once she'd had the chance to cool off, she might have seen it from my point of view. Which would have been a stretch, since I'm not even sure what that is myself.

As I walk down the stairs, I notice Bruno by the front door and roll my eyes. Isaac is the only person who knocks on the front door these days; any friends I had got the message when I gave them every excuse under the sun not to see them, or eventually stopped replying to them altogether.

I edge the door open and stick my head through the gap, shielding my damp body behind the door. Isaac notices my wet hair and pulls a face.

'This isn't a great time,' I say. 'I was in the bath.'

'Oh,' he says, 'sorry. I just need to talk to you.'

I shoot him a look. 'Again?'

'Yes.'

I sigh loudly and step back to allow him inside. He rubs Bruno's ears and I perch on the armchair, hugging the dressing gown around my swollen body. As I look back up at Isaac, I almost want to laugh. He's practically wincing at me.

'Will you stop looking at me like that?' I say, half laughing. 'You're acting like you've never seen a pregnant woman before.'

'I haven't seen one as big as you,' he says. 'No offence,' he adds quickly, and I wave my hand at him. 'Are you sure you're not about to give birth, though? I mean, you're just so pregnant now.'

I raise my eyebrows at him.

God, I feel sorry for any woman he ever has a baby with if these are the compliments she can expect.

'Two weeks,' I say, 'well, two and a bit. Most go longer with their first, though. I'm fine. What's up?'

He snaps his eyes away from my bump and drops into the sofa.

'I think you're wrong about Katy,' he says simply.

I try not to groan. I can't be bothered to go through this again.

'Also,' he adds sheepishly, 'I'm not supposed to tell you this, but you're just so *pregnant* and I—'

'Tell me what?' I interrupt, my heart picking up its pace.

Isaac's shoulders droop and he runs his hand through his hair.

'I'm only telling you because I'm worried you're about to, like, give birth or something,' he says, the words pulling their way out of him.

I wait for him to finish, trying to ignore the fear that is twisting my gut.

'Also, when she left, I didn't think it was going to happen. But I've heard from Ellie that she's on her way back here tonight.'

'Katy is coming back here?' I repeat. 'Why?'

'She's throwing you a surprise party,' Isaac blurts. 'She was worried something was going on with you and she wanted to cheer you up.' He raises his eyebrows at me. 'She knows you better than you think.'

I stare at him, trying to digest this news.

'Katy is coming here?' I say slowly. 'Tonight?'

'Yes!' Isaac says quickly, leaning forward. 'And I think that just shows how much she cares about you.'

'What time?' I say.

'I don't know. Ellie has just texted me to ask to borrow some eggs for the cake.'

'Ellie?' I say. 'Ellie is coming?'

'All your friends are coming!' Isaac cries. 'Everyone wants to see you, that's why Katy organised it! Even Peggy is coming.'

I try and swallow the thick lump in my throat.

'Right,' I say slowly, 'great. So everyone can see how much of a failure I am in one go, right? They can all gossip simultaneously about how sad it is that poor Rachel's husband left her. Isn't it so sad that Rachel slept with a guy who then wanted nothing to do with her? Isn't it terrible that Rachel will be a single mother and will spend the rest of her life alone?'

My voice rises as the words pour out, the anger and shame pulsing through me and landing on Isaac. He stares back at me, his mouth open.

'That's not true,' he mumbles. 'That isn't what people—'

'You have no idea what this is like for me,' I say coldly. 'No one does.'

'That's only because you won't let us in!' Isaac cries, throwing his arms in the air as he jumps to his feet. 'You won't give

283

anyone the chance to help you, not even Katy! It's like you're trying to punish yourself.'

I glare at him, my eyes burning with tears. He stares back at me, desperation beaming from his face.

'You can't lie about this forever,' he says eventually. 'I just wanted to let you know. Why are you so convinced she won't care?'

'Because that's the way we've been for years,' I mutter. 'Not really making the effort with each other, giving each other half-arsed answers, lying to each other. Look at all those lies she told about her flat and her job. Why couldn't she tell me the truth? I'd be asking her to be there for me because I need her, even though I was never there for her when she needed me.'

I break off, my heart racing as I catch the words falling out of me. Isaac is blinking at me, speechless, but now I've started, I can't seem to stop.

'She begged me not to cut our dad out, and I did. She begged me to go to London with her, and I deserted her.'

'She doesn't see it that way,' Isaac says in a small voice.

'And now!' I cry, a laugh pumping out of me as tears swell up in my eyes, 'now she knows that I didn't even share Grandma's ashes with her when we were going through the worst pain in our lives. I was too selfish. How can I ask her to help me? I don't deserve it.'

I clench my hands together, my eyes fixed on the floor as anger throbs through me. Eventually Isaac fishes out a packet of Smarties from his pocket and places them on the coffee table.

'I think she'll surprise you,' he says quietly.

I don't look at him as he ruffles Bruno's ears and then walks out of the house. As the door slams shut, my body jumps and the tears sitting in my eyes break free. Katy is coming back, and has arranged for all my friends to be here. The friends I have ignored for months and completely shut out. The friends who have known Danny and me for years and always called us 'the perfect couple'. They will all gather together here in celebration, only to be shocked when they see how much of a mess I am.

My phone vibrates next to me and I see Katy's name flash onto the screen. A stab of panic jolts through me and I get to my feet. Fear takes over my body as I realise I will never be ready to tell her, I'll never be strong enough for her to reject me and as I grab my empty suitcase, I realise that I'm not strong enough to do this at all.

CHAPTER THIRTY-FIVE

KATY

I stare down at my phone as the taxi rolls slowly through the village. The place is asleep under the blanket of an inky sky, and only the small light in Rachel's front room signals me in the right direction, like a lighthouse waiting for a ship. But she's not there.

Hey, sorry, realised I left something important in your flat so have to go pick it up! Hope you don't mind.

Worry curls through my body as I read the message for what feels like the hundredth time and questions twist through my mind.

What is she talking about? What on earth could she have left behind that is so important I couldn't have posted it to her?

But there are louder questions that scream at me through this text message. She's not asking if I'll be in, or if I mind her staying. She must know I won't be here, which makes me wonder if she knows I was coming back to Wales to surprise her.

A cold thought drops into my mind.

Which makes me wonder whether she's trying to avoid me.

The driver clicks off the ignition and I break from my trance and look out of the window. As I see the blue gate and the strings of ivy that weave up the house, I feel a pang of warmth in the pit of my stomach, like being enveloped by a warm hug. I push open the car door and want to laugh with relief as for a moment the salty air swishes around me and I feel as though it's going to steal my anxieties away and drop them into the sea like a stray leaf. I dig my hands into my pockets and pass the driver some change, smiling at him gratefully.

I wanted to come back for the surprise party, but more than that I wanted to be able to speak to Rachel about everything. I wanted to try and understand why she kept Grandma's ashes, and justify why I've been lying to her about pretty much all of my life choices since I moved away. It didn't cross my mind that she wouldn't be here.

I fish the spare key out of my pocket and slot it in the door. With ears like a bat, Bruno springs up at the bay window and lets out a loud howl. I smile at him.

'Hey, boy,' I say as I push the front door open, 'bet you weren't expecting me back so early . . .'

The words die in the air as I flick the light on and stare at the living room. When I arrived here last week, everything was perfect. It was like a hotel. Now, there are clothes strewn across the floor, stacks of plates are piled up on the coffee table and muddy footprints have been stomped into the carpet. My foot crunches on something as I take a step forward, and as my eyes follow the sound, I realise I've stepped on the only photo of Rachel and Danny, an ugly fork now cracked over their smiling faces. I pick it up, trying to keep Bruno at bay as he leaps around me. Did I do this, or was it already broken?

My mouth is dry as I stare around helplessly, fear echoing in my ears. I dial Rachel's number and it immediately clicks to her sunny voicemail. I sink into the sofa and flinch as something pushes against the back of my legs. I look down and realise I've sat on a packet of Smarties, the cardboard now misshapen under my weight. I hold the Smarties in my hand and stare into the darkness, trying to make sense of what's in front of me.

★

I spent the night flitting in and out of intense nightmares where I was falling down a well and Rachel was watching me, her hand outstretched, but I couldn't reach it. Each time I woke, hot and gasping for breath, I grabbed my phone, but it stared back up at me, motionless. It wasn't until the vibration of my phone rips me out of my dream that I see her name flashing up at me.

Sorry house is state. I'm fine.

I glare down at the message. Oh, she's fine, is she? That's all she's going to say?

I fire a message back immediately.

When are you coming back? I need to talk to you, I thought you'd be here.

Two blue ticks flash onto my screen as soon as I hit send, but she doesn't reply.

I push myself out of bed and stomp downstairs, grabbing my dressing gown and wrapping it round myself.

This is ridiculous. I can't throw her a surprise party if she's not even here! She can't just stalk off into the night *again* with no reasonable explanation! I mean, Christ, what is going on? Is she running from the law? Has she killed someone?

I rip the front door open and hear myself gasp as the icy wind greets me. I grip my dressing gown tighter as I charge down the garden path and up to Isaac's front door.

I don't care how early it is. He knows something about my sister and it's about time he bloody told me. Also, he loves knocking on my door at the crack of dawn, so it's time for him to experience it himself. And do you know what? If he gets angry, I won't even care. I'll say, listen here, *mate*—

The door flies open and Isaac looks at me, bewildered. His eyes are half open and to my alarm I realise that he's just in his boxer shorts. For a moment I forget my anger as hot embarrassment shoots up my body.

Bloody hell, does he always answer the door like that? He'll push our poor postman into an early retirement!

'Katy?' he says, scrunching his eyes as he tries to adjust to the light. 'What are you doing here?'

'I came back to see Rachel,' I say hotly, my skin prickling as the wind continues to bite at me. 'I wanted to check she was okay, but she's not here, again. What's going on?'

At this, Isaac's eyes open fully.

'She's not here?' he repeats. 'She's not in the house?'

'No!' I cry, flapping my arms in the air. 'She said that she left something important at my flat and that she needed to go back, but that isn't like her at all!' To my alarm, fat tears begin to swell in my eyes. 'None of this is like her! Her house is an absolute state and she's being distant and weird and I don't understand.'

I break off, staring up at Isaac desperately. 'I know there's something going on with her but she won't let me in. Is it Danny? Has he left?'

Isaac goes to respond, but I'm not finished.

'Did you see her?' I gabble. 'When she came back?'

Slowly he nods, his mouth twisting uncomfortably.

'Was she okay?' I say. 'Did she seem okay?'

My heart hammers in my chest as I stare at him imploringly. Eventually he shrugs.

'I didn't know she was leaving,' he says quietly. 'I told her about the party; it must have freaked her out.'

I feel my jaw drop.

That can't be it. She's run away because she's scared of the surprise party?

'What?' I say helplessly. 'That's why she's gone back to London? I don't understand!' I cry, tears now escaping freely down my face. 'I don't understand any of this. It doesn't make any sense.'

'Hey.' Isaac steps forward and pulls me into a hug. My damp faces presses against his bare chest, and for a moment I allow myself to sink into him.

'Come on,' he says, 'come inside for a minute. She might have just needed some space. I'm sure she'll be back.'

I nod weakly and follow him inside, his words drumming through my body.

She does need some space; my sister needs some space from me.

CHAPTER THIRTY-SIX

RACHEL

Like clockwork, Jasmine's face pops up at the cabin window just like I knew it would. It's just gone 6 a.m., and the last message from Katy is still blinking up at me from my phone. Every time I read it, I feel as though I might throw up.

I didn't think about much before jumping into a taxi and asking it to take me to Chiswick. I could have gone anywhere. I could have driven ten miles up the road and stayed in a Holiday Inn; why did I decide to go hundreds of miles to a place I barely knew? But when I was throwing everything into a bag and running into the rain last night, the lodge felt like a physical pull. I needed to be back where nobody looked at me with anything but kindness, no questions asked. Just for one more day, that was what I needed.

I rest my head in my hands as a headache thumps around the back of my neck. I should have stayed. I should have stayed and spoken to Katy. I knew that the moment the car sped out of the village and towards London, but as we slipped onto the motorway and flashes of amber light seeped through the windows, I couldn't bring myself to tell the driver to turn around. I couldn't even bring myself to ask to be dropped at the station; I just needed to get to London.

I look up as I hear a small knock on the window. Jasmine's eyes are gleaming at me expectantly. I push the feeling of fear to the back of my mind as I carefully manoeuvre my way to standing. As soon as I open the door, she explodes into chatter.

'Rachel!' she cries. 'You're back! Katy was here yesterday because she got back from her holiday and Mummy said that you weren't staying here any more, only Katy, but now you're here! Is Katy there too? Are you back because you missed us? I got full marks in my spelling test yesterday and Mummy said she was so impressed she would buy me a doll to say well done.'

I try and smile at her, but a sudden hot flash of pain shoots through my body, forcing me to double over and clutch the door frame.

Oh my God.

'Jasmine,' I say, trying to keep my voice steady, 'go get your mum.'

Jasmine nods and races up the garden.

Panic floods through my body as I cling onto my stomach. What's happening? Why is this happening?

Is there something wrong with the baby?

I glance up as Fiona comes racing down the garden. Her silk dressing gown flies behind her and Jasmine gallops alongside her like a faithful steed. I see her confused eyes scanning my body as she reaches me.

'Rachel!' she cries, her voice high with bewilderment. 'What are you doing here? I just sent Katy back to Wales so that she can be with you when the baby is born!'

I try and flash her a smile, but my face is still contorted in pain.

'Oh my God,' she mutters under her breath. Her eyes snap back up to me and I flinch. 'Are you in labour?'

My fingers curl around the door frame, unsure if that's a question that needs answering, and then before I can stop myself, I burst into tears.

'I can't be!' I cry desperately. 'I'm not due for another two weeks! That's what the doctor said. I don't know what's going on, but it hurts!'

I try and swipe the tears off my face, and Fiona suddenly stiffens as though my words have commanded her to stand like a guard ready for orders.

'Right,' she turns to Jasmine, 'go get William and tell him to get dressed, now.'

'But Mummy, I—'

'*Now*,' Fiona says sharply, and Jasmine skids back up the garden. Fiona reaches forward and grabs my damp hand off the door frame. 'Right,' she says calmly, 'it's okay. This is unexpected, but you're not the first person this has happened to, and it could just be Braxton Hicks, but we're going to get you checked out anyway. William was two weeks late and he decided to arrive when I'd just sat down for a meal with Tristan's parents.' She fixes her eyes on mine. 'First of all we need to call your husband and tell him to get to London as soon as he can.'

Her words wind me, and I scrunch up my face. My mind

293

races, trying to think of a suitable explanation as to why I can't do what she's asking, but I can't lie any more.

'I don't have a husband,' I manage, the truth ripping through me. 'He left me. This isn't his baby. I'm on my own.'

For a second I feel Fiona waver. I force myself to look at her, desperate to catch sight of any hint of her reaction now that I've finally admitted my secret. A shadow of sadness creeps over her face for a second before a still, calm expression takes over. I fear she's going to try and question me, angry that I've lied to her, but she doesn't.

'You are not on your own,' she says, her grip on my hand tightening. I blink back at her. 'Who do you want with you?'

I hear my answer before I think it. 'Katy. But she won't be able to get here,' I cry. 'She doesn't drive and there are works on the train line and she doesn't know. I still haven't told her anything.'

Fiona narrows her eyes at me. She whips her head over her shoulder and yells up the garden.

'Jasmine! Make sure you and William have your shoes on.'

My stomach flips over as Fiona turns back to face me, a flicker of adventure gleaming in her eyes as she gives my hand a firm squeeze.

'We're going to Wales.'

★

I wring my hands and stare out of the car window as we shoot up the same motorway I travelled down less than twelve hours before. As soon as Fiona took charge, it felt as though she had removed a huge weight that had been sitting on my shoulders.

Finally, someone else was taking control of the situation. She didn't let me have much of a say in it and I was too blinded by fear to question her.

She piled us all into her four-by-four and sped us towards the motorway, trying to hush Jasmine, who was practically levitating with excitement at the idea of missing school to go and see my house. As soon as I realised Fiona was going to pull the children out of school to take me to Wales, I tried to argue, but she batted me away, saying that they hadn't had a sick day all year and her mum wasn't around to pick them up if we weren't there. My next worry was how Fiona could miss a day of work, but she shot me a look that silenced me pretty quickly. There are some perks to being the boss, I guess.

'I'm really sorry,' I say quietly, keeping my eyes fixed on my hands. 'I feel fine now, I don't feel like I'm in labour at all.'

This is the worst part, the fact that almost as soon as we left Chiswick all my pain seemed to vanish and I started having a simmering fear that I just had some unpredictable gas.

'It's better to check,' Fiona says matter-of-factly. 'Thankfully it's your first, so even if you are in labour, we've got time.'

'Oh?'

'I was in labour for thirty hours with Jasmine.'

I wince.

Thirty hours? Jesus Christ.

'So,' Fiona says, turning down the radio, 'are you going to tell me why you turned up at the lodge unannounced?'

Automatically I feel my mind spring into action to come up with a feasible story, but every idea sinks through my brain with all the strength of damp tissue paper.

'I found out Katy was throwing me a surprise birthday party.'

Fiona flicks her eyes towards me and then immediately fixes them back on the road.

'Is that it?' she says eventually. 'You travelled hundreds of miles not to attend a party?' She laughs, pushing her hair off her face. 'Gosh, I know sometimes we want to avoid a night out, but that's real commitment.'

'It's not like that,' I mumble. 'Nobody knows I'm pregnant. I haven't told anyone, and she'd planned to have everyone at my house. I just couldn't face it . . .' I trail off feebly, my body hot with embarrassment as I hammer another nail into the 'I'm a failure' coffin.

Fiona flicks the indicator and slides the car into the fast lane. As she does so, she glances in the rear-view mirror and a small smile plays on her lips.

'Look,' she whispers. I follow her gaze and see William propped up in his car seat, his chubby face lopsided as he sleeps peacefully.

'He always falls asleep on car journeys,' she says fondly.

As I watch William sleep, the fear roaring in my body melts away. His left hand is clutching a toy giraffe and his thick eyelashes flutter slightly against his full cheeks as he dreams effortlessly.

'They're the best thing that's ever happened to me,' Fiona says quietly. 'I never thought of myself as a mum before they arrived, and now I can't even remember my life without them.'

Instinctively my hand touches my stomach and I feel a shock of emotion.

'Why are you so scared of everyone knowing the truth?'

I move my eyes away from William and fix my gaze on an inky-black car that is skimming along the motorway parallel to us.

'Because I've lied,' I say simply. 'I'm not the person I've been pretending to be. I've always been Rachel and Danny.' Fresh tears pop out of my eyes and I brush them away quickly. 'I'm scared what people will say.'

'Katy?' Fiona says.

I nod, pushing the tears off my face. Fiona notices, and reaches over to squeeze my hand.

'Well,' she says, 'I think there's only one way to find out.'

My phone vibrates in my hand. Without thinking, I answer, and Isaac's voice tumbles down the phone.

'Rachel,' he says, 'it's me. Where are you? We're all really worried. Katy's asking me all kinds of questions and I don't know what to say.'

My grip tightens on my bump. I feel a swell of emotion, and take a deep breath.

'Tell her I'm coming home.'

CHAPTER THIRTY-SEVEN

KATY

'Did she say what time she'd be here?' I ask.

Isaac nods and drops onto the sofa. Bruno takes this as an invitation to be stroked and flops his body next to Isaac's feet.

'Yeah,' he says, 'about an hour.'

'Right.' I nod, my eyes flicking up to the clock. 'Okay. Well, that's earlier than the party was supposed to start, but that's okay, I'll text Ellie.'

As I pick up my phone to punch in a message, I notice Isaac staring at Grandma's ashes. I moved them downstairs this morning; I hated the idea of them being hidden under my old bed like some sort of secret. As I look at the urn, I feel an unwanted flash of anger.

'She asked us to scatter them on the cliff,' I say, leaning my weight against the kitchen counter as the kettle bubbles behind me. 'That was the last thing she asked us to do. She wanted to watch over us.'

'And you couldn't do it?' he says.

I shrug. 'I could have done. I needed to. After the funeral, I asked Rachel about it every day for weeks, but she told me our mum had taken the ashes, so after a while I gave up. I tried asking Mum myself once or twice, but when she said she didn't have them, I just assumed she was lying.' I give a light laugh. 'She lies about everything else.'

Isaac leans on his elbows as Bruno rolls onto his back, his legs stuck in the air like oddly shaped twigs.

'Maybe Rachel couldn't do it,' he says.

As I begin to reply, there is a knock on the door. I feel myself jump.

Is that Rachel already? We're not ready for her! Nobody is here! She's early!

Isaac stands as Felix appears at the window. Bruno scrabbles to his feet and bounds towards the door.

'One sec,' Isaac says. 'Sorry, I told him I was here if he needed anything.'

He disappears into the porch, shutting a confused Bruno out. Bruno starts to whine and I sink to my knees, holding out my arms. He pads over, dropping his body weight onto mine as he attempts to sit on my lap. I laugh.

'It's okay,' I say. 'How did we not get on when I first arrived, huh? Now we're best of friends.'

I give his ears a stroke and he looks at me.

'Everything will get back to normal soon,' I say quietly. 'Don't worry. It will all be okay.'

I cup Bruno's face with my hands, suddenly unsure as to whether I'm speaking to him or myself.

'Sorry about that.' Isaac reappears.

I get to my feet and drop two tea bags into a pair of my hand-made mugs. Isaac's is big, more like a bucket than a mug, and is painted different shades of blue with a buttercup-yellow blob in the corner, smiling down like the sun. Mine is much smaller, and light pink, with a girl's face reading a book. It's not until I really look at it that I realise I've chosen the mug I made Rachel for our sixteenth birthday.

'So,' Isaac says, trying to keep his voice light but failing, 'what did your boss want in London? Did you get that job?'

I hand him his mug, trying to stop my cheeks flushing pink.

'Yes,' I say, 'I did. I start next week.'

He cradles the mug in his hands and nods.

'Great,' he says quietly, 'good for you. Well done, Katy.'

'Thanks,' I say, perching on a kitchen chair and keeping my eyes fixed on the steaming mug on my lap.

'So you'll be back to breakfast at the Shard in no time then?' he says, giving an odd laugh as he flicks his green eyes towards me.

My body aches as I watch him trying to make light of the situation and not admit what we both know: that me accepting the job means we will still be apart, and when we're apart, we can't be together.

'Yeah,' I say, a limp smile pushing its way onto my face, 'something like that.'

I jump as I hear the front door clatter open and Peggy's sing-song voice as she bustles in.

'Hello!' she calls. Her arms are laden with carrier bags. 'I made all the party food.' She starts unloading plastic boxes onto the kitchen table. 'Cheese puffs, jam tarts and sausage rolls.' She beams at us both. 'Now, what time is she getting here?'

For a second I notice a small glance between Peggy and Isaac, but quickly dismiss it.

'She's on her way,' I say.

Peggy nods. 'Perfect.'

★

'Okay. So if you hide behind the sofa, and if you maybe just squat there for a bit, is that okay? And then maybe . . . oh *Bruno!*'

I grab Bruno's collar as he tries to jump on one of Rachel's friends. Isaac laughs and leans over, gently moving Bruno towards him behind the kitchen table.

'Look, you just stay here,' he says, forcing Bruno onto his lap and wrapping his arms around his middle. 'Okay, buddy? She'll be here soon.'

I flash him a smile of thanks and look around the room. Ellie brought six friends with her in the end, and including Isaac, Felix and Peggy, that gave me ten hiding places to find in our smaller-than-average cottage. Well, eleven, if you count Bruno, who keeps leaping around from person to person like he's the bloody guest of honour. I was half tempted to lock him outside, but the last thing anyone needs is for him to run away again.

'Shall we light the candles when she comes in?' Ellie asks, glancing over at the staggering chocolate cake that Maura baked.

'Er,' I say stupidly, pulling my sleeve off my watch to check the time, 'yeah, maybe that's a good idea?'

'Katy.' Isaac's voice comes from under the table, and I glance over to see that Bruno is now fully slumped on his lap. 'Do you think maybe you should see Rachel before the party? Like, meet her at the train station and bring her here?'

His voice carries an edge of urgency, and I frown. Peggy is hovering behind him, trying to look busy by rearranging fondant fancies on a plate, but I can tell she's listening.

I don't actually know how Rachel is getting here. I assumed she would get the train and a taxi like we always do, but I'm sure I saw work on the track planned for today when I arrived last night.

'No,' I say, waving his question away, 'it'll be nice this way. I want her to feel immediately happy, you know? I don't want her to feel guilty when we see each other, or worry that I'm going to have a go at her.'

I feel a stab of guilt as I remember the message I sent when I found the ashes. I can't pretend I'm not still angry, but some things are better spoken about face to face, and I can hardly do it at her party.

To my surprise, Peggy suddenly leans forward and pulls me into a tight hug. When she lets me go, her cheeks are wet.

'That's the spirit, love,' she says warmly. 'She'll be so happy to see you.'

'Katy,' Isaac calls, distracting me from the weirdly intense moment with Peggy, 'I've just had a message from Rachel. She's about five minutes away.'

'Right!' I call, clapping my hands together as excitement shoots through me. 'Places, everyone! Please make sure you're hidden!'

I step forward and hide behind the front door, holding my breath as I watch out of the window.

This is it. Finally I'm about to see my sister.

CHAPTER THIRTY-EIGHT

RACHEL

Fiona flashes me a look of alarm as I fold my body in half, letting out a low groan.

'What?' she barks. 'What is it? Are you okay?'

I take a deep breath as hot daggers of pain ripple up my body. I've been trying to hide them, but for the past half an hour they've become more steady.

'Have your waters broken?' Fiona says, manically flitting her eyes between the road and my legs. 'Has it happened?'

'No,' I wheeze, although if I'm being honest, I'm not sure.

Have they broken, or is my vagina just coming out in a fierce sweat?

'What's wrong with Rachel?' Jasmine pipes up, pulling the large headphones off her head.

'Nothing,' Fiona snaps. 'Put your headphones back on.'

Jasmine jumps and does what she's told. The sat nav sings

out another direction for Fiona and she turns a corner obediently.

'Rachel, if the pains are getting worse, I need to take you to hospital,' she says sternly.

'No,' I snap, my teeth gritted. 'I need to see Katy first.' I flick my eyes up and notice that we're pulling into the village. 'We're two minutes away. I need to see Katy before I go into labour. I need to give her the choice. Look!' I cry, as Fiona starts to argue. 'My house is just here.'

I hold up a limp hand and point to the cottage. My stomach flips as I spot Katy peering through the window and then ducking back behind the curtain, and for a second the searing pain in my body is silenced.

'Are we here?' Jasmine cries excitedly, snapping off the headphones again. 'William, wake up. This is where Rachel lives!'

She shakes him awake and unclips her seat belt. Fiona wrenches up the handbrake and whips her head round to the back seat.

'Stay there,' she says. 'We're not getting out yet.' She stares at me imploringly as I undo my seat belt. 'Let me help you walk in.'

'I'm fine,' I say at once, forcing a smile on my face. 'I'll be back in a minute.'

She blinks back at me and I flash another reassuring smile.

'Really,' I say, 'I'll be fine.'

I take a deep breath, trying to silence the rattling nerves that have sprung to life all over my body. Carefully I push the car door open and step down, pulling my cardigan around my body as I walk down the garden path. Hot tears spring into my eyes as I take out my key and slot it into the door and step into the cottage, my secret finally on full display.

CHAPTER THIRTY-NINE

KATY

'SURPRISE!' I yell, throwing my arms in the air as the front door creaks open. Ellie turns the lights on and everyone jumps to their feet. My heart races as adrenaline thumps through my body, and my toothy smile splits my face.

Rachel's face is still and perfectly composed and for a horrible second I think she isn't happy to see me. Then my eyes fall down her body and my stomach drops.

'Oh my God!' I cry, my eyes widening. 'You're pregnant!'

I step forward and grab her hands, my body shaking as I stare at her. Her brown eyes glisten back at me, a look of sorrow painted on her face.

'I'm so relieved!' I gabble. 'I was so worried that something had happened between you and Danny, but I was wrong: you're having a baby!'

I hover in front of her, an uneasy question swimming in front of my eyes.

Why wouldn't she tell me she was pregnant?

A moment too late, I pull her into a hug, an awkward laugh falling out of me.

This was her secret? Why would she keep this a secret from me?

'You're pregnant!' I say again, although this time it comes with a sharper edge. 'Why didn't you tell me?'

'Sorry, sorry!'

I jump as Fiona appears, holding hands with William and Jasmine.

'They're desperate for the toilet. Hello, Katy, where is . . .?'

I hold a limp arm towards the stairs and Fiona squeezes past us, Jasmine flashing me a guilty smile.

My eyes stay fixed on Rachel, waiting for her to reply, and I suddenly feel Isaac behind me.

'I'm just going to give you two some privacy,' he says quietly, pulling the porch door closed behind us. Without quite meaning to, I snap round to face him as realisation hits me.

'You knew about this?'

He freezes in the doorway, his eyes flitting over to Rachel.

'I asked him not to tell you,' she says quietly.

Heat rushes over me as I stare at him, almost waiting for him to tell me that it's not true. That he didn't know, he hasn't been lying to me for the entire week.

'But why?' I say stupidly, turning back to Rachel. 'Why wouldn't you tell me? You're going to be a family! When is Danny back? Will he have some time off when the baby is born?'

She flinches and pulls her hands away from mine. My heart turns over as a tear escapes her eyes and she shakes her head.

My stomach tightens. How can they make Danny be away when his wife and newborn child are at home? That's not fair, they can't expect—

'It's not Danny's.'

A chill runs through me. Rachel has always been with Danny; I've never known her with anyone else.

'You had an affair?' I manage.

She shakes her head, tears now streaming down her face. I stare back at her helplessly.

'Rachel, I don't understand!' I cry, confusion bubbling alongside anger. 'What's going on with you? Why didn't you tell me any of this? Why have you been lying to me *again*? I don't feel like I even know—'

I break off as she lets out a scream and stares at the floor. A cold bolt of panic shoots through me and I follow her gaze to see a small glistening puddle shining up at us.

Oh my God.

Rachel pulls her eyes up to mine, a look of terror etched on her face. Suddenly I feel a surge of heat rush up my body, and I grab her hands, gripping onto them tightly.

'What is it?' Isaac cries, pulling open the porch door. 'What's happened?'

'Get the car,' I say, trying to keep my voice steady as fear whips up in my insides. 'We need to go to hospital. Now.'

*

If anyone wants to know what the best form of contraception is, it's watching your identical twin in labour in the back of a Ford Fiesta and breaking every bone in your hand in the process.

I mean, Jesus. What happened to *Call the Midwife*, where nice women hand nice clean babies to their nice clean mothers? This is more like *Game of Thrones* and Rachel is about to give birth to a raging dragon.

I quickly modify my face as I realise I'm gawping at her in horror, again.

'Stop looking at me like that!' she snarls between gritted teeth, her head pushed back onto the seat as beads of sweat break out on her forehead.

'Sorry!' I say quickly, forcing an unnatural smile onto my face as I squeeze my legs together, saving my poor vagina from her squeals before it closes up completely. 'It's going to be fine, Rachel. Just breathe, okay? Just breathe.'

What am I talking about? I'm just repeating rubbish I've seen on *Holby City*! I know nothing about giving birth! Nothing!

Oh God, what if we don't make it to the hospital in time and I have to deliver this baby in the car? I can't deliver her baby! I don't even like looking at my own vagina at the best of times!

'It hurts,' she whimpers, scrunching up her face, 'it really hurts.'

'I know,' I say, rubbing her arm with my free, non-crushed hand, 'I know.'

I mean, I don't know. I haven't got a bloody clue. This is the stuff nightmares are made of. I cried when I had my ears pierced, for goodness' sake.

'It's okay!' Isaac calls from the driver's seat. 'We're almost there, Rachel! I know about this sort of thing and you're doing great.'

I gape at him from the back seat.

Know about this sort of thing? How can he possibly know anything about this? He doesn't even *have* a vagina!

'I've delivered a goat before,' he says steadily, even though I can see in the mirror that his face is white and stricken. 'This is all normal.'

'Rachel's not a goat!' I shriek, feeling as though I may burst as Rachel lets out another deep groan.

Christ alive, if we can't get to the hospital in time, it looks like I'll have to deliver this baby. I'm not letting Isaac near Rachel if he doesn't think there's much difference between a woman and a random ruminant.

I mean, he saw me naked last week! What does that say about me?

'Katy,' Rachel rolls her head towards me, her face wet, 'I'm sorry I didn't tell you. I was scared.'

'It's fine,' I say quickly. 'You don't have to explain.'

'I was scared you wouldn't want to know,' she continues, her voice strained. 'I was worried you'd be angry or—'

Her words are swallowed by a scream, and I feel a shock of panic as she arches her back.

'ISAAC!' I yell. 'We need to get to hospital now! How fast are you going?' I stick my head over his shoulder and glare at the speedometer. '*Thirty-five?*' I cry incredulously. 'This is an emergency, you should be doing at least fifty!'

'I can't do fifty in a thirty zone!' he scoffs. 'Rachel, we're two minutes away, just hang on.'

'Just close your legs,' I plead, turning back to Rachel and cupping her face. 'Just for two minutes.'

'That won't help!' Isaac cries from the front seat.

'Oh, sorry I'm not an expert in goat birth like you,' I snap. 'She's not about to give birth to a wheel of Brie.'

'That doesn't even make any sense!'

309

'Stop fighting,' Rachel groans, wrenching her eyes open to stare at me desperately. 'Katy, please, I don't know how much longer I've got. You're going to have to deliver this baby.'

My eyes widen in shock.

No fucking way.

'Isaac!' I scream. 'Hurry up!'

'We're here,' he pants, wrenching up the handbrake. He climbs out of the car and Rachel stares at me, fear flashing onto her face.

'Will you text Dad and tell him?' she says quickly.

Dad?

'Yeah, of course.'

She gives me a limp smile, and I squeeze her hand.

'I'm scared,' she says quietly.

'I'm here,' I tell her, my heart racing in my chest. 'I'm not going anywhere.'

She nods slowly, tears leaking down her face. I wipe them away, my eyes locked onto hers fiercely.

'I'm here.'

★

I stagger out of the hospital room, my eyes twitching as I try and stay focused under the unnaturally bright lights glaring down at us from the neatly placed squares in the ceiling. Rachel has been in labour for hours, and I mean *hours*. If I'd have known that was going to happen, I never would have panicked so much in the car. Every ten minutes or so she seems to let out a shriek of pain and lurch her body forward, and I jump to attention like I've been stabbed by a cattle prod, and the nurse makes some cooing noises and suggests I rub Rachel's back while she rocks on all fours.

I mean, crikey. Maybe Isaac was on to something comparing her to a goat.

I've been sent out on a mission to get some apple juice and Kit Kats. I'm not sure whether Rachel is even allowed to eat while she's in labour, but those were her orders. Although perhaps she's just sending me on a scavenger hunt to get rid of me for a few minutes.

Anxiety twists in my gut as I turn on my heel, following the signs towards the café. Rachel has tried explaining things to me, but every time she speaks, I bat her away. She has more important things to worry about. But now that I am alone, an uneasy feeling reawakens in the pit of my stomach and starts to whirl around like a washing machine.

So this is what's been going on with her. This is why she's been distant and odd for the last few months, and even more so since I arrived in Wales. Her marriage had ended and she's pregnant. And she didn't want me to know.

I chew on my lip as guilt swells in my chest.

How could she go through all of this alone? How could she lock out everybody she loves?

My eyes sting as the loudest question hums in my mind.

How could I not have noticed? I knew something was wrong, but I just thought something was going on with Danny. I didn't even try and ask her. I should have forced her to tell me. I should have stayed on the phone until she told me.

I blink away the tears pricking my eyes and turn another corner. I tuck my hands in my pockets as I walk. It's almost two in the morning. Two in the morning! A part of me thinks Rachel is shrieking like a banshee every ten minutes just to make sure I haven't dropped off, which is very tempting seeing as we're in a building full of beds and clean sheets.

Everyone seems very relaxed and the midwife keeps telling Rachel that she's doing very well. I won't tell you what she did to work that out, but let's just say it was enough for me to go bright red and stifle a gasp of embarrassment.

I turn another corner, trying to take note of the route so I can find Rachel again as quickly as possible. Although at this rate it feels as though she'll never have the bloody baby.

I wonder if they sell cheese toasties in the café. That would be nice. Would Rachel like one of those?

'Katy?'

I jump at the sound of my name and spot Isaac sitting on a red plastic chair. He stands as I approach him, his eyes bloodshot.

Has he been here all night?

'Isaac,' I say, 'what are you doing here?'

For a second he just looks at me, and I feel my heart ache, unable to break his stare.

'How's Rachel?' he says eventually, his voice hoarse. 'Peggy is here too. She's just gone to the café.'

I blink at him.

'Fine,' I reply. 'No baby yet.'

'Oh. Good.'

We sink back into silence and I feel tears creep into my eyes.

God, this is horrible. We can't even speak to each other any more.

'Right,' I say, 'well, I'd better go get—'

'I'm sorry I didn't tell you,' he says suddenly. 'About Rachel.

312

I know I should have done, I knew all along, but she begged me not to. She wanted to tell you herself.'

I feel my throat swell as I meet his eye.

I laugh awkwardly and shrug my shoulders.

'When do you go back to London?' he asks.

'I'm not sure,' I say, trying to keep my voice steady. 'In a few days, I guess. I'll make sure Rachel is settled, then I'll go.'

For a second I think Isaac is going to argue with me, but as he rubs his chin, an odd smile skims across his face.

'Cool,' he says. 'Probably for the best.'

He pulls out his phone and I hover in front of him, suddenly feeling as though the conversation has ended.

'I'll let you know when the baby is born,' I say quietly, turning on my heel and walking towards the café, careful to shield my eyes as the tears I've been fighting fall down my face. As I brush them away, I almost crash into Peggy. She clutches her chest and laughs.

'Gosh, you two look so alike, for a second I thought you were Rachel!' she cries. I try and give her a half-smile back, but the tears are still swimming in front of my eyes, and Peggy takes my arm and guides me into a seat.

'Hey, pet,' she says softly, 'what's going on? Are these happy tears? They don't look like them.'

I shake my head, trying to wipe the tears away as soon as they fall.

Come on, Katy. Stop crying. Get a grip!

'You should be happy,' Peggy says, gripping my thigh and giving it a little shake. 'You're about to become an auntie! It's exciting!'

'But she didn't tell me,' I say quietly, finally managing to stop

Olivia Beirne

crying. 'Why didn't she tell me? Doesn't she think I'd want to be an auntie? Does she think that little of me?'

My body slumps forward and I cover my face with my hands, forcing a deep breath into my aching lungs.

This has been swirling round my mind for hours. Why didn't she tell me any of this? How could she think I wouldn't want to know?

Peggy sighs. After a moment, she unwraps a Twix and hands half to me.

'I think it's more complicated than that, love,' she says. 'I think she needs you to be more than an auntie.'

I remove my face from my hands and look at Peggy's kind eyes.

'I think she needs you back for good.'

I rub my throbbing forehead with the back of my hand.

'But why didn't she just ask me?'

Peggy cocks her head, swirling her half of the Twix in her tea.

'I think she's frightened you'll say no.'

CHAPTER FORTY

RACHEL

I take a small sip of water and smile down at Katy. Her body is folded in half in the chair next to me, so that her sleeping face is resting by my feet like a faithful cat. I did try and tell her to go home at one point, but I think between my wavering voice and my desperation to clutch onto her hand, I wasn't very convincing.

An hour has gone by since I gave birth, and almost as soon as the baby arrived and we knew she was healthy, Katy collapsed into a pile and has been asleep ever since.

Even though my entire body aches with exhaustion, I am far too awake to close my eyes. Little sparks of joy have been whizzing around my body like fireflies from the moment I saw my daughter's face, all pink and scrunched up, confused and agitated at being pulled into the world. As soon as I laid eyes on her, all the anxiety I had allowed to take hold of my body fell away like chains, and every space that had been filled with fear was suddenly bursting full of love. How could I have ever wanted to hide you, I thought, when you must be the most important thing I will ever do? In that moment, nothing else mattered, and suddenly I wasn't afraid of being alone. I was a mother; I had someone who needed me and someone to love unconditionally. That was all that mattered. It was all that would ever matter.

★

I must have fallen asleep, because next thing I know I can feel a light vibration on my legs coming from Katy's wrist. I pull open my eyes, which burn under the white hospital lights, and see Katy unfolding herself from her sleeping position. She looks around, momentarily confused, before flashing me a lopsided smile.

'Hey,' she says, her voice husky, 'how are you feeling?'

'Okay,' I answer.

I'm not going to tell her how badly the stitches hurt, and the way my body feels as though it's been wrung through a mangle. I've scarred her enough as it is, and I'd like my daughter to someday have a cousin.

'Oh.' She smiles down at her watch and picks up her phone. 'Look.'

She turns the phone to face me, and I smile at a photo of Fiona, Jasmine, William and Bruno. William and Jasmine are bursting with giggles as Bruno is mid-lick of Jasmine's pink cheeks, and Fiona is holding the camera, her mouth split into a wide smile. My heart lifts.

'They said they'd stay and look after Bruno,' Katy says. 'I did tell her that he'd be fine for a night on his own.'

I laugh, zooming in on William's screwed-up face. 'They asked to see photos of Bruno all the time,' I say. 'I think they want a dog.'

'Fiona would never allow that.'

'I know.'

Katy sighs and smiles at the picture.

'They've been like a family to me,' she says quietly. 'Fiona really looked after me from the moment I arrived.'

'I know,' I say. 'I felt that way when I was with them too.'

'Did you have dinner round their big table?' Katy says, her eyes glinting as she looks up at me. 'With the kids talking about their day and arguing about homework?'

I smile, warmth spreading through my chest. 'Yeah.'

'It always reminds me of when Grandma was alive,' she says.

She breaks off and gazes down at her phone. I take a deep breath.

'I'm sorry I kept her ashes and didn't tell you.'

Katy shrugs, not meeting my eye. I can tell she doesn't want to talk about it, but I push on. I have to try and make her understand.

'It was selfish,' I say, 'but with Danny away and you in London, and Mum and Dad . . . I just felt really alone.'

'So did I,' Katy says, her voice sharp. 'I wanted her back too.'

'You always seemed to have it all together in London,' I say feebly. 'I thought you had this great, full life. I didn't think you needed her as much as I did.'

'Well I did.'

I nod. 'I know that now.'

Katy continues to stare at her hands. Her collarbones poke out from her pale skin, and I notice that her eyes are sunken, streaks of black staining her cheeks where tears have run down. I feel my insides burn as I look at her.

'When are you going back to London?' I say, my voice shaking slightly as I push out the question I've been sitting on for hours.

'Not sure,' she says at once, not looking up. 'Sometime this week.'

We fall back into silence and I chew my lip.

'Are you happy there?' I say carefully.

She shrugs dismissively. 'You can't be happy all the time, but my whole life is in London. My new job, my . . .' She trails off and I stare back at her.

'It's not the same now,' she says, and to my alarm, I notice her wiping tears off her face. 'You can't turn back the clock and pretend it's the same as when Grandma was alive. We're not that family any more.'

She breaks off as a nurse appears and smiles at me.

'How are you doing?' she asks.

'I'm okay, thank you,' I say. 'Actually,' I add quickly as the nurse goes to leave, 'can I hold her? It's not easy for me to get up.'

She nods and scoops the baby up, placing her delicately in my arms. I hold her tight, her little eyes scrunched up as she sleeps, and gaze down at her, feeling as though my entire body is going to collapse under the sheer love I feel for her. As the nurse leaves, I steal a glance at Katy, who has her eyes glued to her phone, though I can still see tears glistening on her cheeks.

'We could be a different family,' I say quietly. 'The three of us.'

318

Katy doesn't say anything, and I feel the words drift past her as we fall back into silence. I look down at my daughter and then back at my sister.

'Do you want to hold her?' I say.

Finally Katy looks at me.

'No,' she says automatically, 'I can't. I've never held a baby before.'

'It's easy.' I shrug. 'It's like holding a doll.'

'But she's asleep. I don't want to wake her.'

I laugh and roll my eyes. 'Just bloody hold her. I need a wee anyway, so you have to.'

Katy looks at me, eyes wide, before shuffling over and holding out her arms stiffly, as though I'm handing her a loaded rifle rather than her niece. Very slowly, I lean forward and place the baby into them.

'She's so cute,' Katy whispers, her eyes glued to the baby's little pink face.

'I know.'

'What are you going to call her?'

I smile. It's the only thing I've been sure of throughout my pregnancy.

'Violet,' I say simply. 'Her name is Violet.'

CHAPTER FORTY-ONE

KATY

I waggle my fingers at Bruno, his large paws scrabbling against the window as I slot my key in the front door, but before I can turn it, Jasmine pulls the door open.

'Katy!' she cries. 'Katy, we've been on an adventure! Mum!' she yells over her shoulder. 'Katy's here!'

I grin down at her. 'Can I come in?'

Jasmine steps back and lets me inside. Rachel will be ready to come home soon, and I promised I would pick up some comfortable clothes for her to wear. Fiona has volunteered to pick her up if I stay and watch William and Jasmine, as there won't be room for three car seats, even though her car is more like a very glamorous minibus.

'What's this adventure then?' I ask as I sit on the sofa and Bruno comes running up to me.

'Well!' Jasmine cries. 'First of all, I caught Mummy *lying* on the phone to Mrs Peters.'

'Jasmine!' Fiona snaps, appearing at the top of the stairs with William, who throws his arms in the air as he spots me and races down to see me. 'Don't say that!'

'But you were!' Jasmine says. 'You told Mrs Peters that me and William had food poisoning and were very sick.'

'Well, sometimes grown-ups do lie,' Fiona rolls her eyes in my direction, 'but we mustn't tell tales on them, remember?'

Jasmine cocks her head as William climbs onto my lap.

'We took Bruno out on a walk!' he says excitedly. 'And we saw the sea and Bruno tried to go in it!'

This causes them both to fall into a stream of giggles, and I give William a squeeze.

'Listen, why don't you two go and play with Bruno outside?' Fiona says. 'Give me and Katy some peace and quiet for a minute.' She flashes me a wink, and I grin.

'I'm sure they'll keep you busy when I go and pick Rachel up,' she says as the back door slams and she goes to the kitchen to flick the coffee machine on. 'Honestly, they're acting as though they've never been on a mini break before! God only knows how I'm going to get them to sleep tonight.'

I laugh.

'I'm assuming you want a coffee?' she says, looking at me over her shoulder. 'I can't imagine you've had much sleep.'

'Yes please,' I say gratefully, sinking back into the sofa. I feel as though I could sleep for a hundred years, and all I did was hold Rachel's hand and feed her Kit Kats.

I tried to offer her a tangerine instead, as a joke, to get her to finally admit that she wasn't a vegan either, but she didn't find it very funny. In fact, she looked like she wanted to kill me.

'I can't believe you're here,' I laugh, as Fiona hands me a steaming mug of coffee. 'In my childhood home, with my sister having a baby . . . It's so bizarre.'

Fiona cocks her head and sits next to me, folding her long legs under her.

'Yes,' she says. 'Rachel is a good person. She was a welcome guest in our family last week.'

I feel a pang in my chest as I take a sip of the coffee, wincing as it scalds my tongue.

'Listen, Katy,' Fiona says slowly. 'I wanted to talk to you about this job.'

My eyes snap up.

'Have I not got it?' I blurt. 'Have you changed your mind?'

'No, of course not.' She smiles. 'I just wanted to make sure you actually want it.'

She pauses, and I frown at her.

'This is really hard for me,' she says, 'because I have absolutely loved having you as a part of my family for the past three years, but if I'm being honest, I haven't always felt that you've been happy. You're not like the other girls in the office—'

'I can change,' I interrupt. 'I can be more like them.'

'Oh God, no.' She laughs, screwing up her face in mock disgust. 'They're awful; that's the last thing you should do.'

I clasp my coffee, my palms damp.

'I don't understand,' I say quietly. 'Do you want me to leave?'

'I just want to make sure you're doing what makes you happy,' she says. 'You'd be snapped up in a second by an events firm in Wales if you wanted to stay and be with Rachel.'

She says the last bit carefully, and I feel my heart flip.

She reaches forward and takes my hand.

'No rush,' she says softly, 'but I just wanted you to think about it. You seemed like a different person when you came back from your trip; you were so relaxed and happy and I don't want you to lose that. Don't answer me now,' she adds quickly, cutting across me as I open my mouth to speak. 'Think about it.'

My stomach flips over as I force a smile onto my lips, a feeling creeping over me that Fiona knows me better than she has ever let on.

'Now,' she says briskly, putting her mug down and getting to her feet. 'Where can I find this car seat?'

CHAPTER FORTY-TWO

RACHEL

I stare down at Violet, fast asleep in her buttercup-yellow sleep suit with its tiny matching hat. By the time I came back from the hospital, Ellie and the rest of the girls had filled the porch with bags and boxes of adorable babygros, toys and big bars of my favourite chocolate. Peggy had cleaned up after the party and stuck *CONGRATULATIONS!* banners up outside the front door. She'd also left a huge wrapped basket filled with a baby tennis kit, which made me feel *awful*. Where on earth she managed to find it I have no idea, but what I do know is that whether she likes it or not, Violet will have to be the next Andy Murray. Which I guess makes me Judy.

I push my glasses up my nose as Katy appears in the doorway holding up a white T-shirt.

'Is this mine or yours?'

I shrug. 'Don't know. Take it anyway; it won't fit me for months.'

She nods and I follow her back into her bedroom, where her case is flung open and her clothes are waiting in neat piles. My stomach twists as I look at it.

'When will you be back?' I ask, trying to keep my voice upbeat.

We haven't spoken about Katy leaving since I was in hospital. After Fiona dropped me home, we got into our pyjamas and watched *Mean Girls*. Katy even cooked us a curry (something I had no idea she was capable of doing), and the evening felt too perfect to bring it all up again. I didn't want to spoil the first moment we'd had as real sisters for years. I can't ask her to stay; I don't know what I was thinking, imagining she might give up her whole life in London to come and live with me.

'I'm not sure,' she says, not looking up from the suitcase as her face tinges a light pink. 'I'll have to see what time off I can get.'

I nod, sinking onto the bed as she continues to pack.

'Dad is going to come up for a few days,' I say. 'He's got some time off work.'

Katy's face lights up. 'That'll be nice,' she says. 'Have you told Mum about Violet?'

I chew my thumb. 'Not yet,' I say. 'I'll call her.'

'I'll do it with you if you like,' Katy says earnestly.

I smile at her and we fall into silence.

'I'm sorry I can't stay,' she says at last, her voice strained. 'I really want to be with you and Violet. I'm just not happy here. I don't like being in Wales, it brings back too many memories.'

'I know,' I say softly, trying to catch her eye, but she refuses to look up from the suitcase.

I've given up trying to tell her how I think she's happier in

325

Wales than she ever has been in London. The sea air has ruffled her hair, which she usually straightens flat against her head, and I notice that she's only wearing a light swipe of mascara. Her sleek clothes have remained packed in her suitcase, untouched, and she's wearing old dungarees with a yellow T-shirt underneath. She looks more like Katy than I've ever seen on her Instagram.

'Why do you want to live in London so badly?'

For a moment I think I see her flinch.

'I just don't think I can live here,' she says in a small voice.

'You didn't enjoy being here last week?'

She pauses. 'I don't know.'

'What about Isaac?' I say. 'You wouldn't want to see—'

'There is nothing there.' Katy cuts across me. 'He thinks I should go too. I am sorry.' She looks up at me, her eyes shining. 'I promise I will see you more – I'll visit whenever I can – but it's too painful for me to live here. If you need me to help, I can use my annual leave and come and stay. I'm sure Fiona will let me work remotely from time to time too.'

I look back at her, trying to force a smile onto my face.

'Would you mind watching Violet for a minute?' I say. 'I just want to run and grab some milk from the shop. I could do with the fresh air.'

Katy nods silently, still staring down at her suitcase as colour rises up her face.

'Thanks,' I say, jumping to my feet and running down the stairs. Bruno looks up at me quizzically as I skid past, and I shoot him a look.

'Go keep Katy company for a second,' I say, pointing up the stairs. 'She could do with a cuddle.'

As though he can understand me completely, Bruno scampers

up the stairs. I push the front door open and run up the garden path, and then straight down the path next to it.

'You need to tell her to stay.'

The words tumble out of me before Isaac has fully opened the front door. He raises his eyebrows at me, unimpressed.

'What?'

'Katy,' I say simply. 'She wants to stay, I know she does.'

'No she doesn't,' Isaac says. 'She wants to run away, like she always does.'

'Well then, you should stop her!' I say crossly. 'She thinks you want her to leave and I bet that's why she's going. She thinks you don't care about her.'

'I don't,' Isaac says matter-of-factly. 'We're just friends. That's what she said and that's fine with me.'

I stare at him incredulously.

My God, they are both so *stubborn*!

'Isaac, she's leaving in ten minutes,' I say desperately. 'If you let her go, then you've let her go for good. It's taken me years to get a second chance with her.' I fix my eyes on his. 'Don't throw yours away.'

For a second, he just looks at me. Then he reaches forward and plucks his keys off the hook, and my heart lifts.

'I'll give her a lift to the station,' he says coldly, 'but that's it.'

I open my mouth to protest, but he pulls his front door shut and walks down the path with a look on his face that tells me not to bother. I follow him helplessly.

I have my sister back. But while she's unhappy, I'll only ever have half of her.

CHAPTER FORTY-THREE

KATY

'Isaac is giving you a lift to the station.'

I look past Rachel and spot Isaac slouching reluctantly over his car.

Oh great.

'That's okay,' I say quickly. 'I'll get a taxi.'

'Just take the lift!' Rachel laughs. 'For goodness' sake, it's only a lift.'

I look at her. Her face is pink and her smile is wide and free. I haven't seen her this happy in years.

I've barely been able to concentrate on anything since the conversation with Fiona. I've barely eaten. I never thought I would come back to my old village for a holiday, let alone to live permanently. I couldn't wait to get away; I hated it here. All the anger between my parents and the pain as our family split apart, then the heartache of leaving Isaac behind. When Grandma died, I didn't even feel that I had a family to return to. And now I've been promoted! I've finally been offered the job I've been desperate for. It's everything I've ever wanted. So why don't I feel happy? Why don't I feel as though I'm doing the right thing?

'I'll be back really soon,' I say, taking Rachel's hands. 'I'm sure Fiona will give me some more time off.'

Rachel shakes her head. 'You've got your fancy new job to start!' she says. 'You'll be super busy, I'm sure.'

The excitement in her voice spikes through me, and I try and force a smile.

'I'll call you every day,' I say, 'and I'll come back at weekends.'

She smiles, giving my hands a squeeze. 'That sounds great. Don't worry, Dad will look after us. He gets here tomorrow.'

I hover, my hands firmly gripped in Rachel's. I feel a stone sinking through my body, and for a horrible moment I feel as though I'm lying to her.

'We won't go back to how we were,' I say firmly. 'I promise.'

At this, she pulls me into a hug and I hang in her arms limply.

'I know,' she says. 'Now go!' She gives me a hard squeeze. 'Go, or you'll miss your train, and God knows, they only come once every three days. Trust me, you don't want to get a taxi to London.'

I laugh weakly and pick up my bag. Rachel lifts Violet from her Moses basket and holds up one of her clenched hands to pretend to wave, even though Violet is fast asleep.

'I'll be back really soon,' I say earnestly.

I kiss my finger and plant it on Violet's head. Rachel smiles. 'I know you will.'

I step onto the garden path, my chest burning as though I'm

walking away without my heart, but I keep moving until I reach Isaac's car. He takes my case and I climb into the front seat silently, and as we drive away and I wave to Rachel, the tears I've been fighting spill from my eyes.

★

I stare out of the window, fat drops of rain skidding down the glass, as Isaac steers the car down the country lane. It's about an eight-minute drive to the station, and we've sat in silence for the first three. I've been focusing on swiping the tears out of my eyes before they fall down my face and ignoring the voice that is screaming at me to turn around.

'Felix went on a date.'

My stomach clenches as I turn my head. We haven't spoken since that horrible conversation we had in the hospital. I don't know why he offered to drive me to the station, although maybe it's so it won't be too awkward when I come back to see Rachel and Violet.

'Did he?'

Isaac nods, his eyes locked on the road. 'Yeah. He took her to the cinema.'

'Really?'

'I think he wants to take her horse riding.'

I feel a stab in my chest, and pull my eyes away to look back out of the window as the memory of Isaac and me laughing and galloping through the fields replays in front of my eyes.

'That's nice,' I say feebly.

See, a little voice in my head jeers, *you wouldn't have any of this pain if you'd stayed in London. You never have pain like this there.*

I tuck my hands under my legs as a thought enters my mind.

I never felt pain like this in London, but I'm not sure if that's because I was safe, or because I never really felt anything. I didn't ugly-laugh like I have done with Isaac, or feel the warmth of sitting next to Rachel on the sofa, eating crisps in her safe, cosy living room. I didn't feel any pain because I shut myself off from any real experiences. It's almost as if I just existed, fading into the anonymous city. When I first moved to London, that was exactly what I needed, but in the last week, I feel as though I've come back to life, and the closer we get to the station, the harder I'm finding it to remember why I'm so desperate to leave.

'We're here.'

I snap out of my thoughts as I notice that Isaac has pulled up outside the drop-off point at the station. My ears ring as I look at him, but his eyes are still fixed forward.

I unclip my seat belt, my body numb. 'Right. Thanks.'

He steps out of the car and retrieves my suitcase from the boot, placing it in front of me with the professionalism and efficiency of a high-end chauffeur. I steal another glance at him, desperate for him to look at me, but he doesn't. I pick up the suitcase and give a small nod.

'Thank you,' I say again.

'Have a safe journey,' he replies, his eyes fixed on a place over my shoulder.

I open my mouth to reply, but every thought I have fades out of my mind, so instead I turn on my heel and walk towards the station, not allowing myself to look back.

The departures board tells me that the train to London Paddington leaves in four minutes from Platform 2. I take a deep breath and walk towards the stairs, cursing it for being on time and not allowing me to get a coffee and an enormous pastry from Starbucks. It's okay, I'll just have a takeaway when I get back to London, and maybe I'll stop on my way home and buy an entire birthday cake to eat by myself.

As I walk onto the platform, the hot tears are back, biting at my eyes. I blink them away defiantly.

This will get easier. It won't always feel like you're missing part of your heart. This will heal and—

'Katy!'

My head snaps around as Isaac appears, pushing through the crowds of people. At the sight of him, I feel as if I might throw up, and the tears I thought I'd blinked away fall onto my cheeks. His chest is rising and falling and his eyes are flashing, and I feel myself tense.

What is he doing?

'Did I forget something?' I offer.

'How could you do this?' he blurts. 'How could you run away again and leave everyone behind? I've never known anyone like you!'

I hold my breath, thinking for a second that this is a compliment before I realise quite quickly that it's not.

'You're scared of everything! You're running away from the chance of having a family with your sister because you're scared it will break like it did before, but you're not even giving it a chance. You don't give anything a chance!'

I feel myself stiffen.

'Oh?' I say, my voice rising. 'What else haven't I given a chance?'

Isaac looks at me, his green eyes sparkling.

'Fine,' he says, his jaw clenched, 'you want me to say it? Us.

332

You haven't given us a chance. I love you, Katy, I always have done, and I know you love me, but you're too scared of your own feelings to give me or *anyone* a chance. So go!' He points to the train, which has rolled into the platform. 'Get on the train to London and go live your better life. I don't care any more. You win! You—'

But his words are lost, because at that moment, I grab his face and kiss him.

CHAPTER FORTY-FOUR

KATY

ONE MONTH LATER

'I'll tell you what, this is a much more relaxing drive when I don't have to worry about catching a baby every time I change gear.'

I flash Fiona a smile as she flicks her indicator on and turns into the village. I glance over my shoulder at William and Jasmine, who are both sound asleep in their car seats. They were so excited at spending a week with Rachel and Bruno (and seeing baby Violet again) that they fell asleep before we were on the motorway.

Needless to say, I missed my train to London. But I did go back. I had to.

'So,' Fiona says, 'Cassie starts next week.'

She raises an eyebrow at me over her sunglasses.

I had to go back to hand my notice in and pack up the cabin to move back to Wales. It was like Isaac had seen inside my soul and was pulling out each of my fears one by one. By the end of his rant, I couldn't see why I was afraid of any of them, when the idea of being anywhere but with him and Rachel was the scariest thing of all.

'Oh?' I say. 'How are you feeling about it? What's she like?'

'Well,' Fiona sighs, 'she won't be as good as you. But she is an actual nanny, which is a start.'

'Are we here?' Jasmine pipes up loudly from the back seat. I swivel round to face her and grin.

'We thought you were asleep!' I say, poking her stomach.

She grins. 'I was just pretending. I've been awake this whole time.'

Fiona raises her eyebrows. 'Sure you have.'

As the car slows down, Bruno comes skidding out of the house and starts yelping, with Betsy yapping at his heels, fighting to be heard. William jolts out of his sleep at Bruno's loud barks and Jasmine squeals at the sight of him.

Fiona clicks the ignition off, and I see Rachel pushing the buggy down the garden path, Dad walking behind her, his arms outstretched and his face split in glee, as though my arrival is a big surprise and he can't quite believe it. I step out of the car and laugh as Bruno gallops up to me and nearly knocks me over.

'Hey,' I grin, 'hey, boy!'

Bruno is about to leap on William when a strong hand reaches down and grabs him by the collar. I look up and see Isaac beaming down at me.

'Hey,' he smiles. 'How was your journey?'

My heart lifts, and when he kisses me, my entire body fills with warmth at his touch.

'Good.' I grin. 'Much better than the train.'

'Mummy!' Jasmine cries. 'Mummy, shall we get Katy's boxes out now?'

Fiona laughs. 'Give me a break, I need a coffee first!'

'I'll make you one,' Isaac offers, giving William a high five as he leaps into the air.

'Now, does anybody here like chocolate cake?'

I laugh as Peggy sticks her head out of the bay window, holding a wooden spoon and looking quizzically at the children. Jasmine and William fling their arms into the air and Peggy raises her eyebrows in mock surprise.

'We'll only be gone for half an hour or so,' Rachel says apologetically, 'so please make yourselves at home.'

'Oh don't worry,' Fiona waves her hand, 'Bruno will keep these two busy, and Isaac makes a lovely coffee, if I remember correctly.'

I laugh as Isaac flashes me a wink before gesturing Fiona and the children inside the cottage.

'Now don't be too long!' Dad says, wagging his finger. 'The rugby starts at four and Vi is desperate to watch it, aren't you, love?'

He grins down at Violet, and I give him a quick hug.

Rachel turns to face me and smiles.

'Are you ready?' she says.

I nod and hook my arm in hers, and we start walking towards the cliff, taking the route that is a steady incline rather than the steep stairs. I turn my face towards the sun as the spring air swirls around my face. I can hear the frothy sea lapping against the rocks and there is a smattering of laughter coming from the drinkers in the Sailor's Ship. We walk in silence, both of us deep in memories. Eventually Rachel stops.

'Here?' she says.

We've reached a field overlooking the sea. The green stretches for miles and the salty air ruffles the blades of grass. In the distance I can see the cottage shining under the light of the low sun. As I look down at our home, I feel my heart swell.

I nod as Rachel clicks the brake on the pram and bends down to retrieve Grandma's ashes, tucked away in a basket. For a moment, she holds the urn close to her, and I notice tears shining in her eyes. I reach forward and touch her arm.

'She'll always be with us,' I say quietly. 'She'll always be a part of our family.'

She gives a small nod and carefully removes the lid. She holds the urn to the sky, and then turns to me.

'You do it,' she says.

'Are you sure?'

'Yes.'

Slowly I take the urn out of Rachel's hands and hold it in the air. As soon as I tip it, a fresh gust of wind takes the ashes away, scattering them across the field and into the sky. As I drop the urn to my side, Rachel links her arm in mine and rests her head on my shoulder.

'You're right,' she says softly. 'We will always be a family.'

EPILOGUE

To Fiona Cunningham from Katy Dower
Sent 15 July at 12:06
Hi Fiona,

Thought email was the best way to send over this photo of Violet. I can't believe she's rolling over! Are you and the kids around for a video call this week? We miss you, the house has been very quiet since you left last week!

Also – I GOT THE JOB! I start as events executive at the Firefly Hotel at the end of the month. I'll make sure I check the fire alarms before the first event I do (LOL) xx

To Super Bike Customer Service from Katy Dower
Sent 18 July at 17:43
Hi there,

Please could someone advise on how to return the Super Bike? Mine is in mint condition, never used. I would like a full refund, please.

Many thanks,
Katy Dower

House Swap

To Rhys Dower from Katy Dower
Sent 2 September at 13:06
Hi Dad!

Here is the link to sponsor me and Rachel in the fun run! I'm so excited, we start training next week. Let us know what time you're coming up at the weekend.

Katy x

To Rhys Dower from Rachel Dower
Sent 19 September at 02:46
Hi Dad,

Does it ever get any easier feeding in the middle of the night? I thought I'd cracked Violet's sleep schedule, I even bought myself a new eye mask as a celebration!

I've been thinking about it a lot since you last came to stay, and take some time to think about it . . . but why don't you come back and live here? You don't have to move into the cottage, I know it has a lot of memories of you and Mum, but you could live nearby. This might just be the unrealistic thoughts of a severely sleep-deprived new mum, but let me know what you think. Hope you're having a nice week, love you.

PS Katy isn't doing the fun run any more. She said she's twisted her ankle xx

To Rhys Dower from Katy Dower
Sent 5 November at 13.07
Hi Dad!

Got to be quick as I'm at work, but Isaac said we can be there at about midday on Saturday to help with the move. He also wanted me to tell you that they're showing the rugby on Sunday at the Ship. Thought it might be nice to go there for a roast? Violet loves the rugby, even though Peggy keeps trying to get her into tennis (no idea why). Let me know! Xx

To Katy Dower from Rachel Dower
Sent 20 December at 14:08
Katy – please finish work early. I can't think of any ideas for Elf on the Shelf (I know V is only a baby, but I really think she's enjoying it). Also, I want to open the Baileys and watch *The Holiday*.

To Rachel Dower from Katy Dower
Sent 20 December at 14:11
Spoken to boss and can leave in twenty! Maybe hold off the Baileys for me though . . . Isaac and I have a little surprise for you all xx

ACKNOWLEDGEMENTS

As always, I need to start by thanking my Super Agent, Sarah Hornsley, who has believed in me from the very beginning and saw this book for what it could be. Even though I had no idea what that was. An enormous thank you, as always, to my wonderful Editor Jess Whitlum-Cooper. I feel very lucky that I get to write books with you two in my corner, championing my characters and waving your magic.

Thank you to everyone at Headline for all of your incredible work. Jane Selley, my fantastic copyeditor, Kate Truman my wonderful proof-reader, Shadé Owomoyela, Marketing guru and Antonia Whitton, Publicist extraordinaire.

This book required a different type of research to my last two, so thank you to the marvellous mummies-to-be and mummies-who-are, who helped with Rachel's conundrums, worries and mishaps: Keri, Katie, Ciara, Tash, Kristie, Libby and Becca.

To Ziggie and Gemma, two friends who walked in rain, shine and snow, and kept me smiling, laughing and suitably horrified at various pregnancy stories. Also, I must thank you both for keeping me fed when I'm in the depths of an edit: nobody has a chocolate and biscuit collection quite like either of you.

To Arianna, who always laughs at my jokes, even when I've said it four times and Kiera, my soul sister. Thank you also to Claire, I'll forever be grateful that you took me under your wing in year seven.

To three authors who have always championed me endlessly: Lynsey James, Daisy Buchanan and Emma Cooper. Your kindness and support have helped more than you'll ever know.

Book bloggers from all over the world have been monumental for me throughout my book life so far, but in particular I must thank Megan Palmer, who gives me random boosts of confidence when I've forgotten how to spell my own name.

To my cheerleaders, Alex, Catherine, Maynie, Alice, Hayley, Katy, Georgia, Jamie, Andrew, Adam, Luke, Laura, James, Anna, Emily and Loren.

To my grandparents, sitting and talking about books and theatre with you both is one of my favourite things.

To Chris, my rock, who keeps me silly in the most serious of scenarios.

And finally, to my family. My sister Elle, my brothers Dominic and Tom, my incredible mum and my dad, who never lets any of us take life too seriously.

Would you open a love letter that wasn't meant for you?

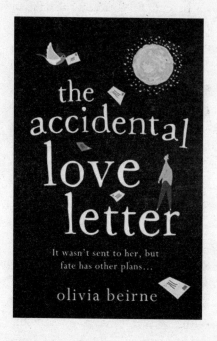

'A hilarious, heart-warming read' Daisy Buchanan

'A charming, uplifting read . . . Delightful' Roxie Cooper

Available now in eBook, audio and paperback
from Headline Review!

If you enjoyed *House Swap*
then you'll love *The List That Changed My Life* . . .

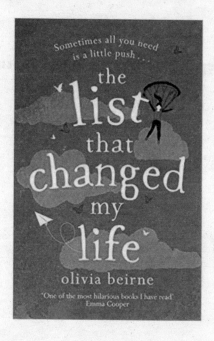

'One of the most hilarious books I have read for
a very long time'
Emma Cooper

Available now in eBook, audio and paperback
from Headline Review!

Keep in touch with Olivia Beirne!

www.oliviabeirne.co.uk
olivia.beirne
/Olivia-Beirne